TICKET TO PARADISE

THE CAJUN EMBASSY BOOK ONE

CHERIE CLAIRE

Dedication

To my husband, Bruce, and our early years in Los Angeles where we spent many wonderful weekends escaping to beautiful Ojai. And to our later one-time home, Santa Clarita, for being an oasis when we needed it.

CHAPTER 1

artin stared numbly at the waves winking at him in the early morning sun, coming alive when his cell phone began playing the guitar riff from Hotel California. He wondered how long he had been parked on the shoulder of the Pacific Coast Highway, wondered how long the ocean had been laughing at his failed flight into exile.

He had wakened early and made his escape before his sister had entered his room, grabbing his toe in her unbroken daily ritual. Ever since Cassie had hit bottom in the film industry and moved into his once-spacious condo, Martin was never late for any meeting. But this morning, he had eluded her, got as far as Ventura before the cell phone's buzzing interrupted his peace. Rubbing the bridge of his nose, knowing that Cassie would not give up, he pushed the talk button.

"Hey, stinky face."

"Where are you?" his sister demanded. "And how did you know it was me?"

"It had an irritating ring to it."

"Funny. You're at the beach again, aren't you? What's with you and the Pacific Ocean these days?"

Martin started to explain how a quick trip down Highway 126 to Ventura cleared his mind of the ongoing stress of keeping his family business afloat, but it was a useless explanation. Cassie had an easy answer for all his troubles. So did his brother Paul. Only Martin didn't want to hear it. "What's up?" he asked instead.

"How do you know it's me?"

"Cassie, how is it possible you're a graduate of USC and you don't know about caller ID?"

"I hate cell phones."

Martin couldn't argue with that one. The portable interruption was the bane of his existence. "Then why are we having this conver...?"

"John Withrop called," Cassie said. "Said you are meeting at ten thirty this morning, wanted to know if you could make it ten instead."

Martin hadn't told Cassie about the meeting with the bank, hadn't wanted her to know how dismal Christmas sales had been.

"Sure."

"Why are you meeting with John?"

"Usual business," Martin lied as he watched a pair of pelicans sail down the beach, oblivious to the world's troubles.

Cassie wasn't convinced. "Martin, we can settle this once and for all with three signatures."

Martin closed his eyes, wishing he could will away the problems surrounding his newspaper. Tell the *Los Angeles Daily Times* to go to hell. Convince his siblings that since he had promised to keep the family legacy alive nothing short of death would deter him from that pledge.

They had heard it all before. Just like he had heard their pleas repeatedly.

"I'm on my way," he answered before she could inquire further. Disconnecting the conversation, Martin turned off the phone and threw it on the backseat. Some day he would have time to enjoy a sunrise, have time to stop and breathe the salt air most Angelenos take for granted. The first thing he would do is fling his damned cell phone into the Pacific.

IMAGE WAS everything in Southern California. Like his colleagues in the nearby movie industry, Martin Taylor knew how to push insecurities aside and offer the world a confident persona. Swinging open the boardroom door as if he had emerged from important business, Martin warmly greeted John Withrop, vice president of the Bank of Santa Helena and a life-long friend.

"John, good to see you," Martin said.

"Good to see you again, son." John grabbed Martin affection-ately by the shoulders. "How's your mom? I never see her out anymore."

Martin grimaced thinking how true that was since his father's funeral. "She doesn't socialize much since dad's gone."

John rubbed his chin, no doubt calculating how long it had been since the death of Martin's father. "Perhaps we'll see her at the New Year's party?"

"Perhaps."

"But that's not why I'm here."

The headache that usually arrived after lunch, the daily advertising reports and the first editorial meeting came early. There was only one reason why John would pay him a visit during the busiest time of a banker's day.

"*The Banner*'s not for sale," Martin bit out too quickly. "You of all people should know that I would never sell this family-owned newspaper to a media conglomerate."

John removed his jacket and draped it over a chair. "Martin," he said solemnly. "I've seen the holiday reports."

The reminder of the bleak Christmas ad sales felt like a knife in his gut, but he wasn't going down without a fight. Martin headed toward the credenza and poured himself a coffee, thankful that his secretary had brewed a fresh pot. Coffee was his ultimate ally and he liked it strong.

"Can I get you something, John? Cassie brought in some French roast, your favorite."

John followed him to the credenza, leaning back on the massive piece of furniture that Martin's father had purchased from the *Daily Democrat*, a community newspaper that had fallen under bad times in the 1950s. Ironic, Martin thought.

"Have you even looked at their offer?" John said. "You are losing money daily."

"It's a slow period." Martin attempted to sound a hell of a lot more positive than he felt, since Christmas was usually their finest hour. "Advertising is down for many reasons -- one of our department stores moved to inserts, the Times' damn new bureau in town. But there's a Kohl's opening soon and I have some excellent reps working to establish a..."

"Martin," the older man interrupted, placing a friendly hand on his shoulder, "there is no more time."

When Martin gazed over at the man who had graduated next to his father and been a sponsor at his christening, Martin felt remorse for his lies. Still, he had made a promise. "I'm sorry, John. But I'm not selling."

John's eyes turned steel gray. "I understand how you feel. Don't you think it pains me to see you sell your father's blood and sweat? But you don't have a choice."

Time was still on his side. More importantly, Martin owned the Taylor family determination that, in the past, had moved mountains. "I have most of the money. Give me a few more weeks and I'll pull this around."

John squeezed his shoulder like his father used to and Martin knew that what he had to say would be his last. "It's not working, my boy. You tried your best to turn this paper around, and you've done an admirable job, but..."

"Technology is expensive, John. You know that. I needed that loan to..."

"To buy the computers and software your father never had the foresight to purchase, I know. And you're right, it was expensive, which is why you have that enormous balloon payment in ten days."

Martin rubbed the bridge of his nose, trying to will the pounding—and the problems—away. "After those upgrades, we didn't have anything left over to fix that worthless excuse for a printing press and it broke twice last month."

"Which is why," John continued, "you haven't collected a salary during the last six months."

Martin said nothing, thinking how minuscule that sacrifice had been. A year of his salary would not constitute one-fifth of what was due.

"I am right, am I not?" John asked.

"Doesn't matter." Martin placed his now empty cup on the credenza and offered a smile worthy of a studio executive. "I own my condo. I make enough freelancing to keep me in groceries and everything else I write off as a business expense."

John grimaced, his green eyes filled with sincerity. "You can't possibly make that payment, Martin. You only made half of the last one and you know the bank can't carry you again."

"I will find the money," Martin insisted, and he felt that confidence in every inch of his being.

John shook his head. "Where? You already sold your father's house. What other assets do you or your mother own? Your back is against a wall."

Martin attempted a rebuttal but there was no argument to the facts at hand. Confidence and faith were not assets on a bank statement. A silence lingered between them, one that threatened to swallow Martin whole.

"Martin," John finally said, "You are killing yourself trying to hold a failing company together, a business you had no part in creating. You are too talented to throw your life away at a losing battle. You deserve better than this."

For a moment, Martin concurred. He did deserve better. He wanted better.

But he had made a promise.

"I won't sell," Martin said sternly.

John patted him on the back, and then headed for the door. "I'm sorry, my boy, but you don't have a choice."

As the door closed behind the bank president, leaving Martin alone with his thoughts, he wondered how a day could start so peacefully and end up so aggravating. He wondered how and when he had fallen into such an impossible trap. Either way, he was doomed. If he stayed the course, the bank would repossess the newspaper and sell it to the *Times* on its own. If he sold the newspaper, he would emerge with a hefty inheritance and benefit his mother and siblings but he'd be selling his family's legacy to a cutthroat media empire. Turning his back on his father's promise.

The only way out was to find half a million dollars. And the only place Martin knew that offered that kind of reward was the California State Lottery.

Lizzy Guidry wondered how a day could start so peacefully and end up so aggravating. Before dawn she had taken her morning walk, relishing in the fog hugging the Santa Helena Valley and breathing in the heavenly scent that was Southern California in early winter: eucalyptus and pepper corn trees and the tangy scent of sage on the chaparral. She had to impress three county commissioners that day and after her trek up the mountainside felt empowered to meet the task.

Then came the letter. If only the mail had been an hour later, she would have missed it until that night, missed worrying about her future until after the dreaded meeting. But timing was not on her side that day. As of January first, the rent on her grandmother's room at the Mountain View Nursing Home would increase by three hundred a month. Three hundred dollars she did not have.

Happy New Year, she thought, pocketing the note in her running jacket.

"Don't they have to give you thirty days notice," Peter had asked when she returned home. "If I were you, I wouldn't pay it."

Lizzy cringed, mentally screaming that she was as far apart from Peter Dark as a chigger bug was to California. Of course, he wouldn't pay the increase; he didn't pay for anything! How had she managed to let her ex wiggle his way back into her good graces and her apartment? As her best friend Holly Phillips always said, Peter Dark could talk her into ice cream on the coldest day of the year.

When Peter followed up his lecture by asking for more money, Lizzy thought how the chigger was a good analogy when it came to her ex. Like the pests that inhabit her native South, chiggers dig deep under a person's skin until they are warm and comfortable, but they irritate the hell out of the host, causing a red welt and a nightmare of an itch.

She had handed Peter her last twenty, hinting that now would be a good time to make a fresh start. She had taken him in during the holidays, after his acting spot on a small cable sitcom had been cancelled and he had lost the lease on his Burbank apartment. But his agent had called the day before and things were looking up. Two auditions were scheduled and she wanted him gone.

"I'll be out of here by the time you get home," he had promised her, planting a kiss on her left cheek.

At least one thing had gone right that morning.

Driving home from the failed meeting, Lizzy listed the catastrophes in her mind, amazed at how so many could appear within one morning. Her car had failed to start, and by the time she had it running she was twenty minutes late and the freeway was packed with post-holiday shoppers.

When her cell phone rang, she spilled coffee on her new designer blouse, a blot that ran straight down her breastbone and permanently stained the expensive silk.

"Damn," she yelled, and then answered "Elizabeth Guidry" while pushing the talk button, then speaker so she could maintain one hand on the wheel while dabbling her blouse with a Kleenex.

She was greeted by two women laughing. "Hello to you, too."

"I didn't think you heard that."

"Are we interrupting something?" Dewey asked.

Lizzy was dying to speak to her Columbia journalism school buddies, nicknamed "The Cajun Embassy" because they had all hailed from Louisiana, but her psyche wasn't in the right place. The threesome reconvened every year for Carnival in New Orleans and this would be the first year Lizzy would miss the fun.

"It's not a good time, y'all," Lizzy said, dreading having to tell them the bad news. "I'm on the 5 and the traffic's horrible."

Only Dewey would understand that scenario; she worked for an entertainment magazine in Hollywood.

"What's the 5?" asked Maggie, who wrote for a regional publication in Memphis.

"It's hell on wheels," Lizzy said with a laugh. "The Golden State Freeway. And right now I'm late to a meeting downtown."

"We won't keep you then," Dewey said. "Just call us later and let us know about Mardi Gras because we're finalizing plans."

Lizzy's heart had fallen into her knees. Mardi Gras was the vacation she took every year and a time to kick back with good friends—the best! This year, however, the money wasn't cooperating.

"Will do," she had said, trying to keep the despair from her voice. "I'll call you later."

When Lizzy finally arrived downtown, she hated desperately for parking spaces, then ten minutes later rushed in the door of the county office building only to break a heel in the process.

By the time she had made it into the commissioner's office, the meeting had been cancelled. Probably for the best, she had reasoned, when she discovered a snag in her hose that hugged the back of one calf. Until she got the phone call from the commissioner's secretary saying they would not consider her ideas again until June.

Lizzy pulled into the Santa Helena's city parking garage, reminding herself to check her oil when the car sputtered into her spot. Turning off the engine, she leaned into the wheel, wondering where she would find three hundred dollars for Nana—or more to get her to New Orleans—or what she would do if her car finally died. She had to ask again. Tom owed her as much.

"You want what?" Tom asked, when she entered his office and approached him about the raise.

She started to retort until the mayor turned and stared out the window overlooking the Santa Helena Towne Centre. She expected resistance, but tension gathered between his shoulder blades as if he were angry.

"Is it because of the meeting?" she asked. "It couldn't be helped, Tom. My car is on its last leg. If I would have had a raise months ago like I asked, this might not have happened."

Tom turned his dark gaze upon her. "It's not about the meeting," he practically shouted.

She had never seen him this way, never heard that tone before. He had always been happy with her work, just strapped to find money in the budget.

Then she sighed, remembering the image consultant he was paying to raise his numbers in the polls. "It's that New York weasel, isn't it? What's Anthony saying about me this time? I already bought new clothes, which wiped out my savings account. Like that's really going to make a difference in the press you receive, anyway."

Tom's eyes flamed. "The press I receive, Lizzy, is exactly the problem."

He threw the *Santa Helena Banner* on to the desk, its page turned to the editorial section. Lizzy leaned forward and her heart stilled. The headline read, "Mayor Whitley expert in all he does."

Lizzy would have been optimistic about such a headline had she not known Martin Taylor and his sarcasm, his constant criticisms of the current administration. It had to be bad.

"Expert in hiding wrongdoings," Tom explained. "Expert in protecting friends."

Lizzy groaned. The District Attorney had been caught fixing tickets for his nephew, a joyrider who loved to speed the Santa Helena back roads in the early morning hours. The mayor had chosen the D.A.'s side, claiming the boy had hurt no one, and Lizzy worked days trying to gloss over the details to the press.

"Expert in double talk," Tom continued. "Expert in failing to meet campaign promises."

Tom had tried to make good on projects he had campaigned for, but the city council refused to budget half of them, nipping funds to the rest. The new crop of council members was on a budget-cutting roll and Tom's propositions had been its victims.

"I'm sorry, Tom," Lizzy said. "But you know I have no control over what Martin Taylor puts in his newspaper."

Straightening, Tom grabbed his coat and headed for the door. "That's your problem, Lizzy. You should have control. Next time you ask for a raise, try doing your job first."

Tom slammed the door behind him, and Lizzy's spirits,

whatever was left of them, sank to the floor. "What more could happen today?" she wondered aloud. Then a line in the editorial caught her eye.

"Let us commend the mayor's public relations director," Martin had written. "Another expert at City Hall who so aptly cleans up the mayor's dirty work. Someone should inform Elizabeth Guidry that she's in the wrong position. She would be better suited as the city's official pooper scooper."

A fire began in Lizzy's foot, the spot she had twisted when her heel had given way, and quickly burned up her spine, following the same path as the run in her stockings. She bolted upright as if the flames shot out the top of her head. "Pooper scooper?"

She had been wrong. The horrid day would not end.

Lizzy limped from the office, passing Holly, the mayor's executive assistant, on her way to the elevator.

"I guess you saw the editorial," Holly said, fighting back a smile.

Lizzy slammed her palm against the elevator button, but the damned thing didn't light. She then pushed it with all the force of her index finger.

"Don't be mad, Lizzy," Holly said. "No one reads that paper anyway."

The elevator doors opened and Lizzy stepped inside, then turned to face her friend. "I'll kill him," she uttered before the doors closed on Holly's grinning face.

LIZZY PULLED into the Mini Mart, thankful that some things were always reliable. After visiting her grandmother in the nursing home, it was close to eight and most businesses were closed in the peaceful valley several miles outside the nation's second largest city. The corner gas station-convenience store was open all night, its neon a beacon to Lizzy and her injured car.

"Hey Lizzy," Jeff called out from behind the counter.

"I need some oil, Jeff," Lizzy replied. "The light came on again."

"You got it." Jeff came around, picked up Lizzy's brand on aisle three and placed it on the counter. "That will be seven fifty-eight."

Lizzy paused, rubbing the bridge of her nose to remember what else she needed. "Oh yeah, Super Glue."

Jeff moved to come around, but Lizzy stopped him. "I'll get it. What aisle?"

"Four." Jeff sent her a wry smile and Lizzy imagined for a moment he was flirting with her. She answered with a grin of her own. Now, a man's attention would be a nice addition to this disastrous day, she thought, even a harmless flirtation.

"Saw your name in the paper today."

The anger she had carefully hidden from her grandmother returned. Tenfold. She hobbled to aisle four and grabbed a small tube of glue, her forehead pounding from the fury.

"Hey, don't take it seriously," Jeff said. "It is kinda funny."

When her burning eyes met his, Jeff cleared his throat and silently added the glue to her total.

A car pulled up and for a moment Lizzy hated being seen with half a shoe, a run in her stocking and a brown stain pasted across her chest. But the way she was feeling, the Queen of England could walk through that door and she wouldn't say boo.

"Well, speak of the devil."

Lizzy turned and watched in horror as Martin Taylor stepped out of his Ford Explorer and waltzed toward the Mini Mart. "It's his twice-weekly ritual," Jeff explained. "He comes in every Wednesday and Saturday to get a lottery ticket."

When Martin crossed the store's threshold, Lizzy wondered

if he had had a day much like hers. His usually expressive blue eyes were filled with worry and his shoulders slumped as if he carried a great weight. But what did she care?

He glanced up and seemed genuinely happy to see her, although he didn't offer his trademark charming smile, the one that made half the women in Santa Helena swoon. "Lizzy."

"Martin," she replied tartly.

He paused, a frown creasing his forehead, then looked over at Jeff, who shrugged. Could it be possible the man failed to remember he had made her the laughingstock of the entire Santa Helena Valley? She wanted to throttle him. No, torture him slowly.

"You're just in time, Mr. T," Jeff said nervously. "I have to shut down in three minutes. Let me take care of Lizzy and I'll get you your lottery ticket." To Lizzy he added, "Lizzy, your total is ten ninety-five."

"Lottery ticket." Lizzy thought her head would explode from the rage. Martin Taylor insults her publicly, keeps her from obtaining a raise that would keep a roof over her grandmother's head and now she has to hurry along so the infernal man could play a stupid game? "You must be kidding."

Martin finally focused his attention on her, still eyeing her curiously as if he didn't make the connection. "If you don't mind, Lizzy, they close the machines this time of night. They pick the numbers at eight."

The nerve of him infuriated her further, if that was possible. Slow torture wouldn't be enough. "Gee, Martin," she answered sarcastically, "how nice of you to remind me. I could use a lottery ticket myself."

Jeff cleared his throat. "I don't think there's enough time."

"Twenty seconds." Martin offered that charming smile, the one that lit up his all-too-perfect face. "I'll be out of your way."

Lizzy took a deep breath. Drawing herself up and placing a steadying hand on her hip, she blocked his path from the cashier. "You'll never be out of my way, Martin Taylor. Not as long as you keep printing those hateful diatribes you call editorials."

Martin cringed. Now, he remembered. "Lizzy, it was only one man's opinion."

"Only an opinion?"

Suddenly, the anger dissipated and Lizzy felt her senses clear. Slow torture was exactly what Martin Taylor needed. "Jeff, I'd like a lottery ticket."

"Quick pick?" he asked, trying to speed things along.

"No," Lizzy said with a smirk. "I think I will pick my own numbers. Don't you think that's the better way to do it, Martin?"

She sensed Martin knew what she was up to; he folded his arms across his chest and sighed.

"Yes," Lizzy said triumphantly. "I want to pick my own numbers."

"You have three minutes, Lizzy," Jeff said.

To his credit, Martin said nothing, just offered a defeated, aggravated smile.

"Four and fourteen," Lizzy said. "I think I'll start with my birthday since I was born April 14. Don't you think that's a good idea, Martin?"

Martin said nothing, continued to stare, his eyes frigid pools of blue.

"How many more?" Lizzy asked.

"Six and a bonus," Jeff answered, "but hurry."

"Twenty-seven for my age," Lizzy said. "Twelve for Martin's age."

Martin's cold eyes narrowed, but he remained silent. She could feel the animosity emanating from him and she felt victorious. And to think she actually found the jerk attractive once.

"Two minutes, Lizzy."

Glancing back at Jeff, she saw a designer name printed on his T-shirt. "Surfers 58" it read.

"Fifty-eight," Lizzy announced.

"You forgot the bonus number?" Martin offered. "How about two for your maturity level?"

Lizzy gritted her teeth, amazed how much anger still brewed inside her. "Fine," she answered, tilting her chin up. "Two it is."

Jeff immediately set the machine in motion and a square pink ticket popped out. There had to be moments to spare, but not enough time for Martin to purchase one. She folded her arms across her chest and met his gaze head on.

"Ten ninety-five," Jeff said. "And one dollar cash for the ticket."

Suddenly, the wind lifting Lizzy to victory disappeared and she crashed to earth. She had given Peter her last twenty that morning.

"Oh God," she muttered, "I have no cash."

Martin stared at her as if she had lost her mind, then ran a hand through his blond hair and shook his head. Before she had time to recover and plot another course of attack, he pulled a dollar from his pocket and threw it on the counter.

"It's on me," Martin said. He turned to leave, then paused as his hauntingly blue-eyed gaze met hers. "Thanks, Lizzy. That was the perfect end to a perfect day."

The hurt and frustration staring back at her nearly made her regret her attacks. She wasn't the mean and revengeful type, but Martin had touched a nerve. One that caused raises to be withheld and placed loved ones in jeopardy. For an instant, she hated thinking she was the cause of a person's bad day, but then she remembered all too clearly who had been the cause of hers.

"Just returning the favor, Martin."

Martin walked through the doors of the Mini Mart, climbed into his Explorer and drove away. After apologizing to Jeff, she placed her lottery ticket inside her purse and followed suit, her heel breaking clean as she crossed the threshold. With one breath, Lizzy reached down, snatched the broken shoe and flung it into the bushes. With equal agility, she disposed of the other. Then she entered her car and headed home.

At least Peter would be gone, she thought. She had that to look forward to. And maybe, just maybe if her horrid streak of bad financial luck would improve she might join her friends for Mardi Gras revelry this year and put this horrid holiday season behind her.

One block from her house, the car sputtered and stalled. A fear began in the back of her mind that she might have damaged the engine, but she pushed it away. She pulled to the side of the road and abandoned the tiny Tercel, mentally making a note to call Jevon in the Sheriff's Office who was good with cars. He would know what to do. Right now, she hadn't the brainpower to think.

Lizzy limped toward her apartment, the coarse cement of the sidewalk ripping her stockings further. A few steps more, she told herself, and she could fall apart within the safe confines of her home.

When she opened the door, the sight before her was more startling than all of the dreadful occurrences that day put together. Peter had left all right. Along with most of her furnishings.

She uttered an expletive, but the word emerged soft and slowly, as if spoken in awe to the force of an incredibly horrific day.

"You're late."

Chartreuse Bellamy was not Martin's idea of a rejuvenating evening, but he had promised to join her for dinner. "I had paper business," he muttered before hijacking the glass of wine in her hands with a grin, then falling onto her couch.

"The roast is burnt," she said matter-of-factly. "You better be prepared to take me out."

Martin rubbed the bridge of his nose, praying for relief from the constant pounding. Chartreuse had been good for a few laughs at the Chamber Christmas party, in addition to being supermodel gorgeous, but she confused ten minutes of flirting with a lifelong commitment. She called daily, insisting on every-thing from romantic dinners to long weekends in Mexico, now that she was between photo shoots and bored. He finally relented on her home-cooked meal when he ran out of excuses.

"If it's all the same to you, I'm not feeling very well." Martin downed the contents of the glass in one swallow. "I think I'll go home and get some rest. I'll owe you one, I promise."

"If you worked out more, you wouldn't be this tired."

Martin laughed, wishing it were that easy, but he couldn't help feeling less of a man by her remark. So many things had been put on hold over the past three years. "I'll start first thing tomorrow," he said with a sarcastic smile. "Right now, I'm going to work myself into bed."

Chartreuse wasn't buying it. She stood glaring with hands on her hips, one covered in an oven mitt shaped like Tweety Bird. "Fine," she said in an injured tone. "I'll throw the roast to the dogs and starve."

"You don't have dogs. And you starve yourself quite nicely without my help." Martin couldn't help himself. The few times they had talked, the pencil-thin woman—a strong wind could blow her away—never stopped whining.

Chartreuse sent him one of those smug, idiotic facial gestures, the kind girls used to bestow on him in grade school. Were there no mature women left in the world?

"Then go home," she announced with a pout that would have looked as authentic on a boa constrictor. "I'll spend my evening alone."

Martin stared at the auburn-hair goddess with long, slender

legs most men would itch to wrap around their waists, but all he envisioned was half a million dollars and the brown-eyed devil who held his ticket to paradise.

"It's Wednesday, Chartreuse," he said. "Eat a microwave dinner and watch TV like the rest of the world. I'll call you tomorrow."

To his surprise, she waved off his promises. "I'm through waiting for you, Martin Taylor. All those excuses about working late, you must think me a fool."

Martin laughed. He placed a comforting arm upon hers. "I assure you, any time you want to see me you can always find me at *The Banner*."

Chartreuse huffed and marched toward the kitchen so Martin placed his glass on to the dining room table and headed for the door. Before his fingers touched the doorknob, Martin spotted a memo on the end table. His chest constricted as he recalled each horrific number written there.

"What's this?" But he knew. The same figures Lizzy had ceremoniously pulled out of thin air.

"Your stupid lottery numbers," Chartreuse said. "I wrote them down for you when they announced them half an hour ago. Like you asked. A half hour ago when the roast was still moist."

Life was incredibly cruel, Martin thought, gazing at the memo with "Life's a bitch and so am I" printed at the top. The one night he misses a lottery ticket—buys it for someone else, no less!—and she picks the winning numbers.

He uttered an expletive, but the word emerged soft and slowly, as if spoken in awe to the force of an incredibly horrific day.

CHAPTER 2

*D*iane Wells waved her hands defensively as soon as Lizzy rounded the corner. "It was a printing error," the nursing home director exclaimed. "The increase doesn't go into effect until February."

The news slowed Lizzy down, but the panic remained. "It's three hundred dollars a month, Diane. Where am I to find three hundred dollars?"

Diane quickly moved around the counter, placed an arm about Lizzy and headed them into the lobby. "Not so loud," she whispered. "Mrs. Rodriguez is sleeping and you know what she's like when she doesn't get her nap."

Had she raised her voice again? What on earth was happening to her? First, she screamed at the policeman hauling her car away, almost to the point of getting another ticket, and now she was yelling at the woman who had created a loving home for her Nana.

"I'm sorry, Diane." Lizzy took a deep breath. "I'm having a string of bad luck and it's three hundred dollars! That may not sound like much to you but I'm a single breadwinner taking care of my grandmother."

There it was again, that high-pitched tone laced with panic. Among all her faults, Lizzy hated losing control the most.

Diane squeezed her shoulders. "We'll work it out."

"How?" Lizzy didn't mean to be unkind, but she had a car to contend with and an apartment devoid of furniture. She had an angry boss refusing to grant her a raise. Three hundred dollars might as well be three million.

"Go visit Nana and we'll talk later." Diane patted her arm one last time before heading back to her desk. "We'll work it out."

Lizzy tried to compose herself before moving down the hallway to Nana's room. Her heart raced, like it did every time she felt emotional and at the mercy of someone else. She prided herself on being independent, of relying on no one, of always being in the driver's seat. Ever since her parents' death and their brush with bankruptcy, Lizzy vowed never to let life grab her steering wheel.

But life had a way of doing what it pleased.

Nana's door stood open and Lizzy paused at the threshold, trying to force a smile. Nana had adamantly urged her to stay away from Peter, reminding her time and again that the handsome actor could not be trusted. But Lizzy had to learn the painful lesson on her own, finding him in the arms of his co-star, a tall, elegant actress with hair three shades of red.

Yes, she prided herself on her independence. Except when it came to a breathtaking smile beneath bewitching blue eyes begging her forgiveness five nights ago, promising the world if only she would let him use her couch for a few days. Rubbing the bridge of her nose, Lizzy wished, not for the first time, that she had her Cajun grandmother's insight.

"Are you going to stand there all day or wait until the cows come home?"

Lizzy gazed up to find Nana studying her. She moved into the room and planted a kiss on a cheek that was far more graceful than its advanced age and years of working in the south Louisiana sun.

"What are you doing here this time of day?" Nana asked. "I just saw you a few hours ago."

"My car broke down last night." She pulled her wrap about her grandmother's shoulders. "I'm on my way to work. Besides, I have a press event later so I won't be able to come by tonight."

"You don't have to come by every night, *'tit-monde.*" Nana took her hand and placed it against her cheek. "I done told you that. Go out and get a date, have some fun, pass a good time."

"I do have fun," Lizzy said. "I had a wonderful time at Christmas."

Nana dropped her hand and met her eyes. "Not with me, *chèr.* With someone your own age."

Lizzy turned toward the window and stared down into the meditation garden filled with succulents and cacti and wondering trails that led past a stream. Nana's nursing home, like the meager house they left in Bayou Rose, Louisiana, exuded a peace she could never capture in her own life.

"You look terrible," Nana said. "What you do, sleep on the floor?"

How true that was, Lizzy thought, but Nana didn't need to know the particulars. "I didn't sleep well."

"Does your insomnia have something to do with that conniving ex-boyfriend of yours?"

Lizzy held her breath. How on earth did Nana know that Peter had used her couch for five days? Nana's gaze narrowed as if she could read Lizzy's mind. "Dave said he saw him coming out of your apartment last week. Tell me you didn't let that bozo back into your life."

"He got kicked out of his apartment. I helped him out over the holidays."

"Lizzy!"

Lizzy began pacing, the familiar panic raising her blood

pressure. "I know, I know. I'm a naive idiot who makes bad choices with men."

"Only when it comes to *couyon* actors who think with other things besides their brains."

Lizzie almost smiled at Nana's Cajun French word for idiot, but thinking back on the previous evening, she wondered if she were a magnet for such creatures. "Seems to be a pattern."

"Hein?"

Despite having lived in Southern California for years, Nana sounded as if she'd walked off her husband's shrimping boat, marsh mud between her toes and a gumbo cooking on the stove. Lizzy savored the Cajun cadence that kept her connected to her parents, made her feel as if she were twelve years old again, skipping among the cypress knees and catching catfish for dinner. A time when she was content and free from fear.

"Peter's gone." Lizzy lifted her chin, feeling her old confident self return. "I assure you I won't make those mistakes again. I'm swearing off men for good."

"Well don't do that, *'tit-monde*. They're not all Peter. Did you call Jevon at the Sheriff's Office? He'll get your car up and running in no time."

Lizzy grinned, thinking of sweet Jevon who Nana placed high on the Richter scale of men. Even if she did fancy the mechanic—which she did not beyond friendship—Jevon only had eyes for Holly. And the car wasn't easily fixed.

"Well, it's a little more complicated than that."

"How come?" Nana stood and grabbed her cane, made her way to the mirror to ready herself for lunch.

"It stalled last night and I left it by the side of the road in front of my apartment. Apparently it was a tow-away zone and…"

The panic returned and Lizzy swallowed to keep the tears at bay. Nana turned and grabbed her in a bear hug, Lizzy relishing the feel of her strong arms from years of working the shrimp boats. The world could go crazy—and had—and Nana could make it all right again.

"Oh, *chèr bébé*," Nana whispered, "it will work out in time. Get that boss of yours to pull a few strings."

"My boss is angry with me," she answered against her shoulder. "That hideous man Martin Taylor published another tirade against him and he blames me for it."

Nana pulled back, a gleam in her eyes. "Is this the one who called you a pooper scooper?"

Anger, like a wild brush fire, poured through her veins, replacing the sadness. Her own grandmother had read the despicable editorial. "I swear I will kill that man."

Nana grinned, a sparkle reflecting in her brown eyes the color of a gumbo roux.

"What?" Lizzy asked.

"Seems to me that when a man goes to all the trouble to include you in an editorial, one about the mayor no less, he's trying to get your attention."

Lizzy huffed. "That's ridiculous. He humiliated me."

"It wasn't that bad." Nana waved her hand as if dismissing a gnat. "It got your attention."

"If he wanted my attention, he could have called me up and asked me out for coffee." An image of their first meeting flitted across her mind.

"What?" Nana asked, sitting down before her mirror.

Lizzy frowned. "He did ask me for coffee, the day I went to the paper and introduced myself."

"Ah, ha."

"That doesn't mean a thing." Lizzy rearranged the combs in Nana's hair. "He stared at my breasts the whole time. Of course, it was right after Peter left and I had gained weight and the sweater I was wearing was rather tight." She shook off the argument. "Doesn't matter. He's a womanizer."

"What does he look like?" Nana said, staring at her granddaughter in the mirror, the sparkle still shining. "And pooh on your weight. You're beautiful."

Thinking back on the numerous times the two had crossed paths, Lizzy had to admit Martin Taylor was quite a looker. As if she cared. "Typical California charmer. Blonde, blue eyes, smile like the devil."

"And you turned him down?"

Lizzy planted her fists on her hips and stared back. "Like Peter, he thinks with the wrong piece of anatomy."

A knock sounded behind them, then a woman dressed in a nurse's uniform leaned inside. "Time for launch," Consuela Rodriguez said in a thick Spanish accent. "Huliene fries, just like you like them, Mrs. LeBlanc."

"Merci, Consuela," Nana answered. When the smiling nurse disappeared, Nana turned to Lizzy. "They sure do talk funny 'round here. Me, I can't understand half they say."

Lizzy stifled a laugh, wondering how much Consuela understood her grandmother, especially when she woke from a nap spouting conversations in Cajun French.

"Go home," Nana said as Lizzy walked her down the hall to the dining room. "Call in sick and soak in a bath for a few hours. You'll feel better once you get some rest."

"Doubtful." Thinking back on the myriad problems facing her, nothing short of robbing a bank would afford Lizzy rest.

Nana stopped and gazed at her sternly. "Peter is gone, isn't he?"

Well, at least there was one bright spot in her disastrous week. Peter was not likely to come crawling back now.

"Yes, Nana. Peter is gone."

So is practically everything she owned.

"Good," Nana said with finality. "Go call this cute newspaper boy and see if he wants coffee."

Feeling dismissed but wanting the last word, Lizzy leaned

inside the dining room. "I told you, Nana, I have sworn off men."

"YOU'RE LATE."

If there was one person Lizzy didn't want to see that afternoon at the education press conference it was Anthony Billers. The New York consultant had been hired to boost the mayor's ratings in the polls, but so far had only succeeded in raising her ire. His ideas were sound, but his arrogant personality and his constant observations about her work grated on her nerves.

"My car broke down and I had to take the bus, which was twenty minutes late." Lizzy shook out her umbrella and tried to tame her wet hair. Months of gorgeous California sunshine and today it rains. Were all her planets in retrograde?

"You missed the press conference," Anthony said as if he were her boss. "And couldn't you have picked a more appropriate outfit?"

Her composure close to snapping as it had done the night before, Lizzy leaned forward so only Anthony could hear, poking him with the tip of her umbrella. "If you don't get out of my face, Yankee, I'm going to show you what a Southern woman is capable of."

Anthony, to his credit, never faltered. "And what would that be, Lizzy? Barefoot and pregnant, married to your first cousin?"

Lizzy stood and brandished her umbrella like a sword, wishing the tip had a point so that she could slice the blackguard's heart out. "Get off my back, Anthony," she whispered, surprising herself at the amount of anger in her voice. What was happening to her lately?

"I'd do as she says," a voice sounded from behind them. "You should see what she does with a lottery ticket."

Anthony pushed her umbrella aside sending her a warning

look, then transformed into a picture of cordiality. "Martin, what can I do for you?"

Lizzy expected to find Martin's typical heart-stopping smile, or that defensive grin he exhibited when people crossed his path or disagreed with his editorials. He could have been a politician with the charming way he handled his reading public. But today, Martin wasn't smiling.

"I need the figures on the school construction. Specifically Via Lopez Elementary."

A smug look came from Anthony as he turned his gaze toward Lizzy, but it was anything but agreeable. Lizzy's heart stopped. All of her press releases and statistics were back in the office.

"I, ah." Damn, she thought. She was losing control. Again.

Sea-blue eyes met hers and for the first time they stared at her accusingly. Was Martin furious over her lack of preparation?

"My car broke down," she began, defensively. "The statistics press release is on my desk but..."

"I'll get them to you right away, Martin," Anthony interjected. "You can count on it before deadline."

Anthony grabbed his raincoat, but stopped and turned toward Lizzy with a harsh glare. "I'm sure Ms. Guidry will be happy to fill you in on any details you may need."

Anthony bolted out the door, heading back toward City Hall, but Martin remained, his expression solemn. She knew Anthony expected her to kiss up to the publisher, but Lizzy couldn't stomach such insincere actions. Besides, this was Martin Taylor. He would print whatever he pleased. Even though his actions the day before had infuriated her, being a journalism graduate she admired his ethics all the same.

She placed her briefcase on the table and hoped appropriate information was inside, anything to keep from looking the idiot.

"I didn't expect to see you here today."

Lizzy turned from shuffling through her papers, a wet tendril falling into her face. "What?"

Martin leaned against the desk in that casual, sexy way he always did, but again the smile hadn't returned. "I thought you'd be on a beach in Hawaii by now."

Hawaii? The man had lost his mind. Lizzy laughed. "Don't I wish."

Lizzy managed to find the budget report for the elementary school through the calamity inside her briefcase. She handed it to Martin, who still stared, but now a frown had replaced his scathing glare.

"You're mad at me because I stole your lottery ticket? Look, I'm sorry. I was furious over your editorial..."

"Did you check it?"

Lizzy paused at his interruption, backpedaling her thoughts. "Check what? The school budget?"

Martin crossed his arms and Lizzy could have sworn he was the one who was furious. "The lottery ticket," he bit out.

Lizzy laughed again but she felt an annoying rush of tears behind. "Oh, the lottery ticket. Of course, how stupid of me. Here I am worried about my car in the pound and not being prepared at the press conference when I have several million dollars waiting at home. Gee, thanks, Martin. I'll rush home and head for Hawaii."

To her surprise, Martin's countenance shifted. He lowered his arms and his face softened. "You didn't check it?"

Now, the tears burned behind her eyes. "Why would I do that?" she asked, fighting them off and the emotions lingering in her words. "I never win anything and the last thing I need right now is another disappointment."

Knowing she would embarrass herself if she looked at him longer, Lizzy thrust the information into his hands and headed for the bathroom and a much-needed cry.

. . .

DEAR GOD, Martin thought. She didn't know she had won. Five million dollars was probably sitting on the bottom of that disaster she called a briefcase, more than likely cast aside like a useless scrap of paper.

Five million dollars!

Of all the luck. Martin had faithfully bought his tickets twice a week, never so much as winning more than five dollars, once the bonus number, and here Lizzy waltzes into the Mini Mart and claims the entire jackpot. Enough to save *The Banner*. Enough to help his family. Enough to put his life back in order.

And it was his dollar that paid for her winnings!

Lady Luck was definitely a woman.

"Young man," an authoritative voice sounded, waking him from his misery. "We have to talk."

The mayor and his entourage of assistants headed toward the door, but Tom Whitley paused long enough to send home a message, a directive Martin read loud and clear in his eyes. "Yes, sir, I think that would be wise."

"Tomorrow morning?" the mayor asked. "Ten a.m. in my office?"

Martin had no idea what his schedule allowed for Friday, but he owed the mayor the courtesy of meeting on his own terms. He didn't regret the words he had written in his editorial, but in hindsight they had been spiteful and abrasive. He liked Tom and agreed with his agenda, but abhorred his recent compliance with the City Council, a group of mealy-mouthed career politicians who fought change at every turn. Martin hoped the scathing editorial would light a fire under the mayor, but instead the piece had created a chasm between the paper and City Hall.

"Tomorrow will be fine," Martin agreed.

The mayor nodded while Holly helped him on with his coat. "Do you think you can halt your libelous remarks until then?"

Libelous? Martin had to smile. "You're a public figure, Tom, and you are open to criticism. It's hardly considered libelous and you know that."

"And what you called my public relations director?" the mayor retorted. "Ruining her reputation? Is that hardly considered libelous?"

Martin paused, knowing that damaging a person's reputation in print could be held accountable, but the comment had been humorous at best.

"He didn't ruin my reputation, Tom."

Lizzy approached the group, her eyes bloodshot and her cheeks puffy. Had she been crying? As much as Martin resented her stealing his winnings, he felt his anger dissipating. He could charm a woman into eating ice cream on the coldest day of the year, but he melted at the first sign of tears.

"I'm sure Martin meant it as a joke," she said softly. "I hardly think I will be unable to work in this town because of some stupid editorial."

Where before she had breathed fire and fury, Lizzy appeared as if she might break. Just then, a wicked idea came to him. Lizzy might need a friend right now, someone she might wish to repay for his assistance, especially since it was his dollar that made her rich. For the first time that morning, Martin felt hope. Perhaps *The Banner* wasn't lost after all.

"Still, use some restraint," Tom bellowed to Martin. "Your father would never have written such a thing."

If the mayor wanted to match fighting words, he hit his mark. Martin felt the wound clear to his soul. His father had commanded respect from the entire community of Santa Helena. Everyone met with his father at *The Banner*, on his turf, including Ronald Reagan when he courted his father's endorsement for governor. His father never had a poor Christmas season, nor did he ever lose subscription sales. Theodore Taylor fought off the *Los Angeles Daily Times* twice in attempted takeovers. And now Martin was practically handing them the company.

Looking at Lizzy in her defeated state, he knew what he had to do.

"Tomorrow then," the mayor said as he moved to leave.

"Tom," Lizzy said, touching the mayor's arm. "My car broke down in a tow-away zone. It's in the pound."

Tom glanced over at Martin. "Then get it out, Lizzy."

Lizzy pulled on the mayor's sleeve, tugging him away. "It's two hundred dollars," she whispered. "I thought you could call Darryl and use your influence to..."

Martin watched as the mayor feigned innocence, no doubt on his behalf, as he listened to Lizzy's tale. "I don't pull strings." Tom glanced in Martin's direction. "You know that, Lizzy. You're on your own."

Holly placed the opened umbrella over the Mayor's head and sent Lizzy a sympathetic look as they headed for the parking lot. When Lizzy turned back toward Martin, knowing he was the cause of the mayor's refusal to help, the tears had disappeared, replaced by an anger he knew all too well. But Martin had a plan.

"I have a friend at the pound," he said. "He owes me a favor."

Swallowing hard, no doubt to combat more tears, Lizzy shuffled past him to the table to retrieve her briefcase. "You've done enough for two days, Martin. Do me a favor and leave me alone."

Martin leaned against the desk, one hip against the side of her briefcase interrupting her actions. "Now why would I do that, Lizzy, when I have a warm, dry car and your ride just left?"

He expected his seductive words to warm her heart, but instead Lizzy bolted out the door, scanning the parking lot for the mayor's car. As she glanced around the half-deserted lot of the Board of Education, rain spotted her face. Whether it was raindrops or tears streaking her cheeks, the sight caused Martin's heart to constrict.

"Damn," he muttered to himself. He hated losing control.

Martin opened the door, feeling the rush of cold air greet him, snaked an arm about her waist and pulled her back inside the lobby.

"Get your hands off me," she protested, although again the fire had left her eyes.

"I have a car," he said firmly, like a big brother. "I'll take you home. It's too late to call the pound but I can pick you up in the morning and get your car."

"I don't want anything from you." She pulled free from his embrace.

"Then allow me, at least, to help you as a form of apology."

Lizzy stopped fighting and gazed suspiciously into his eyes. For a moment, Martin imagined she knew exactly what he was up to.

"I'm sorry about the editorial," he quickly said. "I didn't mean to include you in my condemnation of Mayor Whitley. I just thought you had better ethics than to clean up that clear disregard for the law by the District Attorney's office."

The fire returned, full force. "It's called a job, Martin. Maybe you don't know what that means, having had a newspaper fall into your lap, never having to worry about your next paycheck."

Martin couldn't help himself. He laughed, which only infuriated Lizzy further. The irony being played out before him was too much to bear.

"I assure you, Ms. Guidry," he bit out harshly, his humor gone, "that I do not live on Easy Street."

He meant it as charming sarcasm, but anger and resentment emerged with the words. Martin wanted to follow up with something funny, something seductive to cover his blunder, but Lizzy's features softened and she stared at him with new eyes.

For a moment, he swore Lizzy saw the real Martin Taylor. Not the joking bachelor who caressed women with his beguiling words, nor the brother and son who laughed off the problems surrounding the newspaper to his family, convincing them all he had both his life and his career under control. For a moment, he swore Lizzy saw right through him.

And it scared him to death.

Martin glanced out the window at the pouring rain, anything to escape her gaze. "It's storming pretty hard out there, do you want a ride or not?"

Whatever thoughts were floating through Lizzy's mind, she sobered with his question. "You don't have to be kind to me just because..."

"Where do you live?" He looked back at her, sending her the same authoritative look he gave his sister.

"An apartment building on San Fernando, near the park."

Martin picked up her briefcase and handed her the umbrella. "It's the Ford Explorer."

Neither one said a word on the way to the car, their shoulders bumping as they fought to stay under the protection of the umbrella. Finally, Martin tired of the awkwardness and placed an arm about Lizzy so they remained dry and walked in unison. Her hair smelled of lavender and felt like silk against his cheek and he wondered—again—what she would be like cradled in his arms.

"I can take it from here if you would unlock the door."

Martin looked up to find they had reached the driver's side. Where had his mind drifted off to?

Martin waited until she was inside and dry, then entered the Explorer. He drove the car on to the main highway while Lizzy sat silent, staring out the window.

"Why do you dislike me so much?" Martin couldn't believe he was asking such a juvenile question. He should be seducing her, not worrying about his feelings.

Lizzy turned slightly, enough that he could make out the soft rise of her upturned nose surrounded by a sprinkling of freckles. Her high cheekbones kissed by the sun accented her finest feature: two enormous brown eyes laced with long, luscious eyelashes. It had been those eyes that had entranced him on their first meeting. When she smiled, Lizzy Guidry could stop his heart.

But she didn't smile often in his presence. Although they had hit it off at first, when she had strolled into his office to introduce herself after the mayor's election, something in their conversation that afternoon had soured her. They had laughed, talked shop, and recounted Santa Helena gossip. By the end of the hour, Lizzy had turned defensive and cold, refusing his request for a cup of coffee. A harmless cup of coffee. For the life of him he couldn't understand what he had done wrong.

Unless it was the way his eyes refused to obey him, falling upon her breasts like a schoolboy. He couldn't help himself. Lizzy Guidry owned an adorable face, but she had the body of a goddess. Just the way he liked women too, soft and curvaceous, a woman he could hold on to.

"I don't dislike you," Lizzy finally said. "I'm just mad at you right now."

Mad, he could deal with. "Look, I'm sorry about the editorial. I didn't think calling you a name would hurt so much."

Lizzy's gaze met his and her eyes glistened with unshed tears. Dear God, Martin prayed, don't cry again. He hated when women cried.

"It's not about calling me a name. I need a new car, my grandmother's rent at her nursing home went up three hundred dollars a month, and Tom won't give me a raise because of your stupid editorial."

"Why would Tom hold your raise hostage because of my editorial?"

"Because he thinks I have control over what you write."

Now, Martin became furious. "What I write in my newspaper has nothing to do with you or the mayor. It's called freedom of the press. Surely, Tom knows this."

"Yes, but he's angry now and that doesn't get my car out of the pound or keep a roof over my grandmother's head."

"I'll help you get your car."

"It wouldn't be in the pound if it wasn't for you. I have an oil leak and I was buying a pint last night at the Mini Mart before I got distracted."

"Hey, no one asked you to steal the last lottery ticket."

Martin felt his heart racing, angry once again that she had won five million dollars, money that should have been his. But that was ridiculous. If he had bought the ticket last night, he wouldn't have chosen those numbers. It was an ironic stroke of luck.

Lizzy turned back toward the window, but he saw her wipe a tear away. "You can have the stupid ticket."

He should have agreed. It was a prime opportunity. Martin could take the lottery ticket, announce that he had won and hand her a nice portion of the winnings. Within a day, both their troubles would be over.

Instead, he found himself driving up to the Villa d'Italia.

Noticing they had stopped, Lizzy glanced his way with a questioning frown.

"Hungry?" Martin asked.

CHAPTER 3

*L*izzy had to admit, she was starving, having failed to eat past breakfast. But what she really needed was a soak in a hot bath, as per Dr. Nana's orders. Have another cry, maybe down the cheap bottle of wine Peter had so graciously left her, figure out what to do with her fragmented life. Before she had a chance to reject Martin's invitation to dinner, however, he turned off the engine, grabbed the umbrella and headed for the passenger's side. When he opened the door she tried to say no, but the noise of the rain made conservation difficult.

"They have a great fettuccine Alfredo here," Martin yelled and held out his hand.

While her brain attempted a refusal, her hand unconsciously reached out to his. Martin pulled her forward and underneath the umbrella, placed an arm about her shoulders and led her to the safety of the building overhang.

"It's not necessary," she said.

Martin shook the umbrella, then folded it. "Of course it is. I heard your stomach growling on the way over here."

Lizzy wished she could command her body to stop

betraying her. As hard as she fought to control her emotions, the tears kept coming. Now, she had to endure dinner with Martin Taylor because her stomach hadn't sense to keep quiet.

As if he read her thoughts, Martin frowned and Lizzy thought she might have offended him. "Would you rather I take you home?"

"Don't you have a deadline?" she asked, trying to place blame elsewhere. "Anthony is on his way over to your office."

"I'm not doing an editorial on the school until Saturday. Darren is doing the story tonight and he has all the information he needs. Even if he doesn't, the deadline is eight p.m."

"Then why did you ask Anthony for the stats?"

Finally, the old Martin emerged, a sly twinkle appearing in his eyes as the corners of his lips turned up in a smile. "Just between you and me," he said, leaning close. "I can't stand the man."

Lizzy couldn't help herself. She smiled. And the simple gesture warmed her all the way to her toes, made her feel like a person again. Briefly. Martin took the opportunity to open the door, place a hand at her back and urge her inside.

"Table for two, Mr. Taylor?" the maître d' asked.

"I don't know, Patrick," Martin replied with a grin, gazing around the deserted restaurant. "You think you can squeeze us in."

"Five o'clock on a Thursday." Patrick shook his head in mock exasperation. "I'll do my best."

He led them to a table next to a roaring fireplace, freshly made and burning bright. Lizzy pulled off her wet raincoat and savored the heat.

"How about two glasses of my favorite Sonoma pinot noir?" Martin asked Patrick, glancing back at Lizzy. "Something to take the chill off?"

Again, her body refused to obey her mind's warnings. "Sure."

The chairs surrounding the cozy table were lined in thick

cushions and Lizzy sank deep within their comfort. When the wine arrived, it left a cozy trail down her parched throat. Coupled with the fire kissing her skin, Lizzy wanted to crawl into a cocoon, close her eyes and shut out the world forever.

"Feeling better?"

Martin's sultry voice, as warm and inviting as the tranquil environment, slipped her deeper into her comfort zone. But the realization of who owned that enticing, sensual voice brought her back. Martin Taylor. The man who started her misery.

"Why?" she asked him, straightening. "Why are writing such hateful things?"

Martin began to speak, but Patrick arrived with a basket of bread. "Fresh soup today, Mr. Taylor. Our specialty."

"Sure, Patrick. Make that two." To Lizzy, he added, "You're going to love this soup."

Lizzy didn't appreciate not being asked, but she let it slide. "The piece you did on the District Attorney was downright cruel."

After taking a long drink of wine, Martin finally met her gaze. "You of all people should know that an editorial is a person's opinion. It's called Freedom of..."

"Freedom of the Press doesn't give you the right to be vindictive, abrasive, cold-hearted and mean."

His eyes brightened and he placed a hand on his chest as if he'd been struck. "You make me sound like an ogre."

"You're enjoying this."

Sobering, Martin sighed. "No, I don't want you thinking I'm vindictive, abrasive, and all those other things you mentioned. But it's an editorial, Lizzy. It's my job to point out to the public..."

"How Santa Helena's best is screwing up, is that it?"

She tilted her glass back and downed the rest of her wine, enjoying the sensation it offered. Feeling bold, she ventured further. "It was different when you first started. Your editorials offered logic, reason, and solution. You were the mouthpiece of *The Banner*, the voice of your community. Now, all you want to do is point out how everyone stumbles. Now, you're..."

"Now, I'm vindictive, abrasive and, what were the other two?"

"You're an award-winning publisher. You should hold yourself and the community in higher esteem."

"I'm an award-winning writer," he corrected her. "Ah, cold-hearted and mean, was that it?"

"It's almost as if..."

She was treading on dangerous territory. Sure, the man had infuriated her boss and stolen her raise, caused her to forget her car's oil, and made her look bad in front of Anthony. But *The Banner* was his paper and he could print what he liked. Still, the wine loosened her tongue. "It's as if you hate your job. As if you despise being publisher."

Where before her words had stolen the charm from his personality, now they produced a hollow stare, as if she had kicked the lifeblood from him. She expected a rebuttal, fighting words to match hers, but he grew solemn and still. Lizzy suspected she would hit a nerve, but nothing like this. For some reason, she had wounded him deeply.

"Our specialty," Patrick announced, as he placed two bowls of soup on to the table. "Would you care to order now?"

Martin said nothing, but thankfully his eyes moved to the soup before him. It was one thing to rob him of a stupid lottery ticket, quite another to insult his career and his family's business. Why couldn't she learn to keep her mouth shut?

"Care to try the fettuccine?" he asked softly, refusing to look at her.

Her appetite long gone, Lizzy shook her head.

"I think this will be all for now, Patrick."

The two sat in silence for several moments before Martin

picked up his spoon and began stirring his soup. "Why would you think I hate my job?"

Lizzy wished she were home soaking in a tub, closing her eyes to the problems that continued to haunt her. Why did she have to agree to dinner? "I'm sorry," she said, hoping to change the subject, finish her soup and get out of there. "I shouldn't have said anything. It's none of my business."

"Of course it's your business. It's everybody's business. 'If the newspaper doesn't speak for its citizens, it fails...' "

"...'to live up to its responsibilities,'" Lizzy finished.

They looked at one another, his gaze questioning. "You met my father?"

Lizzy pulled off a piece of bread. "I used to work for him, when I first got out of Columbia. He hired me to cover the School Board."

Martin attempted a smile and Lizzy hoped their conversation would head back to cordiality. She really needed to control her emotions. Badly.

"He used to say that the newspaper was owned by the Taylor family, but the community was its voice." Martin stared off into the fire. "He thought a good newspaper and the exchange of information and ideas were the basis of civilized society."

Lizzy had heard it all before, from the horse's mouth. Working with Theodore Taylor, although an old-fashioned newsman with chauvinistic tendencies who used to bark at his staff, had been a milestone of her career.

Martin grew silent again and Lizzy remembered it had only been three years since his father's death. It was upwards of twelve since Lizzy was orphaned and still she grieved as if it were yesterday. Lizzy reached for his hand, but thought better of it. "I'm sorry, Martin. I had no right to say what I did."

His countenance shifted and he straightened in his chair, like a deflated beach ball receiving a burst of air. "Don't be silly," he said, attempting a smile. "You have a right to criticize the critical."

Grabbing his own piece of bread, he added, "How's the soup? Is it not the best you've ever had?"

They ate in silence, finishing both soup and wine, and then Martin waved off her protests to pay. "I asked you to dinner, remember?"

Lizzy thought of Peter and all the times he had asked her out. Suggested dinner was more like it. "How about we get some Chinese?" he used to say. "Do you have any money?"

Whether it was the memory of Peter or the wine, her head began to pound. "If it's all the same to you..."

Martin rose, grabbing the bill. "We're on our way."

The ride home was equally quiet, the smell of something sweet drifting up from a paper bag on the seat. They arrived in front of her apartment building and Martin pulled up the parking brake. "Let me see you in."

Was he for real? Did he just ask her what she thought he asked? "Excuse me?"

Martin frowned, glancing at her as if she were crazy. "I don't leave women on the curb."

If she hadn't been so tired, so testy, her head about to erupt like Mount St. Helens, she would have been touched by his chivalry. But she was tired and irritated and her apartment held no furniture. Being raised a Southerner, she couldn't let a gentleman walk her to her door and not invite him in for coffee or a glass of wine. Anything.

Better to bolt, she reasoned. "Thanks," Lizzy said opening the door, "but I can take it from here."

Before she made her escape, Martin gently grabbed her elbow. "Here." He handed her the paper bag. "Patrick gave us dessert to go."

How sweet, she thought. For a second, Lizzy imagined their

dinner would have made a nice date under better circumstances.

"I'll pick you up in the morning," Martin added, letting go. "How's eight?"

She reeled through her brain as if it were the rainbow wheel on her Macintosh, searching for the right piece of information. Well, at least the Macintosh she used to have. "What's tomorrow?"

"Your car. The pound."

Her head blew a head gasket, she was sure. Another day of problems, another day wondering where the money would come from. Another day dealing with Martin Taylor. When she looked back to tell him it wasn't necessary, that she would find a way to get her car out of the pound, his deep blue gaze met hers and her body betrayed her one last time. His arm stretched casually along the top of the car seat, almost touching her shoulder while his damp blond hair fell lazily about his forehead. Before she had a chance to shove the image away, she fantasized about what it would be like for him to lean forward ever so slowly, wrap those strong arms about her and let her hands weave their way through his sandy locks while their lips met. She wondered if he was as good as he looked.

"Lizzy?" Martin leaned his head forward to meet her gaze. Her gaze that was resting on his lips. Dear God, what was she thinking? She needed to get out of there. Fast.

"Sure," Lizzy said, climbing out of the car. "Eight is fine."

She thought she heard him say something before she slammed the car door shut. Without turning back, she bolted through the rain and into her building.

MARTIN STARED at Lizzy's retreating form, wondering what he had gotten himself into. Charming women had never been a problem, but this one was an enigma. So far, he hadn't even thought about getting to first base, he was too busy defending himself.

Tomorrow morning he would take her to the pound and retrieve her car, but not before he insisted she check her lottery ticket. Best to get the damn thing over with. She might say thanks, cash in her five million dollars and tell him to take a hike, but that was a chance he would take. He needed this done.

"Of all the women in the world, it had to be her," he mumbled as he headed back into traffic.

Still, the way she had looked at him just then, he could have sworn...

"No," he commanded himself. "This ends tomorrow. I have more important things to think about."

The cell phone buzzed, a six p.m. ritual, and Martin didn't have to be psychic to know what it entailed. Mac had started the weekend tabloid run and one of the four-color presses had jammed. If not all of them.

"Hi, Mac," Martin said into the phone.

"Hey," the pressman returned. "How did you know...?"

"What's the problem this time?"

"Cyan's giving me trouble. I swear this baby has it in for me tonight."

"I'll be right there."

Good thing he had eaten. More than likely it was going to be a long night. Martin hit the end button and threw the cell phone on the seat, dreading the thought of struggling with the giant machine, Mac talking his ear off about his failing bowling league and coming home once again with his clothes and body stained with ink. Rolling his head to relieve some of the tension in his neck, Martin thought back on his early days in journalism, when every day brought an exciting possibility. Back to the days when he covered events, discovered issues and wrote about people who made a difference. Now, he was lucky to get an editorial out twice a week. Even if they were cold-hearted and mean.

"It's as if you hate your job."

Lizzy's words haunted him, exposed him, and forced secret feelings to emerge that were better left hidden. Did he hate his job? Did he resent being one Taylor of three who inherited the legacy? Damn it, he was a writer, not a savior of *The Banner*. Definitely not publisher material like his esteemed father. Lizzy made that all too clear.

But these days he was *The Banner*'s only hope. And so was Lizzy.

He needed that money. He would see her tomorrow, play his hand and move forward. He would keep *The Banner* alive, forget his own desires for now and do what needed to be done. He was the third generation Taylor who owned a newspaper, one that needed saving, and that was all that mattered.

Didn't it?

Around daybreak Lizzy woke to the soft tapping at her window, as if tiny fingers were urging entrance. Years had passed since she and Nana had moved to California and still the delicate sound amazed her. Rain didn't fall in Southern California. God dipped his hands in water and flicked drops on her window.

Los Angelenos claimed it rained. Lovers of cars and the constant hum of the open road, they shut themselves inside and refused to drive as if the water might be as toxic as the smog. Television stations led their news with the story, reporting on every area of the wet Southland until the first commercial.

"Two-thirds of an inch have fallen in the Valley as the storm continues to hover over the city," the newscaster would report as if a hurricane approached.

Two inches used to fall within fifteen minutes back home.

Two inches in one thunderclap that shook Bayou Rose like a five-pointer earthquake. Lizzy remembered driving in rain that fell in torrents, so much water in one short span of time half the drivers would pull off to the side of the road until it passed. And it usually did within minutes. Then the next afternoon, the scenario would repeat itself. If she had refused to drive in the rain back home, she never would have traveled anywhere.

Home. Lizzy pulled the blanket tight around her chin, thinking back on the sleepy bayou town they had left in a hurry. It really wasn't her town, having grown up in New Orleans. Her parents had moved away from Cajun Country before she was born, her father working for Avondale Shipyards on the river at New Orleans, the three of them living in a shotgun house off Magazine Street. But like her mother, she considered Nana's house and the sleepy bayou a place that repeatedly called her back, offering her spiritual replenishment and ties to a lengthy cultural history.

Louisiana—a state where it didn't have to rain for moisture to permeate the air, where every day the weather changed. Lizzy tried to remember what that felt like, the sticky sensation of hot August when her clothes became pasted to her skin or the cold rush of air before a thunderstorm rolled in. Did she miss it? Would she go back if Nana agreed? Unlikely. Ten thousand crowbars would have to pry her grandmother from her beloved nursing home and the friends she had made. And where Nana resided, so did she.

Lying back and feeling the floor beneath her, Lizzy sighed. Her adventure ended here, in Santa Helena. Broke, broken-hearted and alone in the Golden State.

A knock at her door jolted her from her thoughts. Lizzy glanced at the clock hoping she was mistaken, but after rubbing her eyes and looking again, she realized she had overslept through the darkened dawn. "Damn."

She slid off her makeshift mattress and pulled on a robe,

reaching the door by the time Martin had knocked again. She ran a quick hand through her hair to tame its madness, than opened the door.

He looked perfect as usual, casual and slightly un-ironed but clean and smelling as if fresh from a shower. "Sorry," she said, glancing down to make sure nothing was exposed. "I overslept. Usually the sun shines right on my face at seven, but it's raining."

"No problem."

He offered his trademark smile then entered the apartment. While Martin headed left into the living room, Lizzy darted into the kitchen to check herself in the face of the wall clock, but couldn't make out her image. "Do you want some coffee?" She peered through the pass-through.

His back was to her, but she saw him nod. While she produced two coffee cups from the cabinets, the apartment grew silent. Within a heartbeat, he was at her side.

"What happened?"

She turned to find him staring at her with concern, like a big brother finding his baby sister in the hands of a bully. It was eerily familiar, as if they were old friends and he had rushed to her side, sword in hand. But that was impossible; they barely knew each other. What did he care about her problems?

"I, ah." Where to begin? "It's nothing, really."

"Nothing?" There it was again, that fraternal tone. "You have no furniture!"

Lizzy glanced at the bare living room, looking oddly irregular with three bookshelves full of books and pictures on the wall, but nowhere to sit.

"I still have my books," she said with a sarcastic smile. "But then I don't think Peter knew how to read."

"Who's Peter?" Martin crossed his arms about his chest making his jacket strain across his shoulders. Before she had a chance to catch herself, she wanted to hug him for being so protective.

"He's my... He was my boyfriend." Lizzy grabbed her coffee can and poured four scoops into the machine, mainly to escape his piercing gaze. "I let him crash here over Christmas because of some sad luck story. He repaid me by cleaning me out." Lizzy smirked thinking back on their meeting at the Mini Mart. "That's why I didn't have cash the other night. I gave him my last twenty."

She could feel Martin's stare burn into her back so she turned to gauge his reaction. The look he offered had changed from protective to something else, guilt perhaps? What would he have to feel guilty about, unless all blonde, handsome men in California had a conspiracy going? Right now, she didn't doubt it.

"Where's your lottery ticket?" he asked.

"What?" Lizzy laughed. "You don't give up, do you? I told you I have no luck. Look around."

Martin headed into the living room, searching its contents. "You have a newspaper handy?"

"I don't have a subscription." As soon as the words emerged, she wished she could retract them. He grimaced as if someone sliced a knife in his side. "I read it at the office," Lizzy quickly added.

Martin said nothing and headed for her bedroom. "We can check it online. Where's your computer?"

Lizzy hit the on button of the coffee maker, and then searched the fridge for food. "Are you hungry?" she yelled out.

As she predicted, he returned to the kitchen within seconds. "He took your bed?" Martin practically yelled. "What kind of bastard would do such a thing?"

Eggs, onions and potatoes. She could whip up something with this. "I can make you some breakfast. How about a glass of orange juice?"

Martin crossed his arms again. "How can you be so calm about this?"

"He did put my files on a disk before he nabbed the computer. "That was very considerate of him, don't you think?"

When Martin's gaze intensified, Lizzy placed the orange juice on the counter and sobered. "I'm done crying. I'm close to dehydration so forgive me if I sound flippant. If I don't find some humor here, I'm going to go crazy."

He leaned so close she could smell his aftershave, something light but utterly masculine, and he rubbed her upper arms in a comforting gesture. He didn't look at her, just frowned, deep in thought. For the life of her she wished she could read his thoughts.

"I'm sorry," he said so softly, it sent a spell of shivers up and down her spine.

"It's okay," Lizzy whispered back. "I wasn't in love with him, if that's what you're thinking."

She didn't know why she admitted as such—it wasn't any of his business—but something deep inside her wanted the record cleared.

"Have you called Dave?" Martin asked, removing his arms and leaving her oddly cold.

Lizzy returned to her breakfast-making duties, grabbing the eggs from the fridge along with a large bucket of margarine. "No. He and my grandmother are good friends and I'd rather she didn't know about this. She worries enough as it is and Peter was not her ideal choice of a man."

"Smart grandmother, but you have to report this."

Calling the sheriff wouldn't solve anything. Besides, she could handle this on her own. She always did. She turned to set Martin straight, but he had left the kitchen. Peering through the pass-through, she spied him on his cell phone, but before she had a chance to protest, he was connected.

"Dave, this is Martin."

A loud voice answered on the other end; Lizzy could almost make out the sheriff's words. Martin cringed, rubbing the bridge of his nose. "I know Dave. I understand. I'm sorry if you didn't like my editorial, but can we discuss this later?"

Martin glanced up at Lizzy and their eyes met and something unspoken passed between them. For a split second, they weren't enemies, operating on different sides of a political spectrum, but two journalists constantly dealing with the ire of a critical public. She smiled sympathetically and he grinned sadly back.

"Dave," Martin said with finality, "let's talk about this later. Lizzy's boyfriend has stolen her furniture and she needs to file a report."

Lizzy took the opportunity to head into the living room, ready to grab the phone and insist otherwise, but by the time she reached Martin's side, he had hung up. "He's on his way."

"Martin!" she exclaimed. "Dave has better things to do than trace after my few belongings. How's he going to find Peter in all of L.A.? Most people never get back items that are stolen…"

Martin wasn't listening. He was busy pacing her apartment, studying the outline of her living room and dining area. He glanced up briefly, mentioned something about going to his condo and being right back, then left. In a heartbeat, she was alone.

But it didn't last long. Within five minutes, a police cruiser pulled up to the curb, parking in the same tow-a-way zone that had stolen her car.

"You shouldn't park there," she told Dave when she opened the door and he gave her an enormous hug. She hadn't seen him in months and the hug from the giant sheriff felt like heaven.

"Dear God, what the hell has that boy done now?" he bellowed.

Lizzy sighed. "Well, at least I won't be seeing him again. There's a lot to be said for that."

The look Dave offered was anything but humorous. The salt and pepper-haired sheriff had assisted Nana and Lizzy when their car had run out of gas years before on their trip west, when Nana had gazed upon the mountains of Santa Helena and proclaimed it a sign, that this was their new home. He had helped them find a place to live, introduced Lizzy to Theodore Taylor and helped them fight her parents' probate issues. He had been her hero once, and in hindsight, she should have called Dave first thing. Sometimes, in all her moments of martyred loneliness, she forgot there were people who could help. Forgot there were people who cared.

Now, she felt ashamed.

"Want a cup of coffee?" she asked him.

"Love one, sweet pea." Dave followed her into the kitchen, leaned against the counter and pulled out a notebook. "Now tell me everything that happened."

BY THE TIME MARTIN RETURNED, Lizzy appeared in better spirits, laughing with Dave about some past experience and serving up something colorful that smelled spicy and delicious. Her hair was still mussed from sleeping, one strand defiantly standing at attention, and she lounged against the kitchen counter in her robe and crew socks while underneath he could make out a T-shirt and boxing shorts. How did she do it, he wondered. How could she stand there looking so ordinary and casual yet so amazingly sexy?

And why couldn't he do the one simple thing he had set out to do?

All his good intentions to rid her of that lottery ticket disintegrated the moment he walked into her apartment and gazed into those defeated brown eyes. Hadn't he seen the same despair staring at him from his mother's face, a time when he was powerless to help? It wasn't fair. God was having a joke at his expense, knew exactly what buttons to push. Five million was going to be a lot harder to obtain than he thought.

Lizzy glanced in his direction and lifted a cup of coffee. "Want some?"

"Actually, I need to borrow Dave for a moment."

Dave sent him a surprised look but said nothing and followed him out the door. "What's up?" he said on the way down the stairs.

"I've got a bunch of furniture that was my father's," Martin said as he headed toward his Explorer. "It's been clogging up my condo for months now."

He opened the back of the SUV and pulled out a small oak table.

"This is an antique." Dave slid fingers across the grain, admiring the wood. "Lovely piece. Mission, I believe. Your father had great taste."

"Yeah. It's a table to eat on if you ask me."

Dave grabbed the piece and began climbing the stairs while Martin followed with two chairs. "Don't you like antiques?"

"Not particularly." Martin remembered the musty show-rooms his father used to drag him to on Sundays. "It was my father's hobby. Never had much time for his family but every once and awhile he made time to go antique shopping."

Martin placed the chair on the landing at Lizzy's door and took a breath. There was tightness in his chest but it had nothing to do with the exertion. He felt Dave's hand on his shoulder. The two men didn't look at each other, but Martin got the message and was thankful for it.

Suddenly, Lizzy threw open the door, gazing from one to the other to the table. "What's this?"

Martin studied the woman across the threshold, a woman who held the future of his newspaper in a piece of paper possibly crumpled at the bottom of her purse. They had both suffered a devastating week. If anyone was in need of five million dollars, it was the two of them.

But something within the light of those auburn eyes urged him on to richer pastures. He couldn't explain the sensation, but knew there was a bigger force at work here, a friendship waiting to be developed. He would charm that money, of that he was sure, but for now Lizzy needed him. And something deep inside his heart told him he needed her just as much.

CHAPTER 4

*I*t took another trip to Martin's condo to produce two more chairs and a portable TV and suddenly Lizzy's apartment appeared less barren. Glancing around the living room, Martin surveyed the side wall.

"I have a couch that would fit perfectly over there. It's a set. Comes with an easy chair."

Lizzy handed Martin a cup of coffee, glancing uncomfortably in that direction. "I can't accept this. These are expensive pieces."

"They were my father's." Martin shrugged. "And you're doing me a favor. My condo has been suffocating with all this furniture."

"But…"

He knew what she was going to say next, but he didn't want further arguments. Next to being free of the furniture that reminded him daily of his father, who was as overbearing as the heavy wood, the loan would make Lizzy indebted to him. "But nothing," Martin answered with a smile. "How about that breakfast you mentioned."

Lizzy nodded and hurried to the kitchen, while Dave waved

as Martin raised the cup to his lips. "What?" Martin asked.

"Just wanted to prepare you," Dave whispered. "She likes her coffee strong."

"So do I."

A sly grin stole across the sheriff's face. "Not that strong. That stuff will grow hair on your chest."

Lizzy joined them again with a plate of home fried potatoes laced with peppers and onions and smelling spicy. She glanced from one to the other as if she knew what they were talking about. "Would you like some cream or sugar?" she asked Martin. "My coffee's a bit strong for California tastes."

California tastes? He had to smile. Most West Coast residents spent their lives with one hand cradling a cell phone, the other holding an iced mocha. Caffeine was his life. He had even gone as far as importing his favorite coffee via the Internet.

Martin took a sip, while all eyes watched him for a reaction. The coffee was definitely strong, but offered a familiar bite. If he wasn't mistaken, it resembled the same coffee he drank. But that was impossible.

"Tastes wonderful. In fact, it's a lot like the coffee I drink at home."

"Doubtful," Lizzy said, placing the potatoes on the table and letting her fingers savor the elegant wood in the process. "My cousins back home send me that coffee. You can't get that brand out here. It's got chicory in it."

Martin took another sip to be sure he heard right. Yep, it was his coffee all right. "Community."

Lizzy glanced up from placing forks and plates on the table. Back home. Her familiar accent that came through every once and a while, particularly when she became emotional. The name Guidry. The knowledge hit him full-force. His luck was finally turning. He had found his trump card at last.

"Dear God, you're Cajun."

Lizzy straightened with her hands on her hips, the lone hair still poking up defiantly on top of her head. "How did you...?"

"How could you not know is the question?" Dave dumped two more spoonfuls of sugar into his cup. "I get heartburn every time I eat here."

Still gazing at Martin with a puzzled expression, Lizzy managed to slap Dave playfully on the arm. "How did you know that? And how did you know it was Community Coffee?"

"I told you, I drink it at home."

Lizzy reached through the pass-through and grabbed a plate of eggs, toast and a coffee pot, than sat down opposite Martin with a distrustful air. Martin almost laughed, having seen that look before on Cajun faces in Thibodaux, where he spent his formative years in journalism. A time when he had tried his college French on the bayou citizens, hoping to be accepted, and mostly were rewarded with skeptical glares like hers—or hysterics—in return.

"I got hooked on the stuff when I worked for *The Comet*," Martin explained. "It's a newspaper in..."

"In Thibodaux," Lizzy finished.

"It was my first job reporting." A giddy rush stole up Martin's spine, realizing they had something unique in common, something he could use. "I spent three years in Louisiana."

Nodding to the coffee, he added, "I do believe they put more than chicory in that stuff because it has spoiled me for all others. It's quite addictive. It costs me an arm and a leg to get it on the Internet but I've gotta have my Community."

Lizzy couldn't help herself. Her jaw fell open. Six years in Santa Helena and she never met one person from her home state, not one soul who knew what chicory was or that being Cajun was more than adding spice to your food. Yet, here sat the one person to make that connection. And it was Martin Taylor.

"My first year out of UCLA, I got a general reporting assignment for *The Comet*." Martin dipped into the plate of eggs, loading up his plate. "Three wonderful years and the best food I've ever eaten."

Lizzy quickly glanced down at the plates before them and wondered if she had added enough green peppers to the potatoes or if the eggs needed more seasoning.

"Where did you live?" he asked through a forkful.

"New Orleans, but my family's from Bayou Rose." If only she had another onion. And real French bread, rather than her store-brand wheat.

"Down by Montegue, right?" Martin's eyes glistened with the memories. "I used to go fishing down there. Nothing like the bayou first thing before sunrise, all solemn and still."

A wave of nostalgia overtook Lizzy at the image of the sleepy town she and Nana had deserted just before sunrise one morning six years before. The bayou had been solemn and still that day, deathly silent save for Nana's soft weeping and the engine of her ancient Oldsmobile struggling to clear the Bayou Rose bridge.

"Well, if it isn't a small world," Lizzy heard Dave say, but all she comprehended was two reminiscing blue eyes, which deepened after Martin tasted her potatoes. After several chews, he closed them and moaned with pleasure.

"I take it they live up to your memories." The thought of pleasing someone with her cooking, something as simple as home-fried potatoes, gave her a thrill she hadn't felt in a long time.

Martin continued to moan and grin like a schoolboy, but he managed a nod, right before he washed down the breakfast with a sip of her chicory coffee. When he finally came up for air, he offered the grin Lizzy saw him bestow on half the world on a regular basis, the one that charmed its recipient all the way to her toes. And she felt it, like a lightning bolt shimmying down her spine. Thank God she had on socks to ground the electrical charge.

Socks.

Suddenly, her excitement turned to fear. Dreading having to look down at the disheveled sight she must be, Lizzy ran a hand down the front of her chest, cringing as she realized she was still in her pajamas. She quickly checked the tie to her robe to make sure it was fastened and not exposing her breasts to the world, then ran a hand through her hair, wondering what horrid shape it was in. "I must dress," she said, rushing from the table.

"Wait," she heard Martin say. "Where did you go to school?"

There were so many questions, so many things to discuss, but at that moment Lizzy had to regain her composure, re-establish her control. She headed for the shower to calm her unruly hair.

And to tame her wildly beating heart.

"WHY DO WOMEN DO THAT?" Dave asked, as Lizzy hastily shut the bedroom doors behind her. "She looked fine to me."

She looked more than fine, Martin thought, but he shook the image away. "Some potatoes, Dave?"

"Hell, no." The sheriff leaned back in his chair and stared down into his full cup of coffee. "Don't know how you can eat her cooking. Too hot for me."

"It's not about heat," Martin said through bites, enjoying every minute. "It's about cooking spice in your food, just enough to excite the palette and warm your insides. The Cajun cuisine you get out here isn't the real thing. It's food with too much pepper."

Dave wasn't convinced. "I like it bland. White bread, margarine. People weren't made to taste food twice, if you catch my drift."

Martin raised an eyebrow at his old friend. "What does my mother see in you?"

Even though he teased, it was the wrong thing to say and Martin instantly regretted his words. Dave dropped his chair back to the floor and landed the coffee cup hard on the table, spilling its contents. Then he grimaced and stared at some object on the far side of the room. "How is your mother?"

The same as the rest of his family, Martin thought, still reeling from his father's death, still trying to pick up the pieces of their lives. "She's housesitting in Ojai. A good friend of hers is spending a year in Italy. You know my mom, she's taken over her garden."

Dave grinned slightly, but his brow remained tense. "It probably could feed Santa Helena by now."

A silence stretched between them, one filled with an emotion Martin knew only too well. So many dreams unfulfilled.

Quickly and deftly, before Dave caught on, Martin pulled a business card from his wallet and slid it toward his friend. "Her number, in case you need to contact her."

Dave shook his head, but his fingers lingered over the card. "We had an agreement."

"Screw the agreement." Martin got up to bring dishes into the kitchen and allow Dave a chance to put the card away without being embarrassed. "A quick phone call to say hi won't matter."

"She insisted on this, not me," Dave yelled through the pass-through.

Martin began rinsing the dishes and placing them into the dishwasher. Dave was saying something, no doubt explaining his position again, but the water drowned out his words. Just as well. Martin had heard it all before, from both sides, and neither argument was getting either of them anywhere.

"Don't do that."

Before Martin could interpret the voice, a hand grabbed the dish from his grip. "You're my guest," Lizzy said. "Now, go finish your coffee."

Her soft brown hair cut in a bob lingered right before his face as she slid the dish into the prongs of the dishwater. When she brushed his shoulder, he inhaled the scent of lavender soap and freshly cleaned clothes, and for a moment stood helpless at the sight and smell of her. What was it about this woman that disintegrated his calm? Was his nervousness due to the fact that he was planning to deceive her of money? Or was it something else?

"I make a good gumbo." Dear God, where did that come from?

Lizzy straightened, turning her head at a coquettish angle and it was then Martin realized she wore no makeup, her freckles free of that concealing formula women loved to use. Her eyes and enormous lashes, too, sparkled of their own accord. She even smiled at him, one side of her lips twisted in merriment, causing a small dimple to emerge. The sight of her face warmed him more than her spicy potatoes.

"I'll bet you do, Martin."

Like a sledgehammer to the chest, Martin realized he was back at first base. She wasn't buying his charm, nor did she believe him. "I do make a good gumbo," he said in his defense, feeling like a schoolboy trying to enthuse a girl. He couldn't remember when a woman was so hard to impress.

"Well, Sweetpea," Dave said from the living room, "I have to get back to the station."

Lizzy wiped her hands on a dishtowel, then met the sheriff at the front door for a hug. As Martin watched them embrace, his chest tightened. Outside of an occasional hug from Cassie and his mother, it had been a long time since he shared a connection with another human being.

Dave pulled away and looked at Lizzy sternly. "Next time

something like this happens, you call me." Lizzy nodded, but Dave placed a finger under her chin and forced her to meet his eyes. "I mean it, Lizzy Guidry. That's what friends are for."

Tears welled up in Lizzy's eyes and she hugged Dave again. "I'm sorry, Dave."

"The trouble with you, Sweetpea, is you want to carry the world on your shoulders. Share some with the rest of us, okay? That's how people get through the hard times, by helping one another."

Dave patted her shoulders and opened the door, but he paused and looked back at Martin. "And you. Stop printing those hideous editorials or I'll personally drive over to that newspaper of yours and kick your butt."

Martin wanted to argue his point, mention that the District Attorney was still wrong in his actions, but he bit his tongue and nodded. Dave was a good friend and a good cop, and Martin knew he stood by his colleagues as well as his friends. He extended his hand and Dave shook it.

"Any time you want me to help you with that couch, let me know," Dave added as he headed out the door.

Lizzy folded her arms. "What couch?"

"The one that comes with my excellent gumbo." Martin grabbed his coat and her purse, then placed a hand at her back and nudged her toward the door. "Come on, we'll talk about it on the way to the car pound."

Lizzy glanced at her watch. "Aren't you supposed to be meeting the mayor this morning?"

Martin checked his own watch. Ten minutes to ten. "Damn," he said, shutting the door behind them. "We better get going."

She followed him in silence until they reached the front of the building, then Martin held the door open for her to join him. She passed him with an apprehensive glance.

"Do you mind if we swing by your office first?" Martin

asked, opening her door to the Explorer. "As soon as I talk to Tom, we'll head over to the pound."

Lizzy nodded as she entered his car, but Martin felt something wrong with the atmosphere between them. Was she still mad about the editorial? Would he ever get past that indiscretion?

He entered the driver's side and roared the car into action. As he pulled into traffic, he stole a glance in her direction. She twisted the straps of her purse into knots while biting her lower lip. "Lizzy, look, I know you're still upset about what I wrote."

"I'm not upset anymore." She frowned as she straightened out the crease in her pants. "You see, I called in sick when you left to get the table."

It took a moment for the information to sink in, then he began to laugh. Soon, Lizzy was joining him.

"I've never done that before," she said. "My grandmother talked me into it last night, thought a day off would help. But as you can see, I'm certainly not sick."

"Do you want to wait in the car?"

Lizzy pulled the visor down and examined her hair. "No, someone will surely see me. And then it will be worse."

"Do you want me to take you to your apartment? I can come back."

She met his eyes and offered him a sweet, albeit small grin. As simple as the gesture was, for the first time in two days, it gave him hope. "I'll think of something."

They rode the rest of the way in silence, barely moving past polite conversation from the parking lot up the elevator. Lizzy preferred it that way, searching her brain for a plausible explanation to the mayor and the rest of the staff. But when Holly looked up from her desk and spotted them entering the office together, Lizzy felt all logic escape her. How would she explain Martin?

"Holly," Lizzy said to the secretary whose gaze kept

bouncing back and forth between the two of them. "Martin Taylor has an appointment with Tom for ten."

Before Holly had a chance to react, Tom appeared on the threshold of his office and called out Martin's name. Lizzy could feel the tension build in the man standing next to her and, had it been yesterday, she might have enjoyed his discomfort. Instead, she sneaked him a side-glance, one that spoke of encouragement. Martin seemed to get the message, for he smiled grimly back.

"What on earth are you doing with that horrid man?" Holly asked once Martin had left the front lobby. "And why are you here? I thought you were sick."

"I am sick," Lizzy answered with a fake cough. "Can't you tell?"

She headed for her cubicle to check her email and phone messages with Holly hot on her heels. "You came in with that infernal man."

Lizzy plopped into her chair and began sorting through her mail, turning on her computer with her left hand. "He's not that bad, Holly. He's been helping me."

"Helping you?" Holly sat opposite Lizzy, leaning across the desk conspiratorially. "The last thing I heard you say in this building was that you were going to kill him."

During the past few years that Lizzy worked for the mayor's office, Holly Phillips had been a good friend and confidant. But never in all that time had Lizzy seen her comrade speak well of a man.

"How was your date with Jevon?"

Holly cringed as if a plate of Limburger cheese had arrived and been placed under her nose. Here we go again, Lizzy thought. No specimen of the male gender seemed to meet with Holly's approval. "What's wrong with this one?"

"What isn't wrong with all of them?"

Holly began shaking the snow globe on the desk, the one

Lizzy's mother gave her on her fifth birthday. When Holly began passing her frustrations on to the globe, Lizzy grabbed it and placed the keepsake out of harm's way. "Men aren't the enemy."

Holly straightened defensively. "That's funny coming from you right now. You walked in the door with the man who called you a pooper scooper."

Lizzy watched as the snow fell upon the peaceful cottage in the globe, wondering if such an idyllic place existed. "He brought me furniture this morning. And he's taking me to get my car."

"Why would he bring you furniture?"

Lizzy had forgotten she had told no one of Peter's betrayal and she wasn't sure she wanted Holly to know. They shared everything, but this morning Lizzy wasn't in the mood for another lecture on the ills of men.

"It's a long story. And to be honest with you, Holly, I'm not feeling very good." That was partly true, considering her emotional state. "I was going to check my email and then go home, right after Martin gives me a lift to the pound."

To Holly's credit, she accepted her plea without more of an explanation, gave Lizzy a hug and left her alone. Lizzy's email popped up, eleven messages highlighted. But instead of tending to business, Lizzy stared into the snow globe, getting lost in the flakes whirling around the cozy home and the two people holding hands in front.

"WE HAVE TO TALK, YOUNG MAN."

Twenty-four hours had done nothing to remove the sting from Martin's editorial; Tom appeared as angry as ever. But, twenty-four hours had done a lot for Martin's attitude.

"Yes, we do, Tom." Martin sat in front of the mayor's desk

and folded his arms across his chest. "Why would you think that Lizzy Guidry has any influence over what I write?"

The question instantly deflated the mayor's sails. "What are you talking about?"

Martin unfolded his arms and leaned forward across the desk. "What I publish in my newspaper is my decision. You have a problem with my editorials, you speak to me. But, it's between you and me, Tom. Not Lizzy."

Tom quickly regained his composure. "It's more than that, Martin. I believe it's a community-wide problem. You have a chip on your shoulder and the rest of us are suffering from it, Lizzy included."

"The D.A. was wrong."

"Maybe." Tom finally fell into his own chair, sighing. "But this wasn't the first. Last week it was the Chamber of Commerce. The Chamber of Commerce, for crying out loud! People whose only goal in life is to promote our community. The week before it was the City Council."

"They deserved it," Martin interjected.

"Okay, they did, but Martin you have turned into an angry young man and I can't understand why."

Martin rose and began pacing the spacious room. The décor had changed and the typical political photos were new, but the office had remained the same since he was a kid, following his father around like a shadow "to learn the business." He had wanted to cover government then, investigate corruption and reveal wrongdoings. First thing Martin planned to do upon graduation from journalism school was head somewhere more interesting than Santa Helena, some place where real scandals occurred.

Instead, he landed in Thibodaux, realizing the joys of small-town, community life through fresh eyes.

Damn, he thought, he loved Santa Helena. It represented everything good about Southern California: planned subdivisions instead of uncontrolled growth, environmental restrictions to protect the natural habitat, a town center where folks could gather like in the old days with summer concerts in the summer.

His youthful zest for covering scandal had long dissipated. He had no gripes, really, except running the blasted newspaper twenty-four, seven, and never having time to write. He was a reporter, not a businessman.

Did he really hate his work as Lizzy had said?

"It's been a rough month, Tom." Martin ran his finger against the edge of the Federal desk, wondering if all mayors shared the same bureaucratic-looking furniture. "Perhaps my personal feelings are flowing into my work."

He felt Tom's hand squeezing his shoulder, much like Dave had done earlier. Martin had forgotten how comforting friends could be. "Is there anything I can do?"

Martin wanted to ask if Tom had half a million dollars lying around, but until the day of reckoning, he didn't want to disclose his financial troubles to anyone. Besides, there was Lizzy. If his luck held, his troubles would be over by sunset.

"You can help by not blaming Lizzy for my editorials. They raised the rent on her grandmother's nursing home and her car sounds like it needs major work. How about giving her a raise."

Tom appeared uncomfortable talking about such subjects, but Martin wouldn't let the issue drop. "If you fire that idiot you hired to improve your image, I'm sure you'd have the money."

"Anthony is helping improve my image to the community," Tom defended. "You yourself have pointed out all too often at how Santa Helena citizens don't trust City Hall."

Martin had to admit, he had been rather hard on the mayor and his staff in that regard. When all was said and done, it was the City Council to blame for the town's inability to move ahead with projects, but voters only watched the man in charge. He should have blasted the council more, should have supported the mayor instead of throwing cowardly stones like the rest of Santa Helena. He should have encouraged Tom to fight. Martin ran his hand through his hair, wondering how he could make things right again.

"I'll print an editorial. I'll print several." He couldn't believe what he was saying, couldn't believe the ethics violation he was conceiving, but he blundered ahead. "I'll help you raise your ratings, put pressure on the council instead. Just fire that upstart and give your best worker her raise."

Tom stared, equally surprised. Then the deep recesses of his ruddy cheeks blossomed into a smile. "Dear God, Martin. I never thought I'd see the day."

Martin's collar suddenly felt like a noose and his forehead broke out into a sweat. "Yeah, well, I don't usually cross this sacred line. And don't think I'm in your pocket on this one either. I still plan to…"

Tom shook his head, making the reddish curls of his Irish ancestors fall about his face. "I wasn't referring to the newspaper."

What else was there, Martin thought, but Tom kept grinning as if he discovered the meaning of life.

"Dear God, boy," Tom finally said. "You're smitten."

CHAPTER 5

*B*efore Lizzy had a chance to read her handful of emails, the door to Tom's office flew open and Martin buzzed by her cubicle in a huff.

"Ready?"

Martin stood by the elevator, nervously tapping his foot while picking imaginary lint off his sleeve. Lizzy grabbed her jacket and turned off the computer. "Didn't go well?" she whispered as she reached his side.

"Went fine," he said brusquely.

They waited in silence for the elevator to arrive, Martin refusing to look her way. Lizzy decided the best course was to leave him alone in his misery. But when they entered his car and began driving toward the pound, Martin had no trouble speaking his mind.

"I don't have time for relationships."

The statement caused her pause. She raked her brain thinking where that might have come from.

"I work nonstop. You have no idea how much time it takes to run a newspaper."

Lizzy opened her mouth to say something, but for the life of her she had no clue how to respond.

"I can't tell you the last time I've watched television. So, how in hell am I supposed to have time for a relationship?"

What on earth had he and Tom talked about, Lizzy wondered. For some reason, she felt inclined to defend her boss. "I'm sure Tom meant well."

"Meant well?" Martin finally looked at her, absorbing her features as if he saw her for the first time. Then he frowned, no doubt wondering what Lizzy was referring to. She wondered as well.

"I don't know what y'all talked about, but Tom is a good man and if he lectured you about something, he really has your best interests at heart."

Martin stared back at the road in front of him, shifting gears as they drove through the intersection that separated the subdivisions from the industrial park. "Everyone has my best interests at heart—Tom, my sister, my mother—but somehow reality escapes them."

She started to inquire further, but Martin changed the subject. "Let me do the talking when we get to the pound. My friend Kevin is the president of the Santa Helena Soccer League and I've given him lots of free advertising over the years. He owes me one."

"Dave said he would call and straighten things out," Lizzy added.

"Great. Then you should have no problem. We'll have you back on your way in no time."

If Lizzy wasn't mistaken, Martin seemed eager to be rid of her. If things were as busy at the newspaper as he had indicated, she had robbed him of a morning of business. "I'm sorry for all this," she said. "Feel free to drop me off and get back to work."

His brow creased as he downshifted and grinded his gears. "Did you bring your lottery ticket?"

The man had been reprimanded by the mayor, then forced

to taxi her through town while his newspaper suffered and all he could think about was the stupid lottery ticket? "What is it with you and that ticket?"

He shot her a look devoid of the usual Taylor charm. He almost appeared guilty. "You have no computer. I thought we could stop by the paper and check the numbers."

Lizzy couldn't comprehend the logic being presented to her, but then in her short lifetime most men never made sense. "You don't have time to watch TV or a relationship, Martin, so why would you want to make sure I checked my numbers?"

Martin gripped the steering wheel and turned into the pound's parking lot. "Do you have the ticket or not, Lizzy?"

"No." She sighed, scanning the parking lot for her Tercel as anxiety took hold of her heart. "It's on my refrigerator. I didn't want to risk carrying millions of dollars around with me. On second thought, Martin, why are we here? Why don't you drop me off at the Cadillac dealership instead."

Martin applied the hand brake and paused at the irony being played out. Why were they at the pound and not at a dealership? How difficult could it be to check one lousy lottery ticket? He gazed over at Lizzy, who stared into the parking lot forlornly.

"Do you think it's fixable?" she asked.

She could buy a fleet of Tercels now, he thought. Yet, she sat before him like a woman on the verge of bankruptcy, worrying about the fate of an old car with an oil leak. All he had to do was come clean, tell her she won the lottery and ask for the money. The air would be cleared and he would get his answer and be done with it, return to the newspaper and carry on.

Realizing he wasn't getting out of the car, Lizzy turned her brown eyes to his, silently questioning. As if his hand acted of its own accord, Martin pushed a lone strand of hair behind her ear. "I'll go find out."

He exited his car, slamming the door behind him. "Smitten," Tom had called him, laughing at his repeated refusals. Sure, he found Lizzy attractive, he always had, but he was doing this for the money. Period. He had a newspaper to save and no time to think about anything else.

"What's up Martin?" Kevin called to him.

"Hey Kevin. I need a favor."

Kevin wiped his hands on a rag, then pushed it into his back pocket. "Cute girl," he said, nodding toward Lizzy.

Martin gave Lizzy a quick glance, grinding his teeth in the process. "Yeah, I'm helping her out with her car. It got towed away Wednesday night because she broke down."

"Of yeah, Dave called and told me all about it."

Good, Martin thought. He could deposit Lizzy in her Tercel and be on his way, then bring her a newspaper with the winning numbers when he returned with the couch. "Can we take the car then?"

Kevin squinted at the sun. "Afraid not. The engine's fried."

Martin heard the car door open and close, felt Lizzy approach. He dreaded telling her the news. If only she realized she had won the damn lottery, then losing her car would be a laughable matter, some funny story to tell the grandchildren one day. "I had the worst luck one Christmas," he imagined her saying. "Everything was a disaster, including destroying my car, but then I won five million dollars right before the New Year!"

"I burned the engine, didn't I?"

Amazingly, Lizzy didn't appear as defeated as he imagined she would.

"I'm afraid you did," Kevin said, as if he was speaking to a child. "You've got to remember to check the oil. If you let the oil go down, like you did the other night, the engine doesn't get lubricated."

Why did mechanics do that to women, Martin thought? He'd never forget the time Joe Stephens patronized his sister, explaining what a carburetor was, only to have his sister lecture him on the complexities of internal combustion.

"She knows the role of oil in a car's engine, Kevin. These things happen sometimes."

Kevin appeared taken aback. "I only meant…"

Martin rubbed his temple subconsciously, waiting for the familiar headache to arrive. God, but he was testy this morning. "I know. She was putting oil in her car but some asshole distracted her."

Both Kevin and Lizzy stared at him in silence and Martin did what any Southern Californian would do when faced in an embarrassing situation; he retreated behind his sunglasses. He pulled his shades from his breast pocket, placed them on his face and avoided their eyes, wishing he had kept his mouth shut.

"You could buy a new engine or a rebuilt one, but it's gonna cost you more than the car is worth," Kevin explained to Lizzy. "But I'll be happy to buy the car from you. I have a daughter who's going to be of driving age soon and this would be a perfect car for her. I can look for parts and rebuild the engine myself in my spare time."

Lizzy bit her lower lip. "How much would you give me?"

"Five hundred seem fair?"

She scratched her head and looked over at Martin. "Five hundred's fair. Kevin's right, you don't have many choices here. You're lucky to have a buyer."

Lizzy exhaled deeply. "Can you give me a day to think about it?"

"You bet," Kevin said, patting her on the shoulder. "It's not going anywhere. Dave took care of the fine, so you have nothing to worry about in that regard."

"Can I get my stuff?"

Kevin led Lizzy toward the acres of car, allowing Martin a moment to regain some semblance of control. He watched her examine her damaged car, shoulders bent by the weight of her financial problems, and fought back the urge to rush to her side and confess everything. No, he had to figure this out, had to plot out a new course of action. There had to be a way for her to discreetly discover her winnings and make Martin the hero at the same time. He couldn't bear her realizing that he knew she had won all along. He hated that she might think badly of him.

He fell into his car seat and sighed, glancing at his watch. In ten minutes he would miss the advertising meeting. In roughly five, Cassie would buzz his cell phone, wondering if he had sneaked off to the water's edge again. God, but he wanted to.

Lizzy quickly returned with a plastic bag. "Okay, I'm ready."

Once on the car seat, she exhaled and deflated, gazing off into the distance, her eyes glistening as if tears were close to the surface. She bit the inside of her cheek, more than likely to hold back emotions, and Martin felt as if a hand had taken hold of his heart. "Want to get some coffee?" he asked.

She continued starring ahead, while she shook her head. "No, I've wasted enough of your time today."

"We could stop by the newspaper. I have my stash of Community there."

"No, thanks. I'd rather go home, if you don't mind."

What was she starring at, Martin thought, peering through the dusty windshield. The only object visible from the parking lot was the freeway sign announcing the entrance to Highway 126, his favorite stretch of escape.

"Right before I graduated from journalism school, my grandfather died and with it his livelihood," Lizzy began softly. "I didn't know things were bad until I graduated college and found out my grandmother had lost the house in the bankruptcy. Amazingly, she saw it as an adventure, piling everything we owned inside her Oldsmobile and heading west. She said we would go as far as the Pacific and then sit on the beach and decide what to do."

That explained why she came to California. "What happened?"

Lizzy wrinkled her nose and Martin feared tears would fall

at last. Please God, he prayed, don't let her cry.

"We didn't make it. Our car broke down in Santa Helena. My grandmother proclaimed it was a sign and we've been here ever since."

For a moment, there was no lottery ticket, no advertising meeting, no Tercels with oil leaks. Martin felt the road stretch before them, offering freedom from the trials in their lives, beckoning them on to the comfort of the ocean. He heard the cell phone ring, but Cassie and the Santa Helena Banner would have to wait.

He revved the engine and pulled out of the parking lot, but instead of heading back toward town, rode under the Golden State Freeway and on to the highway that had become his salvation. As they headed west, the sun warming their faces and the cell phone still performing an Eagles tune, Lizzy finally looked his way.

"I have no idea what you're up to but are you going to answer that?"

Funny, she didn't seem in the least bit surprised. "It's my sister. She wants to know why I'm not at the advertising meeting."

"And why aren't you?"

Martin relaxed for the first time that morning, stretching an arm on the back of the seat. "Because today I have a date."

Lizzy studied him hard for a good moment, then answered his cell phone. "Martin Taylor's car."

"Who's this?" Martin could hear his sister say.

"Tell her I'm incommunicado."

"He's incommunicado," Lizzy repeated, then laughed at something his sister said. The two then began a long conversation, with Lizzy mostly agreeing to whatever his sister was implying and smiling in the process, despite the tears still lurking on her eyelashes.

"Don't believe a word she says," he told her.

"She says you don't want to know the advertising figures anyway, but will you make the afternoon editorial meeting."

Martin winced. Christmas had been as bad as he feared. Whatever thrill of escape he had experienced before now disappeared. "Yeah, I'll be there."

Lizzy relayed the message, then turned off the phone and placed it in an empty drink holder. "I take it we're going to the ocean."

"There's a great Mexican restaurant in Santa Barbara. Serves awesome margaritas."

"Martin, you don't have to do this. Santa Barbara is over an hour away."

"Trust me, Lizzy, I need this as much as you do."

There it was again, that scrutinizing gaze. One look from Lizzy Guidry and he swore she saw right through to his soul. He straightened, pulled up his macho facade that he used when courting women and offered her his most dazzling smile. "Sweetheart, today is your lucky day."

If he hoped to impress, his bravado failed him completely. Lizzy's eyes narrowed and she folded her arms across her chest. "My lucky day would have been not running into you in the Mini Mart."

Martin wanted to choke. If only she knew how utterly ridiculous that statement was. Yet, it wasn't the lottery money he was thinking of when he looked back into those suspicious brown eyes. "Why do you dislike me so much?"

She twisted the side of her mouth into a frown, causing a dimple to appear.

"Besides, the editorial," he quickly added.

"You want me to be honest?"

No, he wanted to scream, but he needed to remove her stubborn defenses. "I wouldn't have asked otherwise."

"I know your type."

"My type?"

Lizzy raised her chin, her arms still tightly wound in front of her. "You're as readable as a book. I knew it the moment we first met."

"How is that possible?" Now it was Martin's turn to be defensive. "You wouldn't even have coffee with me."

"Why would I? You stared at my chest the whole time."

Damn, he thought. That was the reason after all. "You have nice breasts," he said, nearly slapping himself afterwards for such a stupid remark.

"You're black and white."

Suddenly, he was back in elementary school. "I'm not black and white."

"Oh no? First, you have no desire to make a commitment with a woman—you said it before—so you immerse yourself in work. Second, since you don't have time for relationships and TV, you exhume charm to Santa Helena's finest women, picking up every model and actress for miles, but I suppose only for a quick fling."

"Now, wait just a minute…"

"You weren't flirting with Magenta What's Her Name at the Chamber party last week?"

"Chartreuse?"

At this Lizzy paused in her brutal dissection and a smile threatened. "Forgive me, I got the color wrong."

He couldn't help but smile, but he remained defensive. "It was just flirting."

"The blonde at the Concerts in the Park?"

"She lasted a week."

"My point exactly."

This wasn't going the way he had planned and the hairs on the back of his neck began to tingle. "I can explain that…"

"Third," Lizzy continued with renewed energy, "you're probably all hands and tongues from the first date onward. Then, once you get them into bed, you leave as quickly as you can, rushing away before they have time to awaken and realize that Martin Taylor has left the building."

His familiar fruit stand came into view in front of acres of orange and lemon groves. Martin had planned to drive straight through to make lunch, but he desperately needed reinforcements. He pulled into the dirt parking lot, blowing up a cloud of dust, then rammed up the brake.

He turned off the engine, removed his sunglasses, then faced Lizzy who had finally unlocked her arms to brace herself against the sudden stop. Taking advantage of the moment, he slid his arm against the back of the seat, brushing her shoulder in the process and leaning toward her face so close he could smell the lavender.

"First of all, I immerse myself in work because I inherited a newspaper," he said as calmly as he could muster. "If I had had a choice in the matter, I'd be happily writing for *Rolling Stone* and chalking up any number of commitments because, believe of not, I have always wanted someone to share my life with, not to mention the ole American Dream of two kids and a dog."

Lizzy started to rebuke, but he didn't give her the chance. "Second, I do flirt with the likes of Chartreuse and that blonde, whose name by the way is Lisa Treager. Would you prefer I remain celibate for the rest of my life because my father dumped a failing newspaper in my lap?"

She tried to speak, but again, he cut her off. "And yes, I do leave after lovemaking, you got me on that one. I hope to someday find the woman of my dreams whom I will enjoy spending the night with, but until then I will prefer the comfort of my own bed, and waking up in the privacy of my own home without worrying about embarrassing stale breath and morning boners."

At this, Lizzy's eyes widened. "And what?"

"You heard me."

He leaned in closer, their lips only a breath away, his fingers playing with the silky strands at the nape of her neck. "As for tongues…" Deftly he descended and brushed his lips against hers, pausing to deepen the kiss and savor the taste of her. He let the contact linger, inhaling her sweet smell, then he leaned back and straightened, amazed that such a simple movement had stolen the breath from him.

"As for tongues," he repeated, clearing his throat and trying to regain his composure, "never on a first date."

LIZZY FELT THE CAR SHIFT, heard the door open and close, but her mind still lingered on the sensations playing her lips. Dear God, what had just happened?

She expected him to rebuke her comments, to retaliate, maybe, by laying on the charm. But never a kiss like that. It had been chaste almost, sweet and hesitant yet lurking with a powerful, sensual energy. He had tasted of raw masculinity, an aspect of Martin equally surprising, as if he could perform slow and steady, unlike charming Peter with all his promises and quick lovemaking.

"Damn," she said to no one, trying to erase the tantalizing image from her mind. She had been brutal on Martin, accused him of shallowness when for all she knew he might be the epitome of a gentleman. He wasn't the enemy, Peter was. Still, he had stared at her breasts for the simple reason they were nice to look at.

Again, she crossed her arms about her chest. She didn't have nice breasts, did she? Peter certainly hadn't noticed. But the way he had rushed through lovemaking, she was certain it wasn't her body he had craved.

No, she reiterated to herself, Martin's a charmer like Peter and most men who only have one thing on their minds. Hadn't he kissed her just then? What more proof did she need?

Lizzy ran a lazy tongue across her bottom lip, the heady

taste of Martin lingering. It was only lunch, she reasoned. She had never seen Santa Barbara, and for some insane reason she trusted him, knew that underneath that bullshit Martin was hurting as much as she was. Perhaps more now because some insensitive woman had labeled him a male chauvinist pig.

She decided to apologize, leaving the car and entering the fruit stand to find him. He stood by the counter, holding a bag of pistachios, next to a woman creating something frothy in a blender.

"I don't understand women and I never will," Martin said to the woman, his temper rising. "Why do you all feel the need to lump us into a one, generic mass?"

"Don't men do the same?" the woman replied. Apparently, they knew each other for their tone was conversational and casual.

"I don't put all women into one basket." Martin placed the bag on the counter. "I value them for their individuality."

"Good for you, Martin." The woman poured the orange liquid into two go cups. "But, you must admit, you are a charmer."

"I like to flirt, is that such a crime? God, Martha, half the fun is the pre-game show."

Martha began ringing up the items, a smile playing her lips. "Not when it really matters, sweetheart." She paused in her addition and tapped Martin's hand. "The trouble with you, sweetie, is you haven't found the right girl."

Lizzy expected Martin to laugh this off, to comment about working so hard at *The Banner* and not finding time. Instead, he stood staring at a crate of avocados, tension gathering between his shoulder blades as if the world's weight was too much to bear. Remorse filled her again.

"This isn't about that beauty you told me about last week?" Martha asked, breaking the silence. "What was her name? Chamomile?"

Lizzy couldn't help herself; the woman's mispronunciation caused her to bust out laughing. When Martin turned and saw her standing there, he, too, began to smile, but a guarded one.

"Am I speaking of the devil?" Martha asked.

"Heavens no," Lizzy said as she approached the counter. "The woman Martin was speaking about is a high fashion model. I'm about as far removed as Chartreuse Bellamy as a woman can get."

"That's not true," Martin said to the woman, his deep voice causing a shiver to run through Lizzy. "Chartreuse doesn't hold a candle to Lizzy."

Lizzy instantly felt uncomfortable. Either he was being nice to gloss things over or he did find her attractive, like Nana had said. She had a hard time believing the latter, particularly in comparison to breath-taking Chartreuse, so she offered up humor as a defense. "Must be my nice breasts," she whispered.

Now who was flirting, Lizzy thought as Martin relaxed and smiled back. Still, the newly established camaraderie between them was comforting. In better circumstances, and without her bitter resentment toward Peter and his gender, she and Martin would probably have made good friends.

"And you are?"

Lizzy glanced back to find Martha studying them both, a sly twinkle in her eye.

"Lizzy," Martin interjected, "this is Martha Hernandez. She runs Highway 126's finest fruit stand."

Lizzy extended her hand and enjoyed the feel of the older woman's strong grip. "Nice to meet you."

"Martha, this is Lizzy Guidry. She works for the city."

A truce had been offered and Lizzy should have let it lie. But for one moment, she felt her old, humorous self returning and she wanted to embrace it.

"I work for the sanitation department," she said with a grin.

CHAPTER 6

"*H*ow many times do I have to apologize?" Lizzy asked as the giant margarita was placed before her.

Martin threw out the straw and took a drink from the over-sized glass, twisting his face when the salt took effect. "One more time," he said, clearly enjoying the reversal of roles.

"Okay, I'm sorry."

He turned quiet as he had during most of the drive over to Santa Barbara, looking like a schoolboy whose wrists had been slapped. If he had wanted to make her feel guilty, he did a great job.

"I was brutal in the car. I really didn't mean to attack you like that. I'm angry at charming men who are hollow inside, that's all."

Martin created a steeple of fingers before his lips and studied her intently.

"Not that you are hollow inside," she quickly added.

Again, he said nothing, the soft candlelight reflecting in his aquamarine eyes as the courtyard grew darker. Thankful for the distraction, Lizzy noticed the sky turning gray and a chilling breeze blowing in.

"Cold?"

"No, I'm fine." When she shivered, Martin rose and removed his jacket, placing it around her shoulders.

"It's not necessary," she said, even though she felt infinitely warmer.

Martin resumed his seat, his face still devoid of emotions, and Lizzy feared they would return to their stilted conversation. But Martin surprised her. "What are you doing Monday night?"

Her mind whirled, trying to connect the importance of that day. Then she remembered why she had blocked it from her mind. "New Year's Eve? The mall merchants put on that big party. Aren't you going?"

"I always go. Bores me to tears."

"You had a hot date last year."

"So did you."

He had noticed Peter? It was one thing to spy on Martin; the women on his arm could have emerged from the Oscar's red carpet. But why would he think to look her way? Unless Nana had been right.

"Martin, you didn't write that editorial because...?" Heavens, she couldn't possibly ask such a question.

He screwed up his face as if in pain. "So we're back to my apologizing."

"No," she said suddenly. What was she thinking? Of course, he didn't write the editorial to get her attention. That was absurd! "Forget it, I didn't mean to... What I was wondering was...?" How the hell would she get out of this one?

"Yes," she finally said. "I'll go with you to the party."

Martin paused with the glass halfway to his lips, his eyebrows raised, and it was then Lizzy realized he hadn't asked.

As a cloud passed overhead, darkening the courtyard further, Lizzy wanted to take the opportunity to crawl under the table.

"Great." Martin placed the glass back on the table. "That would be awesome."

She tried to read his expression, tried to discern if his approval was valid. "That is what you meant, isn't it? You wanted to know if we could go..."

"Yes," he quickly answered. "I thought we could go together since we both plan on being there."

"What about Chamomile?"

Finally, the old charmer returned and his smile warmed Lizzy more than his jacket. "Chamomile Magenta isn't speaking to me at the moment, but that's just as well. We never had anything in common anyway. Plus she confuses my nights at the newspaper with another woman."

"You work nights?"

"Most of them."

"But you're the publisher. Why do you have to be there nights?"

Martin traced a finger around the top of his glass, pushing the salt into the drink. "When I inherited the newspaper, it was in bad need of a technology upgrade. We took out a loan and bought new computers and software, but then had to spend endless hours installing all of it. I couldn't afford too many tech people, so I learned a lot of the process myself, then did half the work after the IT people went home."

"Is this upgrade finished?"

Martin grimaced. "Funny thing about technology and not having IT people. It saves you a lot of time, until it breaks." He shrugged and attempted a smile. "But it's not just that. The press is on its last leg and I know the little secrets that keep it going, things my father taught me. We have a skeleton crew right now, so if one person's out sick, the whole place suffers and sometimes I have to cover a School Board meeting or lay out a page. I have several loans with the bank so there's a lot of paperwork there. Hell, there's always a lot of paperwork."

Funny, in all her years at *The Banner* and the little money it paid, she never imagined upper management suffering. Martin's father never seemed to hurt for cash, always drove a nice car and lived in a Victorian listed on the historical register. That famed Taylor house was sold last year and rumors swirled about the stability of one of the state's last community newspapers. She wondered if Martin had been forced to sell his family home.

"Can I help in any way? It's been a few years since I penned an article, but I believe it's like riding a bicycle."

When Martin reacted with a warm smile, she began to feel the wall disintegrate between them. "Thank you," he responded genuinely. "But the best help you could give me is saving me from boredom at that party."

Lizzy returned the smile, wondering what dress she could haul out of the deep recesses of her closet. She hadn't planned on attending the annual event, hoping to avoid watching happy couples locked in kisses at midnight.

Suddenly, she thought of Martin's kiss in the car and wondered if a date on New Year's would include another. A blush scorched her cheeks and a trail of fire burned down her neck. Lizzy removed Martin's jacket and handed it back to him. "I'm feeling warmer now."

"Are you sure? It looks like a storm's moving in."

He was polite, she'd give him that. It seemed years since she'd dined with a chivalrous man. No wonder half the women in the valley flocked to him. Too bad he worked so much. The way he discussed *The Banner*, it seemed to drain the energy from him.

"You don't like what you're doing, do you?"

Whatever calm had descended upon them, the storm clouds blew away. The light in his eyes extinguished while he furiously used the straw to stir his margarita. "I always expected to take over the newspaper. It's my family legacy, been a Taylor tradition for three generations. I just never expected it to be so soon and at a time when people stopped reading newspapers."

Recognizing that feeling of heartache and grief, Lizzy reached for his hand.

"I knew I would inherit the business one day, but after I had a family and kids, not at the prime of my career." He glanced down at their hands and slipped a thumb over her wrist, as if to keep her hand from slipping away. "You never expect your parents to die. They're supposed to live forever."

"I know," she whispered, feeling that familiar ache overtake her heart once more.

Martin frowned as if some profound thought occurred to him. When their eyes met, she shivered. "Where are your parents?"

The dampness rolling in with the afternoon fog permeated her bones, chilled her soul. She clamped down her teeth to keep them from chattering, while she fought off the urge to flee. She tried to remove her hand from his, but he held on tight.

"Lizzy?"

"They died when I was fifteen," she said, surprised she had managed that much. Twelve years and the horror felt like yesterday. "They were killed in a car accident."

His countenance shifted, as it did with most people who learned of her loss, which made her want to hide all the more. Only Martin's pity was different, sympathetic yet concerned. Regardless, she didn't want to relive the accident, wished they hadn't brought it up.

He attempted to speak, but thankfully the waiter arrived, a friendly man named Gabriel wearing an enormous sombrero. When Martin's attention shifted, Lizzy withdrew her hand and placed it safely in her lap.

"Are you ready to order?" the waiter asked.

Martin sent her a questioning look, as if asking if she wanted more time to think, more time to talk about the accident. But discussing her parents was the last thing she wanted to do.

"What's your special?" she asked Gabriel.

"Seafood quesadillas with shrimp and crabmeat," the waiter replied. "Comes with rice and beans and fresh guacamole."

"Sounds great." Lizzy handed the waiter her menu, pulling her sweater about her shoulders as the wind picked up.

"I'll have the same," Martin said, "but I think we need to move inside."

The waiter took his menu and began picking up their silverware. "Big storm coming in. They say it's a nasty one."

The minute they entered the restaurant and found a table by a roaring fireplace, the sky opened up, pounding the empty courtyard with its fury. "Perfect timing," Martin said, holding out her chair.

"It's going to be a terrible drive back to your meeting. I hope we make it."

Grinning, Martin lifted his sleeve and exposed his watch, which read two forty-five.

"You're kidding? Where has the time gone?"

He took the opposite seat, the wild fire now dancing inside his pupils. Even with his hair disheveled by the wind, Martin exhumed charm as if he owned the patent. He offered her the trademark Taylor smile, but this time she felt as if the gesture belonged only to her.

"Time flies when you're having fun in Paradise," he said as he raised his glass in a toast.

THE TWO STOOD outside the movie theater, staring at the water pouring off the awning. Waves of rain pelted the street while an occasional car sprayed puddles against the side of the building, drenching everything in its path.

"What do we do now?" Lizzy asked.

She had called Nana and Martin had phoned the newspaper, both explaining their situation, then ducked inside the retro theater for a Hitchcock double feature. But that had been hours ago. They had expected the storm to let up in the meantime, not increase in fury.

"Where you heading?" the theater manager asked.

"Santa Helena," Martin replied.

The manager shook his head. "Highway 126 has been closed for hours. Mudslide. Your best bet is to drive into L.A. and then head north up the Golden State Freeway."

Lizzy knew such a route would take hours. The best solution was to find a hotel and wait until morning, but Lizzy dreaded suggesting such a thing.

"My brother has a beach house near here," Martin offered. "It's pretty rustic, a place where he and his med school buddies hang out. But we could stay there until the weather improves."

What choice did they have? Lizzy thought. But again, she trusted him, couldn't explain why. Maybe it was the two-hour lunch they had shared talking about everything from Martin's early days in Thibodaux to her unique relationship with Nana. Then she discovered he loved old movies and preferred the middle front, almost to the point of neck strain, her favorite spot. All in all, despite the police report and the loss of her car, it had been a wonderful, relaxing day.

"How far away is this beach house?"

Martin fought back a laugh. "Not far, up the road in the poor section of town. And it's not exactly on the beach. Hell, it's not exactly a house."

"I don't care." Lizzy tugged her sweater tight across her chest. "As long as it's warm and dry."

Martin pulled the newspapers from under his arm, several free weeklies he had snagged at the restaurant. He unfolded one like a tent and handed it to Lizzy and she placed it over her head. "Ready?"

"Ready as I'll ever be."

The newspapers were useless as the water soaked through every inch of their clothing and permeated their hair through the paper. Martin finally threw his in a trash bin as they raced down State Street, but Lizzy stubbornly refused to let hers go, if nothing else to give her something to hold on to in the howling wind. When they reached the parking lot, his Ford the lone car in a sea of puddles, Lizzy gave up, dropping her arms and letting nature have her way.

"I'm going to get your seat all wet," she yelled through the noise.

She couldn't make out Martin's answer, but she suspected he was laughing. He let her in and she climbed inside, watching the storm's fury from the safety of the windshield, feeling like Tippy Hendrin in *The Birds*.

"It won't be long," Martin assured her as he climbed inside the driver's seat. "Let's see if we can get this heater blowing."

By the time the car finally heated up to a comfortable temperature, they had reached the house. The tiny structure was nestled between two more prominent houses, nearly engulfed by its prosperous neighbors. There was a garage below and a stairway on the side leading up to the second story that looked like a one-room apartment.

"I'm afraid we have to climb those," Martin said, following her gaze. "Paul rents out the garage to help pay for the rent. You wouldn't believe how much they ask for this dump."

"Sure I would." Southern California was notorious for high real estate values, especially near the coast, but residents got a lot for the money considering the gorgeous year-round weather. Except on rare days like this, Lizzy thought with a smile.

"Ready?" Martin asked, and on a silent cue they both bolted toward the upper floor.

Lizzy didn't think she could get wetter, but the rain inundated her further. Then Martin had trouble seeing the lock on the darkened stairway, causing them to wait on the threshold while he fumbled to open the door. Finally, Lizzy laughed, and Martin joined in, their hysterics making him drop the keys.

"Maybe we should jump in the ocean to keep from getting wet?" Martin asked.

In that moment, Lizzy's heart lurched. It was the same joke her father used when thunderstorms would interrupt their day on the Mississippi Gulf Coast. Before she had time to ponder it further, Martin opened the door and ushered her inside.

Her knee bumped what felt like a table and she heard Martin cuss while he groped in the darkness. "The lights don't work," she heard him say over her shoulder.

"Are you sure?" Lizzy could barely make out the room's contents but reasoned she stood in the kitchen area. She decided to head to the left, in what looked like an open area, only to bang her shin on a low-lying piece of furniture.

"Careful." Martin placed a hand at her back. "I know where the fireplace is. You stay put and let me try to find the matches."

Lizzy watched his shadow inch across the room, then heard the rustle of papers and the falling of items. Martin let out a string of expletives, then laughed.

"You okay?"

She heard the sound of a match being scratched against stone at the same time the light illuminated Martin's face. He appeared pleased with himself, looking at her like a Boy Scout doing a good deed.

"Do we have any dry wood?" she asked and his smile disappeared. He quickly looked around the fireplace, exhaling when he spotted a pile. Martin threw a few logs inside the fireplace, then dropped the match on top. Just before it extinguished, he lit another and glanced around, hoping to find a way to start a fire while holding a short-lived match.

Lizzy reached his side and began sticking newspapers between the logs, then Martin dropped the match and within seconds a fire blazed. Knowing it wouldn't endure, they quickly gathered up more wood and paper and started building something that would last. After several matches and lots of trial and error, accompanied by more laughter, they finally built a well-blazing conflagration.

"We need to get out of these clothes," Martin said.

Lizzy leaned into the searing blaze and discovered the same feeling Martin had. No amount of warmth could penetrate layers of wet clothing.

Martin glanced around the room, then disappeared into the shadows. "My brother and his buddies have been coming here for years. Surely, they must have something lying around."

A thick, warm robe and wool socks is what Lizzy hoped for, but instead she was hit in the head by a male jogging suit.

"Will that do?" Martin asked from the darkness. "It might hang to your knees but at least it's dry."

She pulled the pieces of clothing from her head and examined them, a sweatshirt with UCLA blazoned across the front and a pair of gigantic cotton pants. "Is your brother related to Shaquille O'Neal?"

Somewhere in the dark recesses of the room she heard Martin laugh. "Close. I'm going into the bathroom to change so you can have some privacy." Then, in a breath, she heard a door close.

Feeling rather exposed, despite the darkness surrounding her, Lizzy quickly pulled off her wet clothes and threw them in a pile, then tugged on the enormous sweatshirt and pants. It smelled of perfumed bleach, something unexpected from a man.

"Are you dressed?" Martin yelled from the bathroom.

"If you can call it that."

The door to the bathroom opened and a towel slapped her in the face, followed by a chuckle in the dark. "Why do I get the feeling you treat your sister this way," she asked him.

Martin joined her in front of the fire, grinning as he leaned his head forward and rubbed his hair dry with his own towel. He wore a pair of snug shorts and an unbuttoned short-sleeve shirt that exposed a broad chest. Try as she might, her eyes kept following the line of blond hair that ran over a ripple of muscles to his navel.

"I don't work out."

His voice distracted her thoughts, and when she looked up, he was buttoning his shirt subconsciously. "What?"

"I don't have time, although I try to get a swim in at least three times a week."

Why was he so defensive? Lizzy wondered, as she watched his long, muscular legs stretch out in front of the fire. For an instant, she imagined sliding a hand around those thick, tanned thighs, then quickly brushed off the intrusive thought. "Why does everyone in California feel the need to visit health clubs every day? Lots of people don't have time to work out. Me, I go for a walk several times a week. Does me just fine."

Martin shrugged, leaning back on his elbows. "Something Chartreuse said."

Was the woman blind? Had the fashion model actually found fault with him? "Martin," Lizzy said, trying to keep her voice steady so he didn't read more into what she was about to say, "you're perfect."

How did she manage to do that? Martin thought. One minute he's in the bathroom convincing himself to breach the subject of lottery again and the next minute she's gazing at him with those enormous brown eyes, making him thankful to be a man. Every time he focused his mind back to those millions,

Lizzy made him want to kiss her. And kiss her soundly. The sweet taste of her lips still lingered in his mind.

"Did you just give me a compliment?" he asked her.

When she smiled, Martin noticed a tiny dimple appear in her right cheek. How had he missed that adorable trait? But then she had presented so many wonderful new aspects of herself all evening.

"Well, I am capable of being civil, despite my bitchiness these past two days. In fact, I'm really not that way at all. I swear."

She pulled the giant shirt forward and its hem reached below her hips, yet Paul's sweatshirt failed to hide all the blessings of her curvaceous figure. He grabbed a sleeve and began rolling it up her arm until her hand appeared. "Didn't your mother tell you not to swear?"

He meant it as a joke, but the minute the words took flight he realized his blunder. While he searched for a clever comeback, Lizzy offered her other arm. "Yes, she did. She was a stickler for being polite, always insisted I mind my pleases and thank yous. No one was allowed to sit down in our house without being offered a drink, for instance."

Martin suddenly realized he hadn't offered her anything. "Speaking of, can I get you something? I think Paul has some brandy somewhere."

"I wasn't insinuating anything, but brandy sounds heavenly. By the way, where are we going to sleep?"

He headed toward the kitchen in search of liquor, but sleep was the furthest thing from Martin's mind. There was so much room inside that sweatshirt, his hands could easily slip inside. No doubt she wore nothing underneath.

Martin closed his eyes to shake off the thought. Pulling two glasses out of the cabinet, he mentally chastised himself. He had to take it slow, couldn't rush this one with his usual charm. Half a million or not, Lizzy was a friendship he wanted to nurture and retain, not destroy in one hasty night.

"The couch is a day bed."

Lizzy rubbed the towel through her hair, then tossed it back, running her fingers through her scalp to tame the mass, all the while gazing at the futon couch that contained what looked like an oversized twin mattress. He knew what she was thinking. "I can sleep on the floor," he added as he handed her a glass.

"It's not necessary." The dimple deepened, while a blush played her cheeks. "I'm sure in my state of dress I'm perfectly safe from every man on the planet."

Martin poured them both a brandy. "Hardly."

It was the wrong thing to say; he wanted her to feel safe in his presence, not suspect seduction and retreat back within her defensive shield. To her amazement, Lizzy grinned mischievously and tilted her head. "Are you trying to tell me, Martin Taylor, that under all this material I still have great breasts?"

A seriousness he had never experienced before rose inside him as he watched the firelight play against her auburn hair. Something seized his heart, a feeling akin to protectiveness, and nothing seemed to matter but the adorable pug-nosed angel standing before him. "Lizzy," he said, amazed that his voice, too, had changed tone, "you're perfect."

She said nothing, only stared, the smile fading from her lips. They stood facing each other, locked in that moment, wondering where the future would lead them. And it arrived playing *Hotel California*.

Lizzy jumped at the sound of his cell phone ringing, glancing around the darkness to find the intrusive instrument. Now was a perfect time to fling it into the Pacific, Martin thought, but Lizzy retrieved the damned phone from the pocket of his discarded clothes and answered it.

"It's Cassie," she said, handing it to him. "She says it's important."

Martin pressed the phone to his ear and before saying a

word heard Cassie expel a litany of problems. "Slow down," he told her. "What's going on?"

"Editorial says they can't find your opinion piece," she replied. "We've looked everywhere and Mack's getting ready to print out that page."

Shit, Martin thought, he had forgotten he had an editorial due that day. "What time is it?"

"Quarter to eleven. Where are you and do you have any idea what happened to it?"

Just then the lights flickered on and the room illuminated. Martin headed for the desk knowing that Paul always left his laptop at the beach house. If the computer's battery was full or Paul had left a power cord he'd be in business.

"Martin, where are you?" he heard Cassie say.

"In a miracle," he answered, realizing that the power coming back on might solve this problem. He checked Paul's modem and found it blinking. Locating the computer, Martin hit the on key and the machine lit into action.

"Cassie, I've got fifteen minutes to deadline. I'm going to try to get this to you by email. If all fails, use a wire story."

"We already have one picked out, but what is going on?"

"I'll call you back."

Martin placed the phone on the desk. "Thank you, Paul."

"What's wrong?" Lizzy asked from the fireside.

"I forgot I had an editorial due today. I need to plug this over to my sister and then I'm all yours." He paused and looked up from his work. "I'm sorry to have to do this but the good news is we have power."

Lizzy waved off his protestations. "Don't be. I'm going to check out the bathroom and steal a toothbrush, then find some blankets."

Martin wasted no time pounding the keys, penning an editorial that vindicated the mayor and apologizing for his insensitive remarks to a certain member of the mayor's staff. He then went on to list the mayor's many accomplishments since he obtained office, ending with a plea for City Council members to end their bickering and start working toward the good of the community.

After quickly proofing his work and running a spell check, Martin opened Paul's email and sent the piece to Cassie. He waited a moment, then called *The Banner*.

"Got it," Cassie told him. "But why are you using Paul's email?"

"It's a long story, one I'll be happen to relay tomorrow." For some juvenile reason, Martin didn't want his sister to know where he was or whom he was with.

"You're not at the beach house, are you?"

"Gotta run. You have to get that to Mack ASAP."

"Right," Cassie answered, "but I want a full explanation tomorrow."

He turned off the cell phone and sighed as the rush of adrenaline retreated. It was then he realized the room had become strangely quiet, only the occasional popping of a log breaking the silence. Lizzy was stretched out on the couch, fast asleep, her sublime face being kissed by the dying embers of the fire.

What was he going to do? Sitting on her refrigerator was his ticket to salvation, the answer to all his problems. Yet, how was he to tell her now, and where would this eventually lead them?

Martin rubbed his forehead, trying to erase the headache pulsating between his temples. The day had been delightful, one of the best he had ever spent with a woman, yet he couldn't let their new friendship interrupt his plans. He had a paper to save and half a million dollars to raise. There had to be a way to inform her of her winnings and keep him on her good side. He could come out of this a winner, couldn't he?

Then a lightening bolt hit. He was on the Internet. All it took was printing out one page from the California Lottery website and all his troubles were over.

He logged on to the main page, then surfed to the list of winning numbers. There, glowing at him in the dark as if to mock him, were the numbers Lizzy had announced with such dramatics Wednesday evening. Smiling at his cleverness, Martin leaned back in his chair to reach the printer, feeling for the on button and flipping the switch.

Suddenly, the room descended into darkness as they lost power once again.

"Are you having a good laugh?" he asked the ceiling.

Lizzy shifted on the couch, pulling the blanket up to her chin. "Is everything okay?"

Martin expelled a heavy sigh, turned off the computer and joined her by the fireside. "Just talking to God. Who doesn't appear to be listening."

Lizzy lifted her head and propped it on an elbow. "What?"

"Nothing." He gently nudged her back on to the couch and tightened the blanket around her. "Get some sleep."

"There's plenty of room up here."

When he looked down, Martin noticed she had placed an extra pillow by her head and her body was pressed against the far side of the couch. "I appreciate the thought but I don't want to..."

"Nonsense," she answered sleepily. "I won't seduce you, I promise."

Martin climbed in while Lizzy pushed closer to the day bed's backboard. He turned his back toward her, facing the fire, hoping she wouldn't notice the effect her body was having on his. He felt her relax behind him, snuggling into the curves of his body, which only added to his discomfort.

"You're so warm," Lizzy said.

"I knew it. You only want me for my body heat."

Lizzy giggled. "And I thought I was being subtle."

A silence fell between them and Martin watched the dying embers blaze up when the wind came howling and a draft blew across the room. "Why were you talking to God?" he heard a soft whisper.

He turned to look at her, but found the tight quarters awkward. He stretched an arm over her head to free up some room and Lizzy shifted closer to his chest to allow them both comfort. Now, she stared off into the fire, while he studied the way light fell upon her cheeks and the way her hair smelled of spring.

"You smell like lavender."

"It's my shampoo, although I'm surprised the rain didn't wash it out."

He gently moved his hand to stroke her hair, discreetly pulling his fingers through the silky strands. "It smells heavenly."

Her free hand gripping the blanket relaxed. "Why were you talking to God?"

Martin gazed at the ceiling fan above his head, wondering how much to divulge. He wasn't allowed to speak of the impending sale, yet Lizzy must have determined for herself that *The Banner* was in trouble. "It's been one of those weeks."

"My grandmother always says there is no problem without a solution."

Her grandmother sounded like quite a woman, and one related to his mother. "Are you going to introduce me to this lady some day?"

Lizzy placed a hand on his chest, then lifted her head and rested her chin there. "If you don't like what you do, you can change your circumstances."

He knew she meant well, but nothing was that simple. "It's a little more complicated than that."

Lizzy stared at him for a moment longer, than returned her head to the crook of his shoulder. This time, she left her hand on his chest. "Sometimes the most complicated problems are the easiest to solve."

He continued to stroke her hair, watching her body relax as she drifted off to sleep. His problems were easy to solve, one lottery ticket and his loans would be met. Yet, lying there with Lizzy in his arms, he ached for a different solution. One that required complete surrender.

CHAPTER 7

*L*izzy cuddled next to the warm body, amazed at how strong it felt, how masculine the scent. How wrapping her arms around it provided such comfort. Then the bed shifted and the warmth disappeared, replaced by an ominous knock on the door.

When Lizzy rose and headed toward the noise, she was fifteen again, standing in the hallway of her New Orleans home, her hair hanging past her shoulders and the feel of her Beauty and the Beast slippers warm on her feet. She froze at the sight of the policeman's silhouette in the door's window, knowing why he had come and how her life would change forever.

"No," she wanted to scream but the words came out in a whisper. Run, she thought, but her legs refused to obey.

Just then, the door opened, but the policeman wasn't the man who had come to tell of her parents' deaths twelve years before. Peter stood on the threshold, his sly smile shining back at her through the yellow glaze of the porch light.

Lizzy bolted awake, her heart pounding. And if the dream hadn't been scary enough, the site of the giant man standing next to her was. This time, she did scream.

"Whoa," the giant said, approaching with his hands in front of him, palms outward.

Martin flew out of the bathroom, a toothbrush jutting from his mouth and a towel around his shoulders.

"Friend of yours?" the giant asked him.

Apparently they knew each other, but Martin's gaze remained on Lizzy. "Are you all right?"

Once Lizzy had a chance to think, she realized the giant was either Martin's brother or one of the med school buddies. She gazed up at the dark-haired man with deep, soul-searching eyes and saw the resemblance to Theodore Taylor. "Sorry, bad dream. You must be Paul."

He warmed instantly and held out his hand.

"Paul, this is my friend Lizzy, or Elizabeth Guidry," Martin said. "Now, if you two don't mind, I'm going to finish brushing my teeth."

"I'm sorry I screamed," Lizzy said, and Martin answered with a frothy smile before heading back into the bathroom. "Bad dream, that's all, and then I woke up and saw you," she said to Paul.

Paul sat down in an easy chair that matched nothing in the room. "Do you want to talk about it?"

If he hadn't appeared so sincere, Lizzy might have laughed. But something about Paul told her he meant well and his feelings would be hurt. "It's just a recurring dream I have."

"Something unfinished you need to face." Paul leaned back in the chair. "What's it about?"

She couldn't believe this stranger, even if he was Martin's brother. Why would he be interested in her dream? Then a thought came to her. "Martin said you graduated from med school. Are you by any chance a psychiatrist?"

Paul's eyebrows raised, a mixture of surprise and pride. "Yes, I am."

A psychiatrist, a filmmaker and a publisher, what a fascinating family the Taylors were. "Well, I doubt you'd be interested. It's pretty basic, actually."

Paul's countenance never changed. "I'd love to hear it. Dreams are my specialty."

Lizzy pulled a pillow to the back of the day bed to support her back and then relaxed, her heart still racing. For twelve years she had been plagued with the nightmare, what harm would it do to see what Paul made of such a dream? And for some reason, she felt comfortable talking to him, perhaps because he was a stranger.

"My parents died when I was a teenager," she began. "They had gone out for their anniversary and left me at home. I'm an only child so I stayed up for them. I guess that sounds weird."

Paul shook his head. "Not at all."

"They were my world." Lizzy paused, trying to catch her breath through the lump that had suddenly lodged in her chest. This was the point where she shut down, pushed the painful memories back inside and feigned a smile, but somehow talking to Paul helped. For some reason, speaking to this giant stranger lessened the hurt.

"All my friends used to hate their parents, always putting them down at school. But I adored mine. I wasn't very popular, didn't socialize much, but I didn't mind. My mom and I spent a lot of time together. My father adored me, used to call me his angel. The three of us took car trips on the weekends, went to movies, the theater."

She couldn't believe she was talking so much. A voice inside her head warned her to stop, that she was treading into dangerous territory.

"What happened that night?" Paul asked.

Lizzy didn't want to talk anymore, but she had waded halfway into the water and Paul was waiting on the other side, expecting her. "They were killed in an auto accident. Drunk driver. I keep dreaming of the policeman who came to tell me the news. It's always the same. I'm standing in the hallway of my home and hell is on the other side of the door."

This time she had to stop. Tears lurked dangerously close to the surface and she wasn't about to cry in front of a stranger, even if he was Martin's brother and a licensed psychiatrist.

"The world changed when your parents died," she heard Paul saying, but her eyes focused on the pattern of the Southwestern blanket in her lap. "Everything you loved and found safe and comforting disappeared when that policeman came to your door. Your dream is your fear that that might happen again."

Lizzy took a deep breath, amazed that an impartial person could make such simple sense of it all. Maybe what she had said to Martin the night before was right. Even the most complicated problems had simple solutions.

"In this dream, the policeman was my ex-boyfriend." She smiled grimly thinking of its significance. "I guess that's apropos since he left and wiped out my apartment this week."

Suddenly, Paul turned concerned and Lizzy spotted a resemblance to Martin. "What an asshole."

Lizzy giggled, thankful for the emotional relief of laughter. "Aren't you supposed to be emotionally detached from your patient's problems?"

Paul grinned back, his brown eyes lighting up, and it was clear he owned a good share of the Taylor charm. "You're not my patient. Maybe something else if Martin has any sense."

Something crashed in the bathroom, and Lizzy wondered if Martin could hear their conversation. "We're just friends," she said quickly. "We got caught in the storm last night."

The way Paul's eyes were glistening, she knew he didn't believe her. "Want some coffee?"

"Love some."

Paul moved to the kitchen, but paused in the middle of the room. "Quit hogging the bathroom," he yelled out, and suddenly Dr. Taylor disappeared and Martin's brother arrived.

. . .

MARTIN LEANED against the back of the bathroom door, still reeling from the knowledge of Lizzy's trauma. Everything had seemed so easy the day before. Cash in her lottery ticket and all her troubles—and his—would disintegrate. Now, after listening to her heart-wrenching story, he wasn't so sure, since she now trusted him and such a disclosure might ruin that faith. He felt twice the heel even considering charming her out of the money.

No wonder she was so defensive; she had lost everything that fateful night and was now the breadwinner of her small, transplanted family. And what had she said about her grandmother, that they were forced into bankruptcy when her grandfather died, which was why they left Bayou Rose?

Martin sighed and gazed at the ceiling again, wondering why it couldn't have been Chartreuse who had won that damned lottery ticket. He had no qualms about charming her out of money and would have enjoyed wild sex in the process. But then he wouldn't have had last night. He wouldn't have experienced the pleasure of Lizzy's company, one of the most relaxing, enjoyable evenings in a very long time.

Martin pressed his hands against the sides of his head, anticipating the pain to come. What was happening to him? He didn't have time for relationships, had a newspaper to save. Women the likes of Chartreuse were what he needed, not someone who demanded a commitment. Someone he'd want to share the rest of his life with.

Dear God, where had that thought come from? And Paul had insinuated Lizzy becoming something else. What was happening to him?

A soft knock sounded on the door and Martin jumped. "I hate to bother you glamour puss," Lizzy said on the other side of the door, "but I have to pee."

The sound of her lilting voice, the casual cadence of her

tone, made him smile. He felt comfortable around her, and obviously she felt the same. When she had screamed, nothing had mattered but rushing to her side, making sure she was safe. When had he ever felt that way with a woman?

And yet he wanted to steal her money. Worse, to erase whatever trust he had built with her.

He opened the door and found her hair pointing in all directions, the result of sleeping with it wet. He couldn't help but smile, couldn't help wondering how someone so frazzled could look so good.

"Sorry I missed it," she whispered with a sly grin.

"Missed what?"

She passed him at the door, nudging him into the living room in the process. "Your stale breath and morning boner."

Heavens, but she was flirting with him. Despite all his affirmations to remain unemotional, Martin couldn't help being thrilled at the prospect.

And getting in the last word.

"I'm sure it's nothing compared to the shape of your hair."

Her smile disappeared as she turned toward the mirror, letting out a muffled groan. Before Martin had time to tell her she still looked delightful, Lizzy slammed the bathroom door. "Hateful man," she muttered, but Martin could hear the humor in her voice.

When Martin reached the kitchen, Paul handed him a steaming cup of coffee. "Cute girl."

"Uh, huh."

Their eyes met and Martin knew where the conversation was heading. "She's a friend."

"Uh, huh."

"We came out here for lunch and got caught in the storm."

"Lucky you."

Lucky him indeed. "I don't have time for a relationship, Paul. You know that."

Paul grimaced and Martin worried the familiar lecture would be forthcoming. "Whose fault is that? Cassie said we could practically retire on the amount. Then you'll have all the time in the world."

Martin sipped his coffee, missing the bitterness of his chicory blend. "I'm not selling."

"Martin, think about it, will you?"

"Think about what, Paul? The paper's been in our family for three generations. It's our legacy."

Paul placed his cup on the counter and turned to pour another. "It's your legacy."

Martin couldn't believe his ears. "You're asking me to give up everything Pops and Dad worked for? You're asking me to sell a business that's almost a hundred years old so you can pay off your school loans?"

Paul turned abruptly, nearly spilling his coffee. "That's not fair. I'm asking you to give us all a life. We're all struggling here and that damn newspaper is on its last leg. What harm would it be to come out ahead?"

Martin sighed and leaned his head back against the door-frame in bad need of a paint job. "I promised him."

"Promises?" Paul asked, his voice rising. "This is about promises?"

"I swore to Dad this paper would never be owned by the Times," Martin argued. "You know how much he hated Wendell Steiger. You saw what they did to that community chain in the northwest valley. If this paper doesn't bring in the money they expect, they will shut it down."

"Then let them." Paul's eyes glistened with an anger Martin rarely witnessed. "Let it be their problem for once."

Martin gazed at his tall brother in disbelief. "How can you feel this way? That newspaper was Dad's sweat and tears."

Whatever rare anger Paul exhibited, pain now replaced it.

"Remember the time I pitched that no-hitter? The championship game? The one where we took the state pennant?"

Suddenly, Martin understood. "Yes."

"He promised to be there. He promised me."

Martin didn't know how to react. Their father had broken endless promises. By the time Martin had entered high school, he had given up waiting for his father to make time on Martin's turf, had resolved himself to seeing him at the paper instead. But it had been harder for his siblings who had no interest in the business. Still, Martin knew that pain of neglect well.

"Remember the time you broke your arm falling out of the top bunk? Dad had an advertising meeting so he couldn't come to the hospital."

Yes, he remembered, relived the disappointment as if a fresh knife had ripped through his heart. "It doesn't matter, Paul. Mom was there."

"Yeah." Paul raised his cup to his lips. "Mom was always there."

The two men drank their coffee in silence, until Paul exhaled deeply. "I want you to be happy. And looking at you now, working as hard as you do, I know you're not."

Happiness? He truly didn't know the meaning of the word. He experienced brief moments of happiness, like the time he wrote a piece for *Rolling Stone*. The editor loved the profile, had asked for more, and for a time Martin held the world in his grip, imagined he had finally found his true calling.

Two days later his father had died from a heart attack.

"I can't sell," he said as much to himself as to his brother.

Paul shook his head, then placed his cup on the counter so hard the coffee spilled out the top. Just then Lizzy entered the room, jumping at the noise.

"Knock some sense into him, will ya Lizzy," Paul said, and then stormed out of the room on to the porch. His boots hit the stairs so hard the floorboards shook.

Martin hated that Lizzy had witnessed their argument. He ran a hand through his hair and avoided her eyes. "I'm sorry about that. It's a family matter."

"Do you want to talk about it?"

Yes, he thought, but he wasn't allowed to speak of the impending sale. Still, maybe it was time to clear the air between them over the lottery ticket. "Lizzy, there's something I have to tell you."

"Okay." She inched closer, brushing a strand behind her ear nervously. "But would you like a hug first?"

Before he had time to digest her words, she slipped her arms around his waist and leaned her cheek against his shoulder. She no longer smelled of lavender, but something more masculine that belonged to Paul. And yet, the scent that was all Lizzy permeated his senses and the feel of her body fitting so perfectly into his overtook all reason. He wrapped his arms about her and held on for dear life.

"Nana says a hug may not solve your problems but it makes you feel a whole lot better."

"Thank God for Nana," he muttered, pulling her close. She felt as wonderful as he imagined. "Can I meet her someday?"

Lizzy closed her eyes as she rested her cheek against Martin's shoulder, breathing in a mixture of fresh shower and masculinity. His strong arms wound about her, shutting out the problems of the world, holding her tight in a circle of comfort. How long had it been since she was hugged by a man her own age? Truly hugged, as if the affection really mattered? And this one felt so right.

"Maybe on the drive back you could introduce me?"

Martin had said something, but she missed his meaning, too busy savoring the warmth of his embrace, enjoying the feel of his strong back against her hands. "What?" she muttered into his chest.

"Your Nana. Maybe I could meet her?"

Lizzy pulled away as if someone had doused her with cold water. Suddenly, she recalled what Nana had said about Martin and his intentions, reminding herself that it was the last thing she needed at a time like this. Paul had been right. She was scared her world would change again, that someone might rock her currently unstable existence. Only the person standing at the door wasn't Peter.

She ran a hand through her hair subconsciously. "Where's my coffee cup?"

She found the mug Paul had given her by the sink, then poured it full. "Was it something I said?" Martin said behind her, touching her shoulder.

"No." She faced him and offered her best noncommittal smile, but he didn't believe her.

"What just happened?"

"Do you want some breakfast?" She gazed around, but the kitchen appeared devoid of food. "I'm not that hungry. We probably should be getting back."

Martin watched her litany, but she knew he was wondering how someone semi-intelligent and mature could react as rash as she had. She had a hard time believing it as well, amazed and embarrassed at her impulsive retreat. Yet, those charming blue eyes convinced her to trust him —she had hugged him no less, not to mention spending the night with him on a couch!—and that frightened her to the core.

"I'm sorry," she said, hoping that would clear the air. "I'm a bit jittery this morning, the bad dream and all. Plus, I really need to get back to see my grandmother."

"Sure." Martin placed his cup in the sink and grabbed his jacket. "Finish your coffee. I'll go say goodbye to Paul."

Was it her imagination or did he appear injured? Martin had been so kind over the past two days, insisting on paying for every-thing and acting the gentleman. And here she was casting him off after offering a friendly hug. Lizzy rubbed her eyes, chastising herself for overreacting. But it was so soon. The last thing she needed right now was a blonde, blue-eyed Californian promising the moon only to deliver heartache and steal her money.

Lizzy sipped her weak coffee. Martin didn't want her money, what little she had. The man had a steady income, even if the paper was experiencing dire times. Yet, he had made it clear he had no time for relationships and commitment. Martin Taylor might not clean her apartment of furniture, but he sure could wipe out her heart. She needed neither calamity right now.

She took another sip, then emptied the cup into the sink and cleaned the dishes while her stomach grumbled with hunger. She thought of yesterday's breakfast, when Martin had delivered the beautiful table and four chairs. He wasn't the enemy, she thought. Yet, how could she be sure?

"You don't have to do that," Martin said, entering the kitchen with keys in hand.

"It's only three cups."

"Paul's meticulous about this place. He'll probably clean them again anyway."

She wiped her hands on the dishtowel and turned. When their eyes finally met, she knew her previous actions had wounded him slightly. "A man who can clean. What a catch." She didn't know what she was talking about, but she wanted to return to the relaxed state when their conversations flowed easily.

"I can cook," Martin offered. "I told you I make a great gumbo."

He appeared sincere enough, his pleading blue eyes tugging at her heartstrings. "So, you said."

He grinned a little. "You don't believe me."

"Peter once said there was a great little restaurant in

Burbank that served gumbo and it turned out to be a soup with three types of fish I didn't recognize."

His smile grew slightly, but his eyes still held a trace of sadness. "Lizzy, I'm not Peter."

No, she thought, he wasn't Peter. At least something deep inside her soul agreed to that statement. But it was her mind that refused to believe.

Martin seemed to read the conflict raging inside her and he pulled her sweater off the back of the kitchen chair. "Ready?"

They stepped onto the deck and sunlight drenched them while the sky arched above a brilliant blue. Lizzy pulled her now-dry sweater tight across her shoulder to brace against the chilly wind blowing from the ocean. Was it only yesterday the world languished under dark clouds?

When they reached the car, half of Paul's frame was lost beneath the hood. "He's my baby brother," Martin informed her. "But you'd never know that."

"You need to check the transmission fluid more often." Paul's head emerged and he wiped his hands on an oily rag. "You could use some new belts too."

Martin held out his hand and Paul grasped it, while both men slapped each other on opposite arms in a fraternal gesture. "Thanks. I'll keep that in mind."

Martin headed for the passenger side, but Paul reached there first, opening the door and standing aside, waiting for Lizzy to enter. After a moment collecting herself to such gallantry, she climbed inside. "So much chivalry in one family. I'd love to meet your mother."

Paul leaned on the doorframe. "That's easy enough to do. She's on the ride home." To Martin, who was climbing in behind the wheel, he added, "Why not stop by Ojai? I'll call ahead and have Mom make you some breakfast."

Martin stole a glance to Lizzy, waiting for her refusal. Nana would be expecting her, especially since she failed to show up yesterday. Would a few hours matter on such a beautiful day? "It's on the way home," she offered. "Unless you need to get back right away."

Paul patted the side of the car. "The damned paper can wait. I know she'd love to meet you. She'll be thrilled knowing Martin actually has a date."

Martin started to object, but Paul rounded the car to his side. When he got to Martin's window, he gave his brother a tight squeeze on the arm. "Think about what we talked about, okay?"

Martin started the engine and shifted the car into reverse. "Sure."

To Lizzy, Paul shouted as the car backed out of the driveway. "Get Mom to read your tea leaves."

Martin and Lizzy waved as the Ford took off toward the freeway. "Your mother reads tea leaves?"

Martin laughed, and the sound of it made Lizzy relax. "Coffee actually."

His family was becoming more interesting by the minute. "Your mother reads coffee grinds?"

As he turned a corner and entered the freeway, she saw him smile. "You're a non-believer. It's okay, most people don't…"

"No, it's not that. My grandmother swears she can read a person by holding his hand."

Martin paused, seemingly somewhat shocked at the news. Perhaps he was a non-believer. "Is she accurate?"

"Yeah, she is. She saw right through Peter the first time they met."

The smile disappeared and Martin turned pale. For a brief moment, Lizzy knew she was right not to trust him. But then the moment passed.

They drove through the mountainous back roads toward Ojai, his four by four easily making it through the small patches of snow that had fallen in the night. Most of the snow lay at the higher elevations, but occasionally they would turn a corner and witness a grove of pine trees covered in the powder close enough to touch.

"Do you think we could stop where there's a patch of snow?" Lizzy asked.

"Don't tell me you haven't seen snow before."

She couldn't remember the last time, nine years maybe? "I saw some the first year Nana and I moved here, but we drove to the spot, near Frazier Park, I think. I've never seen it fall."

"That's a crime. When we get to my mom's, we'll have to do something about that."

They reached his mother's place within forty-five minutes, a quaint retreat nestled in the mountains above the artsy town of Ojai. As they drove up the long, winding driveway, the bungalow came slowly into view. Lizzy felt her chest tighten when she finally made out the small Tudor house, almost a replica of the one in her mother's snow globe. There was even snow on the ground by the house's front door.

"Wow."

Martin turned off the engine and jumped out of his seat, rounding the front of the car to her side. When he opened her door, she still couldn't take her eyes off the house.

"Cute, isn't it? It belongs to a friend of the family's. The house has been on the market for months but it hasn't sold. The couple had this trip planned to Italy so Mom's housesitting in case a real estate agent comes by."

For the first time in her life, Lizzy wished she had won the lottery so she could snatch up the sight before her. What was even stranger was the song her mother used to sing when she put Lizzy to bed as a child, something about finding a nest, somewhere out in the west.

"Lizzy."

Martin's voice broke her thoughts and she took his hand and stepped out of the car. "Sorry. This place reminds me of something."

They walked toward the front of the house, but Martin held on to her hand. "What does it remind you of?"

"You'll laugh."

He paused outside the door underneath an overhanging pine. "No, I won't."

"What does Ojai mean?" she asked, changing the subject.

"The town sites in a valley in the cradle of the mountains. The Indians thought it looked like a nest."

Her heart constricted further at his words, but she didn't have time to think further. Martin reached up to the pine shadowing them and yanked at its branches. While they stood in front of her dream house holding hands, a shower of snow fell upon them.

Martin leaned over and kissed her cheek. "Today, all your dreams come true."

CHAPTER 8

"*S*o, the house is your snow globe?"

Martin's mother, Olivia, was nothing like Lizzy imagined. For some reason she expected someone akin to Theodore Taylor: forceful, professional, and aggressive. Instead, the graceful blue-eyed woman appeared more like Mother Nature, wearing her blonde hair long, tied down her back in a massive braid with short tendrils gracing her forehead. Her sweater hung loose, overlapping a free-flowing skirt that hung to her ankles and almost concealed thick woolen socks and a pair of beige Keds.

But it was her azure eyes that captivated Lizzy, sparkling and warm like Martin's. In fact, she found the resemblance uncanny, realizing for the first time that Martin held no similarities to his father.

"I know it sounds silly," Lizzy said as Olivia handed her a cup of coffee. "My mother used to sing me this song, some old ballad Nana sang to her when she was a child. It talked about finding perfect peace in a place out west."

"And let the rest of the world go by," Olivia sang with a knowing smile.

Lizzy couldn't believe it. She had been raking her brain for the past half hour trying to remember the words. "That's it. That's the name of the song, *Let The Rest of The World Go By.*"

Olivia opened the door to the living room and stepped aside to let Lizzy through. "It is an old song. Haven't thought about that one in years. We used to sing it at Girl Scouts."

The two entered the living room and gazed at the mahogany woodwork gracing the stone fireplace and the rustic Craftsman furniture surrounding it. Lizzy ran her fingers across the rolled top desk. "What a gorgeous house."

"A couple million and it's yours."

Lizzy shook her head thinking about the enormity of that sum. "Might as well be the moon."

"Fifty-three acres of fruit trees," Olivia added. "And a guest house by the pool."

"A pool?" This definitely was a dream house.

Olivia led the way back into the hall and the winding staircase. She leaned her head into the kitchen area before moving on. "Come on Martin. I'm going to show Lizzy the upstairs."

Martin joined them, wiping his hands on a dishtowel. "Mom, I've seen this before."

Olivia ignored him, climbing the stairs in her tennis shoes as if she wore glass slippers. What was it about this woman that made Lizzy stand in awe? Martin seemed just as entranced, for he followed her to the second floor without another word.

"This is the master bedroom," Olivia announced at the threshold of the magnificent room. "A separate sitting area, two walk-in closets and a spa bathtub in an enormous bathroom."

The room had been decorated in a rustic country motif, exhibiting shades of soft reds and blues. A giant quilt covered a two-poster bed and there were colorful, homey rugs gracing the wooden floors.

"It's perfect," Lizzy said, feeling as if she could jump into that bed and never leave.

Olivia led them back into the hall, but Martin paused at the doorway, watching Lizzy's every move. She wished she could read his mind for his eyes studied her intently.

"Come see the children's rooms," Olivia called to them.

They crossed the staircase landing to the other side of the house and found two bedrooms joined by a playroom, complete with a crawlspace around the perimeter and a window overlooking the fruit trees. Lizzy sat at the window seat and gazed out at the groves, now covered with plastic sheets to protect them from the cold.

"Perfect for children," she heard Olivia say. "And plenty of room for them to play outdoors."

When Lizzy glanced back at Martin's Earth Mother, she realized Olivia was planting a hint toward her son. Martin sent his eyes heavenward when he caught on.

"Two kids and a dog," Lizzy said, trying to add to his discomfort, but surprisingly Martin looked back at her and smiled.

"Oh, has this subject come up before now?"

Martin's smile disappeared and he sighed. "Think I'll get back to fixing breakfast now."

With Martin gone, Olivia turned her knowing grin to Lizzy.

"We're just friends," Lizzy said.

Olivia gazed at her the same way Paul had, that she understood something they had failed to. "Want me to read your cup now?"

Lizzy glanced down into her mug but she had plenty of coffee left.

"Let's go downstairs and eat," Olivia said, patting her knee. "Then we'll see what it says."

When Olivia and Lizzy entered the dining room, Martin had three heaping plates waiting for them, everything from scrambled eggs and salsa to bacon, sourdough toast and home-fried potatoes.

"Told ya I could cook," he said to Lizzy with a wicked grin.

The women sat at the table while Martin returned to the kitchen for drinks. "I taught them well," Olivia explained. "No helpless men in my household."

"You're a goddess," Lizzy whispered. And she meant every word.

AN HOUR PASSED and still they relaxed over breakfast, no one in a hurry to leave the table. Martin didn't know if it was the magical house or the wonderful company, but he hadn't enjoyed a morning like this in an eternity. Except for the awesome potatoes Lizzy had cooked him the day before, he couldn't remember the last time he hadn't grabbed a bagel and coffee flying out the door.

Lizzy. Her eyes glistened as she listened to his mother explain the process of growing strawberries, occasionally glancing his way and offering a smile. The two were getting along famously, no surprise there, and it warmed his heart knowing his mother approved.

Damn, he thought, rubbing the bridge of his nose. He did it again, made reference to something he couldn't have.

"Are you having those headaches of yours?" Olivia asked. To Lizzy, she added, "That newspaper is killing him."

"The newspaper is not killing me, Mom," Martin insisted, although he often believed it. "I'm fine."

"You're not fine, but we won't speak of that today." She pointed to Lizzy's coffee cup. "Ready?"

Lizzy hesitantly handed her the cup and Olivia studied its contents. Martin knew what would follow, some silly nonsense about finding true love or an opportunity waiting to happen. He didn't doubt his mother was psychic, but reading coffee grinds was a stretch. Most of her predictions were either too vague to identify or way out in left field. She once told their maid who spoke no English that her daughter would be Miss America.

This time, however, his mother grew silent and frowned.

"Oh God," Lizzy said. "More money problems?"

Olivia looked up surprised. "Why no. I see you never having financial problems for the rest of your life."

Lizzy looked skeptical, and ironically Martin began to think his mother might be right on.

"I see a windfall of some sorts." Olivia turned the cup to read the other side. "Maybe someone in your family will leave you an inheritance."

Lizzy still didn't buy it. Martin could tell from her expression there was no one back home in Louisiana who had money. If there were, she and her Nana would have stayed there twelve years ago. If it was the last thing he did that day, he would drag her into her apartment and make her check that damned lottery ticket.

Martin rose to pour himself another cup of coffee from the sideboard, but when he turned and leaned back against it, his mother was staring at him.

"You will have a judgment to make," Olivia said, still looking at her son. Then she turned back to Lizzy and took one hand. "It has to do with the money. But don't judge this person in haste. Things are not as they appear."

Olivia raised her eyes in his direction once more and Martin knew he had been discovered. As a child he couldn't pee without his mother yelling from the other room, "Hit the water!" How she knew he had missed the toilet bowl was beyond him. But then she saw and heard everything, and he kicked himself for forgetting that.

"We should get going." Martin began picking up dishes and leftover plates of food, startling them both. Olivia didn't appear surprised by his announcement but Lizzy did. She jumped up from the table and offered to help.

"I'm sorry," she said, passing him in the kitchen. "I didn't mean to stay so long. It's been a long time since I had family..." She paused, then handed him her plates. "I'll go clean off the table."

Martin mentally reminded himself what a complete ass he was. They were having a good time until his mother reached inside his soul and made him feel like he was five years old and stealing cookies from the jar, which was his problem, certainly not Lizzy's. Especially since the cookies were hers. Now, he had taken away Lizzy's chance at a family breakfast.

He decided to apologize and stay longer, but his mother met him at the kitchen door with his jacket. "Don't worry about the dishes. You two get home before it gets late."

"I have to help you clean up," Lizzy insisted.

Olivia took Lizzy's face in her hands lovingly. His mother liked her, that much was obvious. "No, you don't my dear. I have nothing else to do all day and this will help the hours go by."

Lizzy kissed Olivia on the cheek. "Then do come to Santa Helena for dinner one night. Nana would love to meet you and I'll make something special."

Martin watched the color drain from his mother's face, her one fault surfacing. "That's very nice of you." She pulled at her collar nervously and her tone grew cold. "We'll see. Right now, I'm really busy with the house."

Lizzy nodded. "Sure. When the Richardsons get back perhaps."

"Perhaps."

Martin pulled on his jacket and walked Lizzy to the car, then he hugged his mother goodbye, relishing the feel of the woman who had always been his idol. "I love you, Mom."

"I love you, too," she whispered back. "Take care of yourself, Martin. Don't be such a stranger. And don't let that newspaper win."

He knew she meant well, much like the rest of his family, but he didn't want to think, let alone talk about *The Banner*. He squeezed her, then entered the car. Within minutes they were back on the highway.

"Did I say something wrong?" Lizzy asked.

Martin instantly knew what she was referring to, realized Lizzy felt his mother's cold rebuff. "Don't take it personally. My mother is a recluse. She doesn't go many places."

"That's hard to believe." Lizzy turned up the heater and snuggled into the seat. "She's such an impressive woman, so self-assured."

An understatement, Martin thought, feeling the familiar pain grip his heart. "She wasn't always a hermit. She and my dad were very much in love for a long time, but in the last decade they grew apart. He worked a lot, was never home, and Mom had to shoulder much of the child rearing." He didn't want to relive any of this, but how could one explain his mother's sudden resolve to never leave her house?

"Is that when she stopped going out?"

Martin remembered the brunette coming out of his father's office that weekend, tugging at her skirts and adjusting her hair. It had been years ago and unfortunately not an isolated affair. His mother had known, figured it out one way or another, and the knowledge had floored her.

"My dad was unfaithful and I believe Mom fell out of love with him," Martin said softly. "She didn't say anything, but we all sensed it. Then she started seeing Dave. They were old sweethearts in high school and remained good friends. I doubt anything came of their new relationship, but when my dad died months later Mom fell apart and she refused to see Dave or pretty much anyone else. Guilt is a powerful enemy."

That was an understatement, too.

"How awful for your mom," he heard Lizzy say, but Martin's mind was focused on how one man could hold such a tight grip over a family in both life and death.

The drive back to Santa Helena was uneventful, although the conversations weren't. They discussed everything from family dynamics to City Council personalities, laughing at the idiosyncrasies of Santa Helena's best from two sides of the political fence. Before Lizzy knew it, they pulled in front of the Mountain View Nursing Home.

"Want to come in and meet Nana?"

He stretched out an arm along the back of her seat and leaned close, reminding her of the way he felt and smelled when she had hugged him in Paul's kitchen. Two days ago she swore she hated the man. Now, she hated saying goodbye.

"I have to get back," Martin said with regret in his voice. "It's been two days. Who knows what I'll find when I get there."

Martin's gaze fell to her lips and she wondered if he would kiss her again. For an instant, she hoped he would, but then logic set in and she moved back toward the door. "Maybe another time then."

Reality seemed to invade his senses too. He straightened and nodded. "Right."

"Are we still on for Monday?" God, she sounded pushy.

Martin reached a hand to her face and pulled a loose tendril behind her ear. "You bet. I'll pick you up at seven?"

The simple movement sent waves of electrifying pleasure coursing through her. If one finger on her hair could work such magic, what would his kisses be like?

She didn't have time to think of such things. Nana was waiting. "Monday at seven then."

Lizzy opened the door to be rid of the trance he was placing on her, but she felt a tug on her forearm before her feet hit the pavement. "I had a wonderful time," he said when she looked back. "Thank you for that."

He was so close now, she imagined herself plunging into those pools of blue. It wasn't fair that one man could look so good and be so charming. Somewhere underneath all those mountains of perfection had to be a valley of faults.

"I had a good time too." She really meant it, even if her insides were screaming in fear. His lips were so close, so enticing and she wanted so badly to taste them.

They moved forward slowly, their lips only a breath away, when Diane Wells called out her name. Lizzy sucked in a breath, then backed away from his reach, one foot touching cement. "I have to go. Thanks for everything. It was a wonderful weekend."

"Wait," Martin shouted when she exited the car and was about to close the door. "Can I call you later?"

Lizzy leaned into the door, amazed at how that request sent thousands of tingly sensations through her. "Sure," she said, trying to keep the excitement out of her voice.

She felt Diane touch her shoulder and reality came roaring back. The nursing home director launched into a conversation about Nana's bills, but Lizzy focused on Martin driving away, waving his hand out the driver's window as he disappeared down the street.

"So, you see. Your problems are solved."

This caught her attention. "What?"

"I just told you. The mayor called an emergency session of the City Council this morning and they finally passed all those budget bills. I don't know what he did to get them through, but our funding has been restored and we don't have to raise the rates."

"No increase?" Was she hearing right?

"No, my dear." The petite woman hugged the clipboard to her chest. "And I can't believe you don't know about this. I was positive you were the force behind it all."

Lizzy still reeled from the news. "I was in Santa Barbara the last two days."

"Santa Barbara?" Diane offered a toothy smile. "Hot date?"

"No," Lizzy answered a little too forcefully. "Just a friend."

Diane leaned in close and gave her a wink. "Well, whatever you did to turn Martin Taylor around worked."

The comment made Lizzy's heart freeze. "What do you mean?"

Diane's assistant called from the doorway, telling the director she had a phone call. "Read the paper," was the last thing Diane said before re-entering the building. "Today's *Banner*."

Lizzy entered the lobby but no newspapers were to be found. She headed toward Nana's room, finding her grandmother wrapped in a blanket sleeping in her favorite chair, the house cat lying in her lap. Quietly, Lizzy began petting Madonna, but the calico cat stretched and Nana woke with a start. She began spewing forth a conversation in Cajun French, uttering long sentences Lizzy had trouble following, while the cat darted away.

"Nana, *c'est moi*." Lizzy gently captured her grandmother's shoulder. "It's me. Lizzy."

Nana's eyes focused until she realized where she was. Then she relaxed and patted Lizzy's hand. "I was just telling your grandfather to wipe his feet."

Lizzy kneeled in front of her. "Don't you hate when he does that?"

Nana's dark brown eyes studied her, while she ran a weathered hand against her cheek. "You passed a good time with this newspaper guy?"

She passed a wonderful time with Martin, but she remained conflicted about her feelings. She wanted so badly to rush in and tell Nana that the past two days had been some of the best she had ever experienced, but wasn't sure she could allow herself that pleasure. She wasn't sure she could trust Martin. Or herself.

"What's with you?" Nana intruded her thoughts. "You like him or not?"

Lizzy finally sat upon the floor next to Nana's chair. "I don't know. Yes. I'm not sure."

"That makes a hellova lot of sense."

"He's fun," Lizzy tried to explain. "He's charming. He's good looking. He has these beautiful blue eyes and he's extremely polite. He's got a nice family too."

"Sounds heavenly. What on earth's the problem?"

"I don't know." She gazed up at her grandmother, hoping she might have the answer, but her lips were pursed in disapproval. "I'm not sure I trust him."

"Why not?"

Lizzy stood up and began pacing the room. "I don't know."

"Sounds to me like you don't know much."

Lizzy laughed. "I guess that's true."

Nana grabbed her cane and rose from her chair. She hobbled over to Lizzy and took her hand. "Sweetheart, I have been silent these past years, allowing you your grief, but I think it's time I spoke up."

A tightness stole across Lizzy's chest, both from the tone in her grandmother's voice and the subject matter. "Nana we don't need to discuss this."

Nana squeezed her hand, forcing Lizzy to look at her. "I let you retreat from the world when your parents died, fought the social services people to keep you at home when you didn't want to go to school."

A cloud passed over Lizzy's heart thinking back to those horrid days when she hadn't the strength to get out of bed, let alone attend school. "I know, Nana..."

"And ever since we came to California, all that work to support us. You never had time for socializing with friends."

"I've had the Cajun Embassy. Best friends anyone could ever hope for."

"True, but they're your college friends and you only see them occasionally. I'm talking about here, in Santa Helena, where you hardly date. Except for that deadbeat Peter and I think he was just a means to an end, if you know what I mean."

Lizzy blushed. Was her grandmother talking about sex?

"Peter aside, I never met anyone I wanted to date," she said, changing the course of the conversation. "There's a reason they say good men are hard to find. Peter's a great example."

"No, *'tit monde,* you've built a wall around yourself, and it's keeping you from being happy."

The words sunk in hard, like her grandfather's anchor plunging into the bayou mud. Lizzy had trouble breathing, wanting nothing more than to run away.

"Your parents are gone, sweetheart." Nana squeezed her shoulders again. "And they would be heartbroken if they knew you weren't happy."

"I'm happy." The words were uttered as defiance, but they emerged no more than a breath, followed by a rush of tears. Lizzy looked away, trying to fight them off, but the effort was futile.

She felt Nana's strong arms encircle her, while the tears poured down her cheeks. Whatever wall she managed for the world disintegrated in her grandmother's embrace. "Everybody leaves me," Lizzy whispered as sobs rose in her chest.

They stood that way in the middle of the room for several minutes, Nana rubbing her back, stroking her hair, while all the pain and hurt of twelve long years rushed forward. Was it possible that she had carried her torment around her like a shield, as Nana suggested? Or was she merely being protective of her heart? She truly didn't know anymore.

Lizzy pulled away and tried to compose herself. "We all have to go someday," Nana told her, wiping her eyes with a handkerchief. "It's all a part of life."

"I know." Lizzy blew her nose. "That's why I come here every day. I don't want to miss a moment with you."

Nana inched backwards and fell into her chair, then she

opened her arms and Lizzy knelt before her again, placing her head in her lap as she had as a child. "I love seeing you every day, *chèr*. But, to be honest, you're getting a little boring."

Lizzy glanced up to find her grandmother's eyes sparkling with humor. "Gee, thanks."

"I could use some new company. A man would be nice. Maybe some kids."

Now, she knew where Nana was leading. She rested her head back in Nana's lap and sighed. "Then Martin Taylor is out of the picture. He doesn't have time for a relationship, works too much at the newspaper. He made that crystal clear to me on the ride out to Santa Barbara." A silence followed, allowing Lizzy to feel the enormity of those words. Was she disheartened that he wasn't interested? She certainly felt disappointed. "We're friends. That's good enough for now."

Nana slapped her playfully on the back. "Pooh. Your grandfather told me the same thing, was too busy working on his daddy's shrimp boat, saving up money to go to college."

Lizzy hadn't heard this story before. "What happened?"

"What happens with anybody who falls in love? He decided a life with me was more important than four years at LSU. We were happy every day of our lives together, in and out of bed." Nana giggled, and Lizzy stopped breathing. This was more than she cared to hear. "The fact that I made a good gumbo didn't hurt either."

"Martin's life is complicated, Nana. He inherited a newspaper that takes up all his time." Heavens, she was making excuses for the man. As if he might be a contender.

"Oh, I forgot," Nana said. "You young people have it so different from us."

Lizzy straightened and met her grandmother's stern gaze. "I didn't mean it that way."

"The fact that one poor season and we had nothing to eat in no way compares to the problems of a modern newspaper."

"Nana, I didn't mean it that way."

Her grandmother folded her arms. "How did you mean it then?"

How did she mean it? Was she repeating what he had told her in an effort to keep the wall up?

"I'm just telling you what Martin said. His newspaper has lots of problems and he must work constantly, never having much time for..."

"Trips to Santa Barbara?"

Lizzy smiled at her grandmother's stubbornness. "We got caught in the rain."

She wasn't buying any of it. "And the editorial?"

So, now they were back to that issue. "He didn't write that editorial to get my attention. Why would any sane man insult a woman...?"

"I'm not talking about that one." Nana unfolded her arms, reached a hand by the side of her chair where she kept her reading materials, and produced the day's newspaper. "I'm talking about this one."

Lizzy stared at *The Banner*, realizing it held the editorial Martin had written the night before at Paul's beach house. She took the paper from Nana's hands, but stole a glance at her grandmother before she opened it to the op ed page.

"Now, tell me he doesn't have time," Nana said with a laugh.

CHAPTER 9

*L*izzy stretched out on the cold, empty floor of her living room, reading the Sunday paper of the *Los Angeles Daily Times*, but every time she tried to focus on the developments in the Middle East, her mind kept drifting back to Saturday's editorial in the *Santa Helena Banner*.

The op ed page, folded back to reveal Martin's lead editorial, stuck out beneath the Sunday comics. Lizzy pulled it free to read it once more.

"There comes a time when we all need to be reminded of our true values, of our reason to be," Martin wrote. "This newspaper may be owned by the Taylor family, but the community is its voice. 'A good newspaper and the exchange of information and ideas is the basis of civilized society' and the reason *The Banner* exists. A dear friend reminded me of this fact, something I have failed to remember these past few weeks."

Lizzy sipped her coffee, hoping to dislodge the lump in her throat as she continued reading. Although Martin still believed the D.A. was wrong in his actions, he recanted his harsh words against the mayor and lodged his complaints against the members of the City Council whom he felt were hindering the "great efforts of the mayor's office." He added that his "disregard to the feelings of the mayor's public relations director" was unethical and disrespectful and he formally apologized.

Lizzy ran her fingers across the lines of gray type that held her name, newspaper ink marring her fingertips. "Santa Helena needs to work together," Martin concluded. "We cannot succeed in any business without uniting toward a common goal, the well-being of our community. *The Banner* will now and always be its voice towards that goal."

The words gave her shivers, Martin's heartfelt emotions pouring through. Theodore Taylor never could have phrased it so well, never have captured the passion of such a feeling.

Lizzy sat up and stretched her back that ached from reading the paper across the floor. Although her apartment looked infinitely better with her Mission table and chairs, the other half still appeared forlornly empty. She decided to move to the kitchen table and give her vertebrae some rest.

She gathered the newspaper in her hands but a heavy knock on her door interrupted her actions. "Police, open up," the person cried.

Still holding the newspapers, Lizzy opened her door and shook her head.

"You never fall for it," Dave said, laughing. "How do you always know it's me?"

The man couldn't change his voice if he turned eleven again. Before she could come back with something witty, she noticed a beige couch in the hallway. "If you confiscated that from Peter's place, I think you got someone else's couch."

Someone out of sight tossed a bag on to the lovely piece of furniture and within seconds an out-of-breath Martin appeared carrying matching cushions. "It comes with bagels."

She couldn't help herself. Despite her rational mind urging her to proceed with caution, she felt her face light up like Christmas. To both her comfort and dismay, Martin's face did the same. In that second, her heart constricted with the prospect of love and the fear of commitment.

"Are you going to let us in or have us sit in the hall all day?" Dave asked.

"Sure." Lizzy backed away and threw the newspaper on the table. "Can I help?"

By the time she turned, the men were halfway through the door. They placed the couch along the far wall, then stepped back and admired their work. "Fits perfectly."

Martin was right. The couch filled up the space nicely, transforming the room instantly. When he retrieved the cushions from the hall and placed them on the couch, the apartment looked normal again.

"It's a sofa bed," he added. "Pretty comfortable too. I've slept on it before and can vouch there are no lumps."

Again, Lizzy beamed at the beautiful couch before her, but this was too much. Where before her apartment consisted of tasteful but basic furniture she had purchased second-hand, she now had an expensive couch and antiques. She started to protest, but noticed Martin frowning at the kitchen table. She glanced over and spotted the *Daily Times*, guilt washing over her faster than a mountain deluge in spring.

"I get the *Sunday Daily Times*," she said quickly. "I read *The Banner* at work."

Lizzy never felt so ashamed of herself as she did at that moment. If his newspaper was hurting like rumors suggested, she was part of the problem by refusing to get her own subscription. Martin offered up a polite smile, but Lizzy knew he was cringing inside. She avoided his eyes and headed for the kitchen. "You all want some coffee with those bagels?"

"Have to run," Dave answered, heading out the door. "Just wanted to give Martin a hand."

Lizzy returned to the living room to gauge Martin's need for coffee but he glanced at his watch.

"Have a meeting at nine." He paused at the front door, one hand lifted lazily on the frame while he grinned down at her. "The bagels are for you, sweetpea. But you want to grab a bite later?"

Boy, did she ever. His image filling her doorframe was causing her breath to shorten. "I can't. I have to take Nana to Mass in an hour and then the church is having a family potluck afterwards."

Martin absorbed this and nodded. "I have a coffee table you might like."

She leaned against the opposite frame. "Martin, I can't accept all this."

The hand resting on the doorframe slid down slightly and he moved closer, merely a breath away from her face. "Yes, you can. I told you before, you're doing me a favor."

He was so close and his eyes so blue, she had to force herself to concentrate on what they were talking about. "I'm doing you a favor?"

Something came to mind and Martin stiffened. "Yeah, well, I'd rather not be reminded of my dad right now."

"Why?"

Martin checked his watch again. "Gotta go. I can't miss this meeting. Cassie postponed it from Friday and everyone wants to get back home as soon as possible."

He turned to head down the hallway, but Lizzy grabbed his elbow. "You're very talented, you know."

The old Martin returned, charming smile and all. He leaned forward again, one finger tracing the lines of her cheek. "I am talented. But how do you know this when we haven't advanced to tongues yet?"

He really wasn't anything like Peter. If Peter had made that comment, it would have come out coarse and crude. Hearing Martin say such a thing only made her laugh.

"Are you sure you don't want a bagel?" she asked him, hoping he would stay.

His smile faded, but his finger remained on her chin. "No, I really have to go."

He turned his hand over and brushed his knuckles against her cheek while other parts of her body exploded like fireworks. "You really are adorable first thing in the morning."

Whatever spell he was spinning disappeared in an instant as Lizzy realized in horror that she was standing on her threshold in boxer shorts, robe and socks. Again.

"*Mon dieu,*" she said, always amazed at how her dormant French emerged at the weirdest times. She moved back and grabbed the doorknob. "Bye Martin."

She would have shut the door in an instant if he hadn't moved forward and stuck a foot over the threshold. One hand on the door, he leaned in and kissed her hot and hard, his lips sending waves of passion all the way to her toes. But, as quickly as he offered the kiss, Martin moved away and headed down the stairs.

"Tomorrow at seven," he called up to her.

Now it was Lizzy's turn to lean on the doorframe, wondering if her knees would support her.

"AREN'T YOU HUNGRY?"

Cassie had been kind enough to bring in croissants and cinnamon rolls for the meeting, but after the first round of figures Martin lost his appetite.

"So, what kind of a beating did we take over Christmas?" he asked his business manager.

Kevin MacIntire, who had been with the newspaper for twenty years since his father nabbed him from the UC San Diego business school, tapped his pencil against the desk, a bad sign. "Seven percent, maybe eight."

"That's not bad," Cassie piped up. "Seven percent is like nothing, right?"

Seven percent rang the first bell of the death toll, but Martin couldn't tell her that. He couldn't say anything at present; he was too stunned to speak.

"Christmas is our finest hour," Kevin explained to her. "We make more money during the holidays than any other time of year."

Cassie munched on a croissant loaded down with strawberry jam. "Yeah, but a seven percent decrease is not the end of the world."

"It is when you normally make a twenty-five percent profit."

Cassie slowed her chewing as she contemplated this. "What does it mean?"

"It means our profits are down by a third." Martin rose and headed toward the large window that overlooked the valley of Santa Helena, the community that was slowing pulling out their advertising dollars and giving them to the Daily Times. Or someone else since people weren't reading newspapers like they used to. At the rate they were going, he'd be lucky to meet payroll for the next thirty days.

"Martin." He recognized that tone in Cassie's voice and he didn't want to discuss it.

"I'm not selling."

"Martin." This time it was Kevin speaking, and his voice sounded strangely similar. "How are we to make that balloon payment now? We have no choice."

"I'm working on it."

That was a laugh. He brought Lizzy bagels and furnished her apartment, yet he failed to remember the five million dollars sitting under a magnet on her refrigerator. All he had to do was retrieve the ticket, tell her he would check her numbers. She made it clear she had no faith in winning. He could have brought the ticket to the newspaper, then called her later and told her she had won. After all he had done for her, she would have gladly given him a percentage, enough for them to make it to the next quarter.

But all thoughts of the lottery had disappeared the moment she had opened her front door, standing there in her socks, her hair tossed in a million directions. He had wanted to take her right then, show her what he and that sofa bed were capable of.

"Martin." Cassie woke him from his lurid thoughts, images that were becoming increasingly difficult to push away. "Eat something. You haven't had breakfast yet."

Food. That was it. Why hadn't he thought about it before? What was that saying? The way to a person's heart?

Martin grabbed his jacket and car keys, then headed for the door.

"Where are you going?" Cassie asked.

He paused and kissed his sister on the top of her head. "To get half a million dollars."

OLIVIA STARED at the sweater in her hands, her heart racing. Step out the front door and get in the car, she instructed herself, but her feet failed to obey. Finally, she forced herself across the threshold and locked the door behind her, preventing her escape.

Taking a deep breath that she had accomplished that much, Olivia headed for the car. If she could climb in and drive down the driveway, then on to the highway into town, it would be the farthest she had gotten in two years. Just get into town, she said to herself like a mantra. One step at a time.

But when she entered the car and turned on the radio, she was greeted with the song she and Dave had danced to at their high school prom. The very song that played when he had whispered in her ear that he would love her forever.

The familiar anxiety gripped her heart, but she couldn't

forsake a sign. The universe was telling her something. And when the collective consciousness spoke, Olivia listened.

Breathing in a cleansing breath and clearing her mind of all emotions, Olivia focused on the task at hand. She had to get Lizzy's sweater back to her, had to apologize for her sharp tone yesterday. If what she had read in Lizzy's coffee cup was true, then Martin's happiness depended on them being together and she had to make sure that happened. Besides, Olivia liked her. Very much. Lizzy was the first girl Martin had brought home that she approved of.

Olivia put the car into reverse, hearing the words of Elton John wash over her. She could do this. She would do this.

LIZZY HANDED Nana her cup of punch and sat next to her on the park bench. The weather had turned brisk but clear, the trademark California blue washing down on them all as if the world had turned upside down and the ocean took the place of the sky. Days like these still amazed Lizzy and Nana. But if they mentioned the weather, the natives would gaze around wondering what the fuss was about.

"I still can't get used to how beautiful it is here," Lizzy said to Nana. "The rain blew all the smog away. You can see snow on the Angeles crest."

"That far?" Nana chuckled. "Sometimes I forget there are mountains around here. Good thing we get these rains to clear the air so we can be reminded."

Father Wesley strode by and greeted the collection of families gathered around the park. He tousled the heads of children, shook hands with the fathers and listened intently to the mothers. Then he glanced at Nana and came over for a full Cajun hug.

The priest had always treated them like any other family, but watching him with the others stabbed at Lizzy's heart. As he gave Nana a hug, Lizzy wondered if Father Wesley would ever christen her children or teach them Sunday school. Would she ever attend church functions without feeling like the single girl who takes care of her grandmother? The poor girl who lost her parents when she was fifteen?

She heard Nana and Father Wesley discussing her, Nana mentioning yesterday's editorial and them both laughing at the prospect of Lizzy having a beau. She decided it was time for a walk. "I'll be right back," she said to Nana.

"Don't be gone too long," Nana called after her. "It gets dark early now and I don't want to miss *60 Minutes.*"

Lizzy walked toward the pond and leaned against a tree, watching Marie Cassidy's tow-headed toddler chase pigeons around the edge. When he passed her, she noticed his blue eyes sparkling as he laughed, and an acute sadness overtook her. She used to love the annual family potluck, reveled in the time spent outdoors with Nana and the families of the congregation. Today, she wanted to cry at every turn.

What was happening to her? Was Nana right, had she built a wall around her heart? Would she ever have two kids and a dog and a man like Martin to come home to?

Tears burned her eyes and she wiped them away with the back of her sleeve. Who could blame her? She had lost two parents in one night, then had her boyfriend betray her. Twice! Who wouldn't be afraid of commitment?

The boy rushed past, pausing in front of her and smiling. Lizzy smiled back, wondering what Martin's children would look like. Would her dark Cajun features overtake the blonde? Would one of their kids have amazing blue eyes like his?

Dear God, what was she thinking? The man had brought her furniture and now she was giving birth to his children.

"I'm going crazy," she concluded. "Pure and simple."

But when the Cassidy's child chased another batch of

pigeons and paused at her side again, she pulled the toddler into her lap and gave him a round of tickles.

CASSIE LOADED on more jam with her knife, then bit into her croissant, enjoying the combination of its flaky, buttery crust and that soft interior lined with strawberry goodness. Wiping the overflow on her lips, she caught a glimpse of herself in the mirror, which forced her to put the croissant down.

"When did I get so fat?" she wondered, cringing at the sight of her reflection.

It was only ten pounds. Who could blame her? It wasn't bad enough that every film festival had passed on the documentary and her neighborhood art house had refused to show it, but every reviewer known to Hollywood had trashed her.

Her family had offered kind faces, no one brave enough to criticize her choice of topic.

"Psychic cats," Paul had said, refusing to meet her eyes. "Interesting subject matter."

"Might have been better if you had found more than one," Martin added. "But what do I know about film."

Cassie fought back tears, feeling her father's disapproving gaze fall upon her. She hated working at *The Banner*, felt his presence everywhere, especially in his old office that Martin now claimed. Theodore Taylor wouldn't have been so kind. He would have told her exactly how ridiculous her life was, that no money could be made in filmmaking, especially documentaries. "Who in the world cares about one supposed psychic cat?" he would have bellowed. "Get a real job."

Cassie took another bite, not caring if her Lee jeans were busting at the seams. She was thankful Martin had taken her in, given her a job at the paper, but she hoped he would sell the damned thing, let them all have the money and get on with their lives. Paul could pay off his med school loans and start a practice, Mom could feel less guilty. Martin could go back to writing.

And she? What would she do? Cassie had no idea.

Filmmaking was her only love and she had blown it big time. Not only had she failed in her first film out the gate, but she owed thousands to credit card companies and people blind enough to invest in the award-winning film school graduate. No one in the family knew she had filed for bankruptcy; she was too ashamed to tell them. If Martin sold the paper, she could pay off her creditors without anyone being the wiser.

More importantly, she could leave *The Banner* and escape the critical eyes of Theodore Taylor, whose power over her hadn't lessened in death as he glared down from his painting.

Suddenly, a blur of cotton gauze flitted across her peripheral vision and Cassie imagined her mother in the lobby. She leaned to the right to make sure her eyes weren't playing tricks on her. Getting a better view through the doorway, Cassie realized she was right. "Mom?" she called out.

Olivia glanced around uncomfortably, then moved toward her husband's old office, her usual tidy blonde hair tousled about her face as if she drove there with the windows down. She refused to come in, standing at the threshold like a goddess facing an abyss.

"What are you doing here?" Cassie asked. "I can't believe you left Ojai."

"Martin has done a nice job." She clutched her collar nervously as her eyes scanned the painting, then she quickly looked back at Cassie. "I like the way he brightened the place up."

Martin had completely redecorated his father's office, all the way down to removing the seventies paneling from the walls and replacing the heavy leather furniture with modern pieces. He and Cassie never spoke of their dad much, but she imagined their patriarch had a powerful influence over him as well.

"Why are you here?" Cassie asked again.

Olivia raised the sweater in her hands. "Martin's girlfriend left it at the house. I was returning it."

"Martin's girlfriend?" Wow, when did that happen?

Olivia didn't wish to speak further. Standing in *The Banner's* office seemed too much for her to bear. "I have to go," she whispered.

"Sure, Mom, I understand."

Olivia cleared her throat, trying to fight off her demons. Cassie wanted to help, to guide her mother back into the light, but she was clueless what to do. Hell, she wasn't sure what had forced her mother into reclusion in the first place.

"Do you know where the Mountain View Nursing Home is?" Olivia asked.

Oh God, Cassie thought, she couldn't be thinking of such a thing. "Why?" she asked, trying to keep the panic from her voice.

Olivia grinned, obviously guessing where her daughter's thoughts had traveled. "Lizzy's grandmother lives there. I have to return her sweater and I don't know where Lizzy lives."

Cassie exhaled. She hadn't realized she had stopped breathing. "I'll show you, Mom."

"I don't want to interrupt your work."

Cassie threw the leftover croissant in the trash. "Interrupting my work is what I need right now."

Besides being with her mother on such a remarkable day, when Olivia had finally ventured outside, Cassie wanted to meet this Lizzy. If Martin indeed had a girlfriend, she might be the impetus to getting her brother to sell the paper.

The man needed a life. They all needed a life. And hopefully Lizzy was the key to that happening.

CHAPTER 10

The potluck ran late but Lizzy managed to get Nana settled in front of the TV set precisely when the CBS clock started ticking.

"Are you going to stay?" Nana looked up from her favorite chair. "They're investigating some heavy stuff tonight."

Lizzy hated television news, couldn't rationally explain why, except that old habits were hard to break. She preferred her news in newspaper form, the kind you could later use for crawfish boils, line birdcages. The TV and Internet had their places in the media world, but she still chose the kind between six columns of type.

"Diane said the mayor called looking for me," Lizzy said, using the phone call as an excuse to get away. "I'm going to the lobby to see what's up."

"Does that man know it's Sunday?" Nana turned her focus to the TV set.

"We only work a half day tomorrow. He probably wants to make sure our plans are set for New Year's."

"You shouldn't be working at all," Nana mumbled, her attention slipping away. It was clear Nana wanted the conversation over so she could watch her favorite show.

Lizzy placed a mock hand over her heart. "You love Mike Wallace more than me."

Nana waved her away. "I can't hear." But from the corner of her lips a smile emerged.

Lizzy walked to the lobby and called Tom on her cell. He, too, seemed agitated to be taken away from the television, a football game blaring in the background.

"Doesn't anyone read anymore?" Lizzy joked.

"On New Year's weekend?" Tom replied. "Are you kidding?"

She thought to tell him he had called her on New Year's weekend, on a Sunday no less, but curiosity got the better of her. "You wanted to talk to me, Tom?"

"Yeah. I thought I would tell you this before you came in tomorrow. Just so you know."

"Know what?"

There was a pause as Tom gulped down a liquid and a roar sounded in the background. "Damn Trojans."

"Tom," Lizzy said, trying to bring him back to their conversation. "What did you want me to know?"

She heard another gulp, then a sigh. "I decided to get rid of Anthony Billers. He cost too much and he wasn't doing what I hoped he would."

This little piece of knowledge slowly leaked into Lizzy's brain. So, the New York image consultant was gone. Made her night, but what did it specifically have to do with her?

"Okay. But couldn't this have waited until…?"

"You don't understand, Lizzy," the mayor added. "Now, that I have the extra money in the budget, I can give you a raise."

Lizzy gasped, realizing her money woes, so overwhelming only days before, were over.

"How long are you going to be there?" Tom asked. "Half-time's coming up."

"Why? Are you going to bring me the money?"

"Sort of."

A silence followed and Tom started shouting to someone in the background.

"Tom, forget the USC game for a moment and make sense."

Tom laughed. "Just wait there for a few minutes, okay? I'll be right over."

"I still don't understand."

"Lizzy." Tom's tone grew serious. "This surprise I have to deliver in person."

MIKE WALLACE WAS MUMBLING on about the effects of nicotine, but Nana settled back in her chair and let sleep wash over her. She got the gist of the program, now she wanted a little nap before Lizzy came back and urged her to bed. Young people never understood that naps were more valuable to senior citizens than Social Security. She had earned her right to fall asleep in front of the TV and by God she would collect.

Nana felt a presence beside her, a wispy energy as if a bird had flown in the window. She opened an eye and spotted a lovely blonde woman in a flowing dress standing nervously nearby. Without warning, a chill ran up Nana's spine, something that didn't happen often.

"Can I help you, child?"

The blonde woman smiled, sending delicate wrinkles about her blue eyes. "Are you Lizzy's grandmother?"

This caught her attention and she straightened in her chair. "And who might you be?"

The woman walked cautiously forward as if afraid of every step. Nana sensed she owned a heart of gold, yet some fear was creating obstacles in her life. When the blonde woman inched closer and handed her a sweater, Nana noticed a young girl in the hall, equally cautious about entering the room.

"Good God, y'all, I'm not going to bite."

The blonde woman smiled again. "I'm Martin Taylor's mother. Your granddaughter visited my house yesterday and left her sweater there. I didn't know where she lived so I thought I'd return it to you."

Nana accepted Lizzy's sweater, the one she bought her for Christmas last year. Before the woman could back away, Nana took her hand. The woman protested slightly, trying politely to pull away, but Nana's grip held tight. "Why you so afraid, *chèr?*"

The woman paled, but she stopped resisting. It was then Nana realized Mrs. Taylor held intuitive powers of her own. Still, Nana hated seeing such a beauty in pain, especially one with so much love in her heart.

"Let it go," Nana whispered.

Tears pooled in Mrs. Taylor's eyes and gently trickled down her cheeks. "I cheated on my husband," she whispered, glancing back to make sure the girl hadn't heard.

Nana considered this statement, wondering how this fit into the big picture, since she didn't feel the husband's presence in Mrs. Taylor's palm. Plus, if memory served her, which it rarely did, she thought she remembered reading about the elder Taylor passing.

"Is he still with us?" Nana asked.

Mrs. Taylor shook her head, tendrils of golden hair falling about her pretty face. Young people carried way too much pain, Nana thought, reaching her other hand up to touch her face.

"Let it go," she repeated. "Whatever mistakes you made, you have paid for them enough. Go out into the world and find love again."

Nana released her hand and suddenly felt cold. Watching Mrs. Taylor collect herself made her realize that Mrs. Taylor's inner strength far exceeded her pain.

"I'm Olivia," the blonde woman said, wiping her tears.

"I'm Mrs. LeBlanc," Nana said. "And who is the child in the doorway?"

"My daughter, Cassie."

Nana turned toward this Cassie, whose eyes were as big as walnuts. "What is she afraid of?"

Cassie suddenly straightened. "I'm not afraid of anything."

"Then come here and meet Mrs. LeBlanc," Olivia said. "Don't be rude."

But Cassie was afraid of something, Nana could feel it. She refused to come in the room. "It's nice to meet you, Mrs. LeBlanc," she said. "But I think I need to feed the meter."

The young girl rushed off, which caused Olivia to frown. "I apologize. Ever since she failed with her first movie, she's been acting very strange."

"Young people are supposed to be neurotic," Nana assured her. "Makes getting older and losing your teeth more bearable. One thing about being my age, I have no worries."

Olivia sat on the edge of Nana's bed and her face grew solemn. Now, that Cassie was out of earshot, Nana imagined she might open up.

"I found out my husband was cheating on me," she began, brushing hair behind one ear. "He promised the first one would be his last but he lied. When I learned there were more, I went to a friend's house seeking solace and ended up being as guilty as my husband."

"This friend loves you?" When Olivia looked up, Nana knew it to be true. She also saw that this love was reciprocal. "And now?"

Olivia glanced back toward the door to see if Cassie had returned. "He wants to marry me," she whispered when she saw they were alone. With those words, Olivia's face illuminated as if someone had finally turned on the light.

This time, Nana reached forward and took both of Olivia's hands. "Then what, dear child, are you waiting for?"

. . .

MARTIN PULLED in front of the nursing home, parking in front of the fuchsia VW that looked like his mother's ancient car. He glanced in the rear view mirror to see who the figure was behind the wheel, but it was too dark to discern. Even if his mother had managed to leave the house, which was highly unlikely, the person inside this car was far too short to be Olivia. And what would she be doing at the Mountain View Nursing Home? He picked up his basket and headed inside.

Halfway through the power sliding glass doors, he met Olivia on the way out.

"Oh hello, Martin," his mother stated as if she drove into Santa Helena every day.

"Mom. What are you doing here?"

Olivia kissed him, careful not to upset the pots in his arms. "Returning Lizzy's sweater. Her grandmother—what an incredible woman. Have you met her?"

Martin wanted to follow the conversation, but he was still in shock to see his mother out and about.

"Got to go," Olivia said, before he had a chance to respond. "Come by on New Year's. I'll make some corned beef and cabbage."

Martin started to protest, to demand an explanation, but within seconds his mother disappeared out the door. It had happened so fast, he wondered if had dreamt it all.

A nurse walked by and asked if he needed assistance and Martin inquired about a Cajun woman called Nana. She pointed him in the right direction and Martin hauled his collection to room three fifteen. When he peeked inside and saw that the elderly woman was fast asleep in her chair, he silently entered the room and placed his menagerie on to the bed.

Now what, he thought? Was Lizzy around or would he have to indulge her grandmother alone? She looked so peaceful in sleep, he hated to disturb her, but then he couldn't leave his concoction there without an explanation.

Suddenly, Nana shifted and her blanket fell away. Martin picked up the crocheted cloth and gently wrapped it around the woman, studying her face for signs of Lizzy. There was a slight resemblance, the same upturned nose, the fine straight hair. He wondered if Nana had her sense of humor.

Without warning, the woman's eyes flew open. She seemed to recognize him, which alarmed him more than if she would have screamed. She launched into a lengthy conversation, all in Cajun French.

Think, Martin commanded himself. It had been years since he had begged his roommate in Thibodaux to teach him some of the local dialect. Martin had always been quick to learn languages, and he had picked up Cajun easily, but could he manage to now pull it out of the cobwebs of his brain?

"*Est-ce que t'amènes la pluie?*" she asked him.

This rang a bell. He remembered his roommate's grandmother asking the same thing when a long-lost visitor came to call, something about bringing the rain with them?

"*Oui,*" Martin replied. "*Quoi ca dit?*"

Nana's eyes narrowed, as if she finally realized who he was. "You that newspaper man?"

Thank God they were back to English. And that Lizzy thought enough of him to mention his name. "Yes, ma'am."

Just then, Lizzy appeared at the door, equally surprised to see him standing there. "Martin?"

"Lizzy," Nana shouted. "You didn't tell me he was Cajun."

Martin looked first at Nana, than Lizzy, wondering whether to laugh or rebuke this wild accusation. Lizzy beat him to it, giggling while she did. "He's not Cajun, Nana."

"He spoke French to me."

Lizzy approached them both, studying Martin intently. "You speak French?"

"*Un peu*," he answered with a smile.

"Are you Catholic?" Nana gazed at him eagerly as if the question held the power to part the seven seas or rain gold upon the earth.

He started to answer, but Lizzy interrupted. "Don't answer that." She sent her grandmother a stern glance.

Only Nana ignored her. The elderly woman's eyes glistened as she took him in from head to toe. "You're cute," she said, punching him lightly on the arm.

Lizzy's eyes rolled and Martin laughed. This may be easier than he imagined.

"What brings you here?" Lizzy asked.

Martin stood tall, sending Nana a charming smile. "Your granddaughter, ma'am, is distrustful of my cooking talents."

Nana huffed. "If you can cook as good as you look, son, bring on the food."

Martin reached for the large pot he had placed on the bed, while he heard Lizzy defend her position behind him. "I didn't say he couldn't cook. I said it was doubtful he could make a proper gumbo."

Placing the pot in front of the two women, Martin pulled back the lid and a silence fell. Lizzy and Nana peered inside, taking in the aroma at the same time.

"*Mon dieu*," Nana said. "He is Cajun."

"He's not Cajun," Lizzy insisted, although her eyes never left the pot of gumbo. "Your roux looks pretty good, though."

"It's perfect," Nana declared, sending him a wink. "Nice and dark brown, just the way I like it."

Lizzy crossed her arms, trying to look defensive although a smile teased her lips. "Well, let's see how it tastes, California boy."

Martin placed the pot on the side table, then pulled a collection of bowls and spoons from the basket.

"Too bad we don't have any rice," Nana said.

Martin grabbed the last pot from the basket and proudly displayed the rice in front of Nana. "What's gumbo without rice?"

The two women watched in awe as he placed a scoop of rice into each bowl, then followed it with an ample amount of gumbo consisting of chunks of andouille sausage, chicken, and the Cajun trinity—onions, peppers, and celery. He then topped each bowl off with a sprinkling of filé.

"I make a sweet seafood gumbo too, but I couldn't find decent shrimp this time of year."

Neither woman seemed to mind as they stared into the soup that defined their heritage. First, Nana took a spoonful, then Lizzy. As in on cue, both rolled their eyes, then let out a moan.

"I have to admit," Lizzy said, "this is fabulous."

"Makes me want to cry," Nana said. "I can't remember the last time I had gumbo this good."

"Thanks a lot," Lizzy said between bites.

"Her roux is too light," Nana said to Martin with a wink. "She has no patience."

"It takes too long to make it as brown as she likes." Her comment made Lizzy pause, wiping her mouth with the back of her hand. "When did you find time to do this? I thought you had an important meeting today."

Martin filled his own bowl and leaned back against the edge of the bureau. "Bad news doesn't take long."

Those examining eyes that seemed to speak to his soul fell upon him, but he didn't want to think about the problems surrounding the paper. Besides, he was on a mission, one to solve all obstacles. He slipped a hand underneath his jacket, pulling the bottle of wine tucked inside his waistband, then proudly displayed the item he had smuggled into the nursing home. Nana's eyes twinkled.

"My boy," the elderly woman said, "if you have a loaf of French bread tucked in there as well, you are Cajun."

Martin reached into the basket and pulled out the final item, a French baguette. "Can't have gumbo without wine and French bread."

He handed Lizzy the bread to distribute so he could uncork the bottle, and for the moment when their hands touched, whole conversations seemed to pass between them. He knew what that grateful smile meant and the look he sent back told her he was as happy to make his signature gumbo as she and Nana were to enjoy it.

He pulled the bottle opener from his pocket and slipped the cork free, while Nana asked him a host of personal questions that he dutifully answered. Then he poured them all some wine using the nursing home's glasses so as not to cause suspicion should a nurse arrive. Nana asked for another bowl, wiping the first one clean with a piece of bread. Lizzy continued to study him between bites.

"What was the bad news?" she finally asked.

Martin sipped his wine, always amazed at how her eyes peeled away the façade he offered the world, like a best friend waiting to hear of one's real pain. He hated to use such a worn-out phrase, but it was almost as if they were on the same wavelength. For the first time in his life, he wondered if soul mates existed.

Still, he didn't want her to know the truth. Not yet.

"It's always bad news." Martin shrugged, tossing back his wine. "We should have picked more lucrative professions."

Surprisingly, Lizzy brightened, as if he reminded her of some exciting secret. She leaned forward, a blush spreading across her cheeks. "I have to something to show you."

"In front of your grandmother?"

Lizzy's face broke out in a wide smile, the happiest he had seen her yet. "Believe me, Nana's seen it all. Besides, nothing could interrupt her from her gumbo right now."

"Absolutely not," Nana mumbled without looking up.

Martin wanted to stand there forever, absorbing Lizzy's features as her sweet smile illuminated her face. For one thing, her eyes weren't totally brown, but held a trace of green around the edges, shining up at him underneath long lashes she obviously inherited from her grandmother. Her nose wasn't as upturned as he first imagined, but rising ever so slightly beneath a sea of freckles, so cute he longed to kiss every one of them. And those lips. God, but he wanted to taste them, spend hours savoring...

Wake up, he commanded himself. He was here to get the money, not make love to Lizzy. He had to get her alone, then explain everything. He had a newspaper to save.

"It's outside."

Martin sobered. "What is?"

"The surprise."

Lizzy took his hand and led him toward the door. "We'll be right back, Nana."

Nana mumbled something, but she was too busy enjoying her gumbo. They slipped into the hall, Lizzy still holding his hand. Now, was the perfect time.

"Lizzy," Martin said as they headed toward the front door. "I have to tell you something."

"Okay."

She didn't seem to hear him, too intent on getting him outside. They passed through the front door and on to the sidewalk where he paused, causing her to turn and look up at him. "I really have to talk to you."

She seemed to grasp the gravity of his tone, but she stole a peek at the car parked beside them, a brand new Mustang convertible. Martin took one look at the car and knew why Lizzy was smiling. Gazing at the bright red Mustang, he knew his heart had stopped beating. "You cashed in your lottery ticket."

Lizzy's shoulders slumped and she gave him a playful frown.

"You and that stupid lottery ticket. The car's a present from Tom."

Now, he was really confused.

"Someone wrote this editorial that put Tom in a fighting mood." Lizzy looked down at their entwined hands, grinning at the reference. "Tom coerced the City Council to pass a measure that restored funding to the nursing home so I don't have to pay that increase. Then, he fired Anthony and gave me a raise."

Still holding on to his hand, she smiled and leaned closer. "And, since it's the rainy season and the city won't need the parade car until the Founder's Day festival in April, he's letting me use it until then. Even paying the insurance on it, since it's a city car. I have to use it for business purposes, of course, but perhaps I can find some business in Santa Barbara once and a while."

Martin recalled their night together and thoughts of the lottery money disappeared. Was she hinting that she wanted to go back there again with him? Maybe this time, do more than sleep on that daybed?

"Isn't she a beauty?"

Martin nodded, but the only beauty he could see was the one standing in front of him.

"Now that I have a convertible, does this make me a Californian?"

Martin reached up and touched her cheek. "If I can be a Cajun, then I guess anything's possible."

"Martin." Lizzy never moved, but her smile disappeared. "You said something to the mayor, didn't you?"

Did he? He honestly couldn't remember. He skimmed his thumb across her cheekbone and savored the soft feel of her face.

"You didn't have to apologize in that editorial," she whispered, her voice catching. "It really wasn't necessary, although it seems to have helped me out tremendously."

Martin cupped her cheek with his whole hand, moving closer so their lips were only a breath away. "Lizzy, I told you," he whispered back, "you have no influence over what I write in my newspaper."

In an instant, Martin did what he had wanted to do for days. Hell, since the first time he saw Lizzy in that tight sweater sitting in his father's office. He kissed her. Soundly. Passionately. With every ounce of his being.

And she kissed him back. He moved a hand to her waist to pull her closer at the same time Lizzy wrapped her arms about his neck and leaned up on her toes. They were as close as two people could get, kissing madly on the dark sidewalks of Santa Helena.

She tasted heavenly, a mixture of spicy roux and sweet wine and something uniquely Lizzy. He nibbled on her bottom lip, sucking on it between his own, which caused her to giggle. Then he led a trail of kisses down the line of her chin, up toward her earlobes and into the recesses of her neck, breathing in the sensual scent of lavender.

"This is not our first date, you know," she whispered, and Martin understood her meaning instantly. He met her lips once more and this time she parted them to give him entrance, offering her tongue to meet his. As he deepened the kiss, savoring the inside of her mouth, the plump lines of her lips, he moaned with pleasure.

If this wasn't heaven, he was damn sure close. He slid a hand up the length of her back, pressing their bodies closer, enjoying the feel of her curves nestled between his arms. So this was what men with social lives did, he thought, amazed at how wonderful it was to kiss a woman he also considered a friend.

She moved a hand inside his jacket and he felt her fingers explore his chest and back. At that moment, Martin wanted nothing but to coax her inside that red convertible and pull up the top.

"Want to go for a drive?" he asked between kisses. "Test out the back seat of your new car?"

Something he said triggered fear in Lizzy for her hands stilled and she pulled away. She fell back on her feet, starring at the buttons of his shirt, trying to catch her breath.

"What did I say?"

She tugged her hair behind an ear and moved out of arm's reach. She cleared her throat, suddenly embarrassed by what had happened.

The cold air that rushed between them sobered him more than a plunge in the Santa Helena Lake. The loss of her warmth made him physically ache for more. He reached for her hand, but she moved back a step, refusing to meet his eyes.

"What did I say? I keep making mistakes with you and I don't know why."

Lizzy pulled her sweater down, trying to erase imaginary wrinkles. "I have to go," she whispered.

He wasn't ready to let her go, wasn't ready to say goodnight. He grabbed her hand and held it tight despite her resistance. "Please, Lizzy, don't leave. If I insulted you in any way…"

She finally untangled her fingers from his. "I'm sorry, Martin. It's too fast."

He touched her arm and she shivered. He knew they had moved to the fast lane right off the freeway entrance, but they could start over, resume a steady speed. Couldn't they? He started to argue as much, but Lizzy stepped back again.

"I have to go," she repeated.

Within a heartbeat, she disappeared into the nursing home, leaving him alone on the street as the January night cooled the passionate heat that had flooded his veins. And, for a few incredible moments, had made him feel like a human being again.

CHAPTER 11

There was so much to do before the office closed at noon and the next day brought forth the New Year, but all Lizzy could think about was Martin and their passionate embrace the night before. She shuffled papers before her to look busy, but her mind refused to focus on her work.

Why had she reacted so strongly last night? Sure, Martin had asked the same thing Peter had on their first date, to park in a secluded area and make love in the back seat. With Peter, she had been so inexperienced and so eager to learn, she had let him talk her into wild sex in the back of his car, even though wild wasn't exactly the word she would have used to describe it. Back then, charming Peter could have talked her into anything. And he usually did.

Martin had made it clear he wasn't Peter, and deep down Lizzy knew that to be true. Still, she wasn't ready for a relationship, especially with a man who had no time for one. Did Martin just want sex from her, since he couldn't offer anything else?

Lizzy picked up the snow globe and turned it over, letting the fake snow fall about the cottage that looked so much like the house in Ojai. Even the two people in front holding hands reminded her of Martin shaking that tree so snow could fall on her head. He didn't seem like the type to use her for a temporary affair, but what else could he desire from her?

She was so confused. She certainly didn't want another Peter, another man offering the moon and then pulling the earth from her feet. A charming set of blue eyes who took more than he gave.

But Martin gave unconditionally. Because of him, she now had furniture and a car and leftover gumbo for lunch. Maybe Nana was right. Maybe she had built a wall around her heart, using her fears to avoid commitments herself.

Lizzy dropped her head on to the pile of requisitions. Her financial troubles may be over, but new problems, ones of the heart, had taken their place. And those were harder to decipher.

The phone rang, startling her. "It's a man from Editor and Publisher," Holly cried out over the maze of cubicles.

Lizzy groaned. How many times did a person have to say no to subscription salesmen? "Elizabeth Guidry."

"Ms. Guidry, this is Mark Waterman of *Editor and Publisher.*"

Lizzy sighed, dreading the conversation. "Mr., Waterman, I no longer work for a newspaper so I really have no need for the magazine anymore."

There was a pause, something usual for a salesman. Normally, those people failed to breathe. "I'm not calling about subscriptions. I'm a reporter."

"Oh?" Why on earth was he calling her?

"I've heard a rumor that I thought you might be able to confirm."

"I work in the Mayor's Office, Mr. Waterman, how could I confirm anything to do with..."

"It's about the city newspaper, *The Santa Helena Banner.*"

Lizzy bolted upright in her chair like a bullet fired from a gun. "What about it?"

"I've heard a rumor the *Daily Times* is planning to buy out *The Banner* and I was hoping you could confirm that."

"Where did you hear this?"

Another lengthy pause. Damn the man, why didn't he speak up?

"Is it true?" he asked again.

Was it? Probably, although Martin had steadfastly insisted he would never sell the paper. Still, when the major department stores had abandoned *The Banner* and taken their business to the Times, it had to have been financially devastating for the struggling community newspaper. And Christmas sales had been disappointing that year for everyone, which meant the newspaper suffered as well since it relied on advertising dollars.

"I honestly don't know," Lizzy said, feeling as defensive as Martin had the day she mentioned selling the newspaper. "You'll have to ask the publisher, Martin Taylor."

At this, the reporter laughed. "Won't answer my calls, which makes me think something's up. Do you know if he's in over his head?"

Someone down the hall laughed, obviously sharing New Year's merriment. "I'm sorry Mr. Waterman, but I know nothing about this. Now, if you'll excuse me, we're getting ready to close up the office."

"Well, if you hear anything...," the man quickly injected and rattled off a phone number, which Lizzy wrote on her calendar.

"You bet." Lizzy hung up the phone, her mind racing to put pieces together. If only she had taken out a subscription to *The Banner* she might have known how good or bad Martin's Christmas had been. From the papers she had seen in the office, things were mighty slim.

A round of laughter rose up again and Lizzy prairie dogged above her cubicle to get a look at the source. Holly sat relaxed at her desk, leaning forward and chatting with a woman in her late twenties-early thirties, equally relaxed and enjoying the conversation. Something about this dark-headed woman looked familiar. If she hadn't been short and a bit round about the waist, Lizzy would have sworn she was Paul Taylor's twin.

Holly sensed her staring and turned. She waved, but she blushed as she did, as if laughing with another person was a crime. If Lizzy remembered correctly, rock solid Holly never blushed. In fact, she was sure of it.

"That's Lizzy," Holly said to the other woman, and the other woman waved as well.

Lizzy waved back at the duo, wondering what they were talking about. "Nice to meet you."

"Pleasure's all mine," the woman said, but after taking Lizzy in, she turned her attention back to Holly. They retreated to their heated conversation, both staring at each other like lovesick fools.

No, Lizzy thought, as the revelation flitted across her consciousness, Holly would have told her if she was gay. She and Holly were best friends and shared all secrets. Besides, Holly dated men.

Lizzy fell back into her chair, her mind struggling to right the pieces of this puzzle. Holly had hated every man she had ever dated. Had Lizzy failed to miss the signs?

Righting the papers on her desk, Lizzy tried to force her attention back to the requisitions. How could she finish paperwork when there was so much to think about? First Martin and his hot kisses, then *The Banner* possibly up for sale and now her best friend may be gay. What more could the day bring?

She slouched on the desk, her head leaning on the palm of her hand, while she doodled champagne glasses on the desk calendar beneath the pile. She sensed Holly sitting on the chair beside her, picking up her snow globe like she did every day. Suddenly, Lizzy felt betrayed. "You too were getting along well," she muttered.

Holly said nothing, but Lizzy refused to look around. She

should have told her. The woman had known every detail of her love life with Peter, why hadn't Holly confided to her about being gay, if indeed she was?

"It's amazing. It looks like the house in Ojai."

Lizzy jolted at the sound of Martin's voice, finding him sitting in her chair dressed in a blue business suit and overcoat and looking every bit as handsome. She hadn't meant for it to happen, but a heat rose up from her toes and spread to the top of her forehead like a California brush fire, the hot Santa Ana winds urging it on.

But Martin's attention was on the globe, examining it from different angles. "Where did you get this?" he asked her, finally meeting her eyes and causing other parts of her body to sizzle.

"My mother gave it to me when I was young." She cleared her throat, then gulped down her coffee, hoping to quell her nerves. The thought of his kisses came back all too clear, making it difficult for her to breathe. One day she had been comfortable in his presence and now she quaked like a pig-tailed girl in grade school.

"What are you doing here?" she asked him.

"My sister Cassie said she would only be a minute but that was twenty minutes ago." He glanced at his watch. "We're supposed to be downtown by two."

"Your sister?" Laughter emerged from Holly's desk once again and Lizzy made the connection. "The one who looks like Paul?"

"They're twins."

He was looking at her with new eyes, neither smiling nor offering witty conversation like he usually did. Something was wrong, or he was mad at her for dashing off the night before. Yet, Martin didn't appear mad. He seemed almost vulnerable, if that was possible for a man as self-assured as he was. Had she bruised his ego last night or was there something else? Contemplating that something else made her heart quicken.

"How can they be twins?" Lizzy asked, trying to get her mind off those oceans of blue. "She's so…"

"Short?" Finally, he smiled and Lizzy exhaled. She really wanted to get back to friendly terms, put all those wonderful kisses behind them. Didn't she? She found herself staring at his lips, remembering the power behind them.

She took another sip of her coffee. "Can twins be that different?"

His stare intensified as if he was ready to ask some serious question, but the laughter interrupted him. As if on cue, both he and Lizzy rose up and peered above the cubicle at the happy couple across the room. This time, Cassie perched on the edge of Holly's desk, one leg dangling coquettishly over the side while Holly listened in rapture to Cassie's every word. When Cassie finished her tale, Holly laughed again and touched Cassie's forearm. If they weren't flirting, today was the Fourth of July.

She slipped back into her chair, while Martin did the same. Lizzy yearned to ask if his sister was gay, but that wasn't a question one blurted out. Besides, from the look on Martin's face, she wondered if this had been as much of a surprise to him as it was to her. He sent her an expression that said as much, then he shook his head as if remembering why he had come.

"Lizzy, about last night…"

She really didn't want to discuss it. She would see him later that evening at the New Year's party and would dream up an excuse between then and now, but for the moment she had no sane explanation of why she had run away the night before. Except that she had been stricken with pure, uncontrollable fear.

"A man from *Editor & Publisher* called today." Oh God, she hadn't meant to bring that up, but she needed to get him off the subject.

Martin turned the snow globe over, watching the flakes fall

on the two people holding hands. He seemed disappointed she hadn't let him finish. "Your subscription expired?"

"It was a reporter. He wanted information about *The Banner*."

His demeanor changed instantly. When his eyes met hers, she shivered. "What did he want?"

"He heard rumors that the *Daily Times* wanted to buy you out."

Martin said nothing, simply stared, and Lizzy felt his pain deeply. "Are you selling?" she whispered.

Suddenly, his eyes shifted and the pain disappeared. The old, charming Martin emerged, the one that sometimes scared her, reminding her who he really was. "Hell no, I'm not selling."

He stood up, calling out to his sister, but Lizzy knew that he was either lying or putting up a brave front. She recognized that fear, if only for a split second.

He placed the snow globe on her desk and she watched the faux flakes spin around the happy couple. "The snow globe's a sign," Martin said. "Now you have to buy that house in Ojai."

Lizzy touched the glass, wishing she had the funds to do so. "What would I use for a down payment?" She looked up at him with a teasing glance. "My good looks?"

Martin frowned, almost as if he were mad at her. He pulled both arms around her and began typing on her keyboard, so close she could smell his tangy aftershave. Heavens, but he smelled as good as he looked. While he pulled up the Internet and typed in a URL address, Lizzy leaned into his shoulder, closed her eyes and breathed his divine scent.

But as soon as the California Lottery website appeared on the screen, Martin moved away. She would have laughed that he was still obsessed with that ridiculous lottery ticket, but she was too busy missing the warmth of his body.

He backed away, then headed toward the elevator, grabbing the sleeve of his sister who continued to tell some fascinating tale to Holly. As Lizzy watched them over the top of her cubicle,

Martin pointed to his watch. Then he raised seven fingers. The doors closed but not before the edges of his lips turned up in a smile and Lizzy's knees weakened so bad she had to sit down. And when she did, the emblem of the California State Lottery was staring her in the face.

"Okay, Martin. I get the message."

After a dazzling page announcing the current jackpot, she clicked on the date of last Wednesday and watched six winning numbers appear. Lizzy moved her mouse to the printer icon, but again, the phone interrupted her actions.

"Elizabeth Guidry."

"Lizzy," Dave answered. "Get on down to the station. I found a friend of yours, along with all your furniture."

"THANKS FOR THE RIDE," Cassie said as they pulled in front of the Church of the Angels, a lovely cathedral with a dozen stained glass windows depicting various angelic beings. "I'll see you later at the condo?"

Martin had tried small talk, then subtly inquired about Holly, but Cassie wouldn't budge any information. Yet, he had seen her flirt with the woman, could have sworn…

"Is there anything you want to tell me?" Martin asked.

With one hand on the car door ready to flee, Cassie paused but did not look his way. "Like what?"

He reached up and tugged the long, skinny braid hanging down one side of her head, the one dyed an unusual shade of orange. "I don't know. We don't get to talk much anymore."

"Whose fault is that?"

He heard the accusing tone in her voice and felt guilty for not being there more for her. Not only had Cassie's documentary failed miserably, but she had been forced to sell everything, including her car, and move in with her big brother and work for the family business.

"Next year will be better," Martin said. "Things are going to look up."

At this, Cassie finally turned his way. "How is that possible, Martin? When are you going to admit you are cornered?"

"I'm not cornered." Amazing how talk of the newspaper could boil his blood. Martin felt the heat rise up the back of his neck.

"Where are you going to find half a million dollars?"

"I'm working on it."

Now, he was shouting. What was happening to him? One minute he attempted heart-to-heart talk with his sister and now they were back to arguing about the damn newspaper.

"You didn't tell me you had a girlfriend."

Martin gazed at his sister, who appeared hurt that he hadn't mentioned Lizzy. But hell, there seemed to be oceans of infor-mation she had failed to reveal. "She's not my girlfriend. She's a friend that I'm helping out right now."

"You gave her dad's furniture."

At this, Martin laughed. "Yeah, well, that was no sweat off my back."

The air instantly lightened. If anyone knew what that furni-ture represented to him, it was Cassie. She took one of his hands, then leaned up and kissed his cheek. "Have to go. Mass starts in ten minutes and I want to light a candle for mom. I'll catch you later."

Before she had a chance to pull away, Martin grabbed her hand and held tight. "We'll talk later?"

"Sure," Cassie answered softly, as if she doubted it would happen. Then she pulled her hand free and exited the car, running up the steps past Father Wesley into the church.

Martin watched her leave, wondering both how such a chasm had developed between them and if he would make the meeting on time. He knew he needed to pull into traffic and get downtown, but something held him there, some invisible force that gave him pause.

Or maybe it was the enormous weight pressing down on his shoulders that forced him to stay put. Martin didn't know why he continued to stare off toward a distant grove of oak trees, but an unbearable fatigue overtook him as he thought of what was to come.

Someone tapped at his window and he looked up to see Father Wesley next to the car. "Made up your mind yet?" the priest asked.

For a moment, Martin thought he was speaking of Lizzy, the lottery ticket and the newspaper and which one he would chose if the question arose. But, then he realized Father Wesley was referring to Mass.

Martin raised his wrist and pointed to his watch. "Have a meeting."

The priest frowned, then opened the door. "Do you mind?"

Martin really had to get going, but he couldn't say no to his priest. Especially since it had been months, perhaps years, since he last attended Mass. "Sure, Father."

Father Wesley sat down in the passenger seat and shut the door. "The traditional way to do this, Martin, is in a confessional."

"I'm not here to confess," Martin insisted, although God knew he had plenty of material gathered up since the last one. "I just dropped off Cassie."

"Can't remember the last time you've been in."

Martin offered up a guilty laugh. "Me neither, Father."

"I know things are busy at the newspaper, son, but we could always have lunch if you want to talk."

"I'm fine."

Martin felt anything but and when the priest met his eyes the weight intensified tenfold, so suffocating he had trouble breathing.

"I'm losing the newspaper."

Father Wesley placed a comforting hand on his shoulder. "I was afraid of that."

"My family wants me to sell, but I promised Dad I would never let the Times have the paper." Martin exhaled, trying to relieve the pressure building in his chest. He hated discussing his problems, but was grateful for an ear, especially a non-judgmental one. "I have to raise half million by Friday."

"Is this possible?" the priest asked.

The weight grew heavy again, cutting off his air. "I have a friend who won the lottery. She doesn't know it yet and we've been seeing a lot of each other. I've been trying to get on her good side so that when she finds out she'll want to give me the money. Only…"

A silence fell as if the priest waited for Martin to finish his thought. But there were so many emotions flitting through Martin's brain, he didn't know where to begin.

"Only you've fallen in love with her."

His comment stunned Martin, yet the words to denounce it failed to come. "I like her. We're good friends. She's had some rough times and she suffers from trust issues, so I don't want to hurt her."

"Then don't."

"But she holds the future of my newspaper with a magnet on her refrigerator."

At this, the priest appeared confused, running a hand through his dark hair. "Why don't you just tell her she won the lottery and come clean?"

Question of the hour. As Lizzy had said in Santa Barbara, sometimes the most complicated problems had simple solutions. He could blurt it out and get it over with, tell Lizzy she had won and then ask for the money.

"Perhaps you don't want this to end."

Father Wesley had honed his arrow to the mark of his

dilemma and Martin felt the bite of that shot straight to his heart.

"I feel good around her," he whispered. "I can't remember ever feeling this way about a girl before. She's comfortable. She's funny. She makes me feel good about myself."

"Maybe you should tell her that as well."

Martin remembered Lizzy's reaction the night before at the same time he recalled his commitments. The timing wasn't right for either of them. And for all he knew she didn't feel the same way. Yet, the way she had kissed him last night, had encouraged him on, Lizzy had to have some feelings for him too.

The church bells rang and both men shifted in their seats. "I can't tell you what to do, Martin," Father Wesley said. "But know that God gave us hearts and minds." He patted Martin on the shoulder, then opened the door. "Use them wisely."

He rose, but paused on the sidewalk, one arm resting on the car door as he leaned back inside.

"And Martin," the priest said, giving him that paternal look that always made him feel guilty no matter how innocent he was. "If you hurt Lizzy Guidry, I'm going to have to kick your butt."

With those final words, Father Wesley left for Mass.

CHAPTER 12

New Year's revelry, so visible in every part of town, failed to invade the Santa Helena Police Station. While most of the world celebrated the year's final day and heralded in January first, cops spent a long night dragging in the intoxicated and obnoxious.

At one in the afternoon on New Year's Eve, however, the police on duty were enjoying the lull before the storm, including one cop grabbing a quick nap in the far corner of the room. The place might have been empty and the police free from work had not Peter occupied a place on the bench opposite the jail.

Lizzy approached him cautiously, noticing the tension gathered at the back of his neck. He held his blonde hair in both hands, head bowed, eyes focused on his shoes. She almost felt remorse, knowing what financial hardships he endured as an actor. Almost.

Dave ushered into the room, charging the energy around him like a loose utility wire. He kicked the chair of the sleeping policeman and the man came instantly to attention. Peter, too, jumped and straightened against the back of the bench as if frightened of what was to happen.

"You should be scared," Dave bellowed, reading his body language. "You don't mess with members of my family."

Peter followed Dave's gaze and spotted Lizzy, who gulped hard when the familiar blue eyes met hers. He offered her a smile, a fainter version of the kind that used to stop her heart.

"Where are my things, Peter?"

Peter attempted to stand, but Dave cleared his throat and he returned to his seat. Despite the interruption, he pulled on the charm. "It was a joke, sweetheart. You know I would never do anything like that for real. I was going to bring it back tomorrow. You know, a New Year's prank."

"A prank?" She had to give it to him, the man owned a wild imagination.

"Yeah," he answered, as if convincing himself of his ridiculous story. "That's it. It was just a prank."

Peter glanced at Dave hopefully. "Shall I go unload what I have in my car?" To Lizzy he added, "I've got a bunch of it outside, sweetheart, ready to bring back. You see, I wasn't serious about any of this. You know I would never hurt you."

Lizzy remembered the redheaded actress and felt the knife twist again in her heart. He had hurt her plenty in the past, including bleeding her dry of money. But she didn't want to rehash those ugly facts in front of Dave.

"Can you give us a moment, Dave?"

The sheriff hesitated, then nodded, but he sent Peter a stern look before moving off to the counter and sending the relaxed staff into motion.

Peter took the opportunity to rise and hug Lizzy. "Thanks sweetheart. I knew you'd understand." Lizzy pulled his arms from around her, wondering what she had ever seen in the man. "You're not going to press charges, are you?" he asked with a puppy dog frown.

"You stole my furniture," she whispered heatedly. "Right after you took my last twenty. What do you think?"

Peter grabbed her elbow and led her to the bench. "We can work this out, sweetheart."

"I don't see how." She sat down, but she pulled her arm free of his grip. "And if you call me sweetheart one more time, I will assault you here in front of five police officers."

Peter's eyes chilled, revealing the man Lizzy knew him to be. "Then you'll go to jail with me."

"You forget, sweetheart, that the sheriff is family."

For the first time that afternoon, Peter exhibited real fear. She knew the ignorant sod expected to get away with his theft, never imagined anyone would catch him. He had spent his life obtaining what he wanted with charm and a smile and now his harmful ways had caught up with him and he wasn't used to the feeling.

"It's about Lisa, isn't it? You're still mad about me and Lisa."

Lizzy gritted her teeth to contain her anger. "Finding you in the arms of Lisa O'Reilly was months ago. I took you in when you needed a place to stay. Then you stole my furniture, my computer—everything I own. The day after Christmas!"

Any person in their right mind would have felt some remorse at those startling facts, but not Peter. Lizzy could see the wheels turning in his brain, his insensitive mind groping for a comeback. "I wouldn't have been with Lisa if you hadn't been so cold."

His comments halted her anger, hurt taking its place. He had once accused her of being unlovable, a comment that had wounded her to the core. But she wasn't ready to let him do it again. "You're crazy if you think I'm going to buy that argument."

"You spent more time with Nana than you did with me."

"She's my family, what did you expect me to do?"

"The sheriff is supposedly your family. Why didn't you visit him every day? Use him as an excuse not to go away on weekends."

This time, the fire burning up her spine mixed anger, hurt and pride. "So, spending time with my elderly grandmother, who happens to be my only living relative, gave you a reason to cheat on me?"

She hadn't meant to raise her voice, but she couldn't help herself, the man's logic was astounding. When the other policemen turned and looked, Peter leaned in close. "It wasn't just visiting Nana," he whispered. "You use her like a shield."

Lizzy bit the inside of her mouth to keep from letting the tears come. All of this sounded way too familiar. "What are you talking about?"

"You're incapable of love." His eyes turned frigid, like the deep recesses of the Pacific. "You use Nana as an excuse to keep from getting close to anyone."

If he meant to injure, the man's aim was perfect. Seeing he and Lisa in bed together was no match for this infliction. Even if she had wanted to cry, the sobs wouldn't rise for the blockage strangling her chest.

Dave approached them, holding Peter's report in his hands. "So let's move on, Sweetpea. Do you want to press charges and start getting your furniture back?"

Peter's eyebrows raised and his eyes widened, as if to say, "Now that we have straightened out that this is your problem, let me go."

Lizzy felt weak and damaged. She couldn't think for the pain gripping her heart. She felt Dave's hand on her shoulder and remembered when the salt and pepper-haired sheriff had picked them up on the side of the road when the Oldsmobile breathed its last breath, dropping them off at an apartment complex that took them in on the spot with Dave's recommendation.

At the time, Nana and Lizzy were both shell shocked with

grief, standing on the side of the road paralyzed, not knowing where to turn. When Dave came to their rescue and they settled in Santa Helena, they both took a step forward.

Or was it just Nana who healed?

"Sweetpea?"

Lizzy looked up at the sheriff who had once been her savior and searched his eyes for confirmation that she wasn't a heartless being, a woman incapable of love. What she saw shining back gave her strength. She stood and exhaled, pulling her jacket tight around her shoulders, although her insides still quivered from her pain. "Hell yes, I'm pressing charges."

LIZZY SHOULD HAVE BEEN PLEASED to have her things back, but now that Dave and two deputies had returned her furniture, the apartment felt suffocating. Her couch and dining room table were pushed against a far wall, leaving no space in the living room to move. Until she had time to replace all the individual items, everything was stacked in boxes on top. She did manage to squeeze in her coffee table, an Ikea mahogany piece Lizzy saved up to buy new, and add her own throw pillows on Martin's couch which fit together nicely.

But the apartment still felt overwhelming. Too many things in one tight space. She wanted her life back to normal and now she had that chance, but she dreaded returning Martin's comfortable furniture. Suddenly, the secondhand items she prided herself on finding looked irregular and out of place. Or maybe it was her own life that didn't fit anymore.

Lizzy pulled a pillow close to her chest and finally set the tears free. Had Peter been right, was she incapable of loving a man? Was that why she had reacted to Martin's kisses the night before as if he had the plague? Was Nana correct, too, in her assessment that Lizzy had built a fortress to save herself from more heartache?

The antique clock that belonged to her grandfather announced the half hour, but Lizzy hadn't the strength to shower and dress for the party. Moreover, she didn't want to face happy couples on the biggest date night of the year, then watch them all kiss at midnight. Even if Martin had promised to take her, what then? She wasn't in the mood to decipher his motives, nor worry that she might be pushing him away as Peter and Nana suggested she did with men. Her self-esteem had taken a lashing that day and she certainly didn't need another round, one way or the other.

But it was six-thirty and Martin was expected soon. How could she manage to get out of this one?

Lizzy wiped the tears off her cheeks with the back of her sleeve, but she still couldn't motivate herself to move off Martin's commodious couch. If she did manage to get to her bedroom and closet, she more than likely would change into a robe and crawl into bed. When Martin arrived, she could feign sickness and bow out of their date. She was sick, in a sense, if hearts were allowed illnesses. He went to this boring party every year and she was certain he'd find plenty of company there. It wasn't like he needed her for a date.

Thinking of Martin dancing with other women tugged at her heart and another stream of tears fell. No doubt he would be wearing that tux with the red plaid cummerbund like he did for the Christmas open house. Nothing like a handsome man in a tux, she thought, especially Martin with those sensual blue eyes and that engaging smile.

It was now six-forty and the seconds ticked away. What was she going to do?

Suddenly, the phone rang and Lizzy had to climb over her coffee table, past the computer on the floor, to reach it. "Elizabeth Guidry."

Martin laughed on the other end. "You are at home, are you not?"

The sound of his voice reassured her, although she couldn't comprehend why. God knew he was part of the myriad problems facing her now. "It's a habit."

He paused and Lizzy made out the sound of heavy machinery in the background.

"Are you okay?" he asked.

Now, it was her turn to pause. Had he heard the pain in her voice just then? "It's nothing. I got my furniture back, but it meant dealing with Peter."

"Do you want to talk about it?"

Was he sincere? Did he really care what happened? Lizzy didn't know what to say.

"Did you check your lottery ticket?" Martin asked.

Lizzy slipped into one of the dining room chairs and pulled her hand through her hair. "Dave called the minute you left. I never got a chance."

Another pause followed, the only sound being the inconsistent rambling of a printing press. "Where are you?" she asked.

"Where do you think? I was calling to tell you I've got a bit of a problem at work. I may be a little late."

Good, now she had a perfect excuse. "That works out well, actually. I was thinking that maybe we could call it..."

"Give me an hour or two." One of the printers increased its noise and Martin began to shout. "I've got a broken press but I should have it up and running soon."

"Martin," Lizzy yelled back. "It's not necessary..."

"Can I meet you there?" Apparently, he wasn't hearing her. "I still have to go home and get cleaned up, but I won't be long, I promise."

The noise was so loud now she doubted they could hold a conversation. "Sure."

"Great, see you there," he yelled back and hung up.

Lizzy placed the phone on its cradle and leaned her head against the wall. Now she had to go, had to endure small talk from every city official and business leader when she really wanted to crawl into a hole. But, at least she had two hours to force herself into a shower. She could stop at Nana's beforehand, let her see that red dress she bought last year for her one-year anniversary with Peter. The one she never got to wear.

What would Martin think of her slinky dress? she wondered. So far, he had only seen her in bathrobes and casual business attire. She had to admit, she longed to see him tonight, wanted those strong arms around her now. Was that what he wanted too? It was all so confusing.

Still, the phone call sent her into action. She poured herself a glass of wine, and with a heavy sigh, headed for the bedroom.

"IT'S TEN-THIRTY," Mac announced, looking up from his work. "We're not going to make it."

Martin stared down at his nemesis, an enormous machine that seemed to mock him at every turn. First, the color press failed, causing them to halt the printing of the tabloids and special sections. Then the main press jammed and the entire process halted. For two hours they had been down and another thirty minutes would mean not getting the paper out on time the next day.

New Year's Day. A paper loaded with advertising dollars.

Martin had experienced stress in many forms, from writing on deadline to the death of a parent, but this constant frustration was killing him for sure. He examined the broken press, thinking how easy it would be to set the damn thing on fire, right after he plummeted the monster with a baseball bat.

"Martin." Mac brought him back to reality. "What are we going to do?"

"Try reloading the back feeder. Give it more gas."

All the tricks his father had taught him over the years had been used again and again. Usually, one of them got the ancient machinery started, but not tonight. No matter how many ways they kick started the presses, nothing budged.

"It's not working," Mac said. "She's really dead this time."

Martin never hated anything more than he did that press at that moment, and that realization scared him to the bone. Perhaps Lizzy was right. Maybe he did detest working at *The Banner*.

"How much insurance do we have on this baby?"

Mac laughed, but he eyed Martin suspiciously. "You're not seriously thinking…"

"About killing this piece of shit, hell yes."

Martin picked up a crowbar and circled the press, aiming the metal high above this head. "I have coddled you, nursed you, and brought you back from the grips of death. And this is how you repay me?"

"Martin, put that thing down," Mac yelled. "I'm going to try to start it up again manually."

Martin ignored him, kicking the side of the paper feed. "You are interrupting the one decent social evening I've managed to get in this god-forsaken year."

He heard Mac shouting out, but all Martin comprehended was the machine before him, the one obstacle to his happiness. Even if he did find half a million dollars on his own or Lizzy gave him the money to solve the current crisis, the press would fail for good one day and he would be without the funds to replace it. By then, the Times would probably renege on their offer and force him into bankruptcy. Then they could circle *The Banner* like vultures and pick up the pieces.

At that moment, Martin didn't care. He'd had enough of the temperamental beast. If nothing else, one good blow might make him feel better.

In an instant, the machine thundered to life, papers cascading up the side. Martin turned and found Mac smiling, ink pouring down the side of his forearm. "I guess the one hundred and twelfth time is the lucky number."

Everything returned to normal, but for how long? Martin watched the newspapers move up the individual presses until they merged and folded into one neat package and headed for the docks where the trucks would pick them up in the early hours for delivery. If he moved ever so slightly, would the damn thing shut down again?

"Get out of here," Mac said, slapping his back. "And put that crowbar down."

Martin shook his head. "What if it breaks again? I'll only have to come back."

"If it breaks again, we'll go home and polish up our resumes."

Martin threw the crowbar down as the presses roared into high gear. He knew a conversation now was impossible above the noise. Mac grinned and gestured his head toward the door. Then he mouthed the word "Go."

"I have my cell phone," Martin shouted as Mac installed his earplugs and pushed him toward the door. "Call me if you need me."

Once outside the building, the silence of the late night greeted Martin like a blanket, soothing and comforting with its absence of chaos. He stood on the street corner watching the mist form as he exhaled, letting the stillness calm his mind, pacify his temper.

He glanced down at his watch. Ten forty-five. Whatever peace he had enjoyed breathing in the cool night air instantly disappeared. He had to shower, shave, change clothes and remove the ink from his hands and fingernails. Could he make the party before the stroke of midnight? Would Lizzy still be waiting there for him?

He had to try, had to see her if only for a blessed moment. Martin rushed to his car and sped toward home, all the while waiting for the cell phone to ring announcing bad news. Even when he entered his apartment and jumped into the shower, he placed the phone within earshot, waiting for the damned thing to interrupt his plans once again. But by the time he pulled on his tux, tied the cummerbund and gave his hair one last comb through, the phone had remained silent. Maybe there was a chance he would make it after all.

Eleven thirty-six. He pulled his car near the entrance to the mall and searched for a parking spot, one preferably close to the door. Nothing. Rows and rows he traveled but still no available spots. Was the whole world at the Santa Helena Mall tonight?

Finally, Martin parked in a vacant spot on the far side, then grabbed his phone and headed out. It was a long walk to the party, first traversing the enormous mall parking lot, then dealing with security at the door, then halfway through the mall to its center. When he spotted the fountain and heard the crowd noise, Martin checked his watch. Eleven forty-five. If his luck held and the phone refused to ring, he might actually have a chance. Because if it was the last thing he did that night, he was going to kiss Lizzy Guidry.

LIZZY SEARCHED the mall center one more time, glancing around the massive fountain and Christmas decorations, but no Martin. She had to stop looking, had to start enjoying herself, but it was close to midnight and the last place she wanted to be that night was surrounded by happy, affectionate couples.

And Anthony Billers. The arrogant man followed her every-where, drunk as a skunk in the moonshine shed.

"There you are," she heard him say behind her. Lizzy dreaded turning around, but she needed to get rid of him.

"Anthony, what do you want?"

He put his arms at her waist and pulled her so close she knew exactly what he was drinking. "I want you. You look so amazing in that tight red dress."

Lizzy tried to push him away, but the more he drank, the harder it was to release herself from his grip. Three times she told him to leave her alone but the man refused to get the hint, grabbing her every chance he could. "You need to go home and sleep this off."

A sly glint crossed his eyes and he reached for her again. "Great idea. Your place or mine?"

The current Miss California, a resident of Santa Helena, announced to the crowd that the New Year approached, which caused Anthony to turn his attention elsewhere. In that split second, Lizzy stole away. She slipped behind the wall of water that cascaded down a long series of terraces and kept to the shadows near the closed J.C. Penney. Martin or no Martin, she was leaving this retched party.

But before she could slink away, she bounded into the chest of a tall man rushing toward the celebration. Lizzy grabbed the lapels of his tux to steady herself, but recognized the plaid cummerbund instantly. When she looked up, Martin's blue eyes beamed down at her. But she didn't have a chance for a greeting. Within a heartbeat, his lips were hot upon hers.

His kiss was forceful and confident, as if their meeting hadn't been accidental, as if he had been planning to kiss her this way all night. His hands still gripped her shoulders from when she had barreled into him, but she hadn't the sense to know what to do with hers. All she comprehended was the amazing kiss being bestowed upon her and the way her legs had turned to jelly.

Martin pulled back and looked longingly into her eyes, and she felt that power rush through her bloodstream. She wished she hadn't drunk so much champagne for she imagined her knees might give way at any moment.

"It's not midnight yet," she whispered, not knowing what else to say.

"I don't care."

Something in his voice told her he had a rough evening, that pleasantries were to be dispensed with tonight. Which was fine with her as long as he kissed her like that again. He appeared ready to do just that, their lips only an inch apart, when Anthony found them.

"Oh, I get it," Anthony said, stumbling around the corner. "You got it for the newspaper man."

Lizzy felt the anger burn up her neck; she had enough of Anthony for one evening. Before she could tell him to go to hell, Martin did it for her.

"Go away, dude," Martin said between his teeth. "We're having a private conversation here."

Anthony sent Martin a patronizing smile. "Don't think I'm not on to you, dude. I know what's going on."

"You don't know crap, so back off."

Lizzy had never seen Martin so angry. She wondered if the rumors were true, if indeed the *Daily Times* was breathing down his neck. From the way his hair was tousled and damp, she imagined he had only recently showered.

"I know that once you wrote that editorial, the mayor decides to fire me and give little miss sexy in a red dress a raise." Anthony grabbed the fountain railing for support. "I guess there are no ethics in journalism anymore. Sleep with the publisher and you get what you want."

"Shut up, Anthony," Lizzy said.

Anthony turned to her and let his eyes roam across her bosom, then he tossed his drink on the front of her dress. "Slut."

Before Lizzy had a chance to gasp from the cold drink permeating her clothes, Martin grabbed Anthony's jacket and punched him squarely in the face. The drunk consultant fell on his behind, then his eyes rolled back inside his head and he fell unconscious to the floor.

Neither one said a word as they gazed upon the man lying beside the elegant fountain. If anyone had passed by at that instant, they would have assumed Anthony had fallen asleep from intoxication. But Martin and Lizzy knew better.

"We better get out of here." What was she saying? Leave the injured man alone in the deserted section of the mall?

"Good idea," Martin answered, grabbing her arm and heading for the door.

Before they made it ten feet, however, Miss California began the countdown. Martin stopped and looked back toward the crowd. "Well, I'll be damned."

"What is it?"

Dark and gorgeous Alexis Peron stood on a platform, rattling off numbers as a balloon floated down from the ceiling. "That's the daughter of the woman who used to be our maid."

"She's Miss California. She goes to the Miss America pageant soon."

As Alexis counted down to one, Martin grinned, as if the Queen of England was ushering in the New Year before them. "I guess anything's possible."

His earlier anger gone, Martin leaned down and kissed her as the clock struck midnight, pulling her close against him as he did and stopping the world in its rotation. Then he took Lizzy's hand and led her out of the mall into the cool Santa Helena night and the promise of a New Year.

CHAPTER 13

*L*izzy applied the antibiotic cream to Martin's bruised knuckles, one of which had broken skin. Martin cringed when the ointment met the open sore. "It looks so easy in the movies. I had no idea a face was that hard."

"We shouldn't have left him there."

"We told security they had a drunk on their hands. They'll take care of him."

Martin was probably right. They had fled the mall right after midnight, telling security on the way out that a man had passed out by the fountain.

Still.

"How are you doing? Is your dress okay?"

Lizzy looked down at the terry cloth and cringed. "What is it with you and me and bathrobes? I feel like you keep seeing me at my worst."

His thumb escaped her hand's captivity and began circling the inside of her palm. "You look awesome in that robe." His other hand reached up and tugged at the tie. "Besides, it's easier to remove than that skin-tight dress."

A heady mixture of sexual attraction and fear surged

through her. Lizzy wasn't ready to take that next step with him, but his comment failed to make her uncomfortable either.

"But you missed the way my breasts looked great in that slinky red dress."

She was still bent over his hand, wrapping a bandage around his knuckles, but from the corner of her eye she saw him smile. Then he leaned in so close, their foreheads touched. "I didn't miss a thing," he whispered heatedly.

Wild sensations surged through her, but she had to stop this incessant flirting. One minute she was afraid they would go too far too fast and the next... "Martin," she said, tying the bandage knot with finality. "About last night."

Martin leaned back on the bed, resting on an elbow, his eyes studying her intently. Still dressed in his tux, sans the jacket, the man looked delicious enough to eat. If only the first aid kit hadn't been in her bathroom and the living room hadn't been so cluttered, she would have dressed his wound in there.

"What happened today?"

Today? Weren't they talking about last night? "What do you mean?"

"When I called earlier, you sounded like you had been crying."

The gaze from his sexy blue eyes appeared so sincere, she almost imagined them great friends as well as lovers. But how was that possible when they had met only days before? Yet, he knew she had been crying from only a phone call. She could have balled hysterically in front of Peter and he would have asked for a beer.

"I take it this has something to do with Peter."

Lizzy relaxed, thankful to be able to confess her problems. She leaned back on her own elbow, facing him inches across the bed. "I saw him at the jail today."

A pause followed, while Martin continued his dissecting stare. "Are you still in love with him?"

"Hardly, it was more like an infatuation. Or maybe Nana was right, a means to an end." Martin's eyebrows rose and Lizzy laughed. "Call it a Chartreuse relationship."

Martin visibly relaxed. "Well that's a relief."

He moved a hand between them, flat down upon the bed, but the nearness of Martin made her head swirl. Such large, strong hands, powerful enough to knock a man unconscious. When had a man her age ever stood up for her before? Then she noticed the traces of ink beneath his fingertips.

"Was the press causing you trouble again?"

Martin curled his fingertips underneath, pulling his hand into a fist, but Lizzy caught him and straightened them again. "If I can sit here in a bathrobe, you shouldn't be embarrassed from working hard all night."

She meant to move her hand away, but it appeared destined to remain on top of his, as if operating of its own accord. He must have sensed her indecision for Martin gently touched his thumb against hers, careful not to frighten her away.

"The press refused to obey for hours," he said softly. "I was almost ready to tear it apart but it came alive five minutes before deadline."

"How awful for you."

"Well, the phone hasn't rung yet, so I consider myself the luckiest man on earth at this moment."

His smile warmed her, reminding her once again that the man lying before her was not Peter. Still, they were stretched out on her bed and he had asked her for a drive the night before. It was doubtful he would leave tonight without trying to seduce her again. Would she agree was the big question.

"What did you ever see in Peter?" Martin asked, interrupting her thoughts. "If you weren't in love with him, what attracted you?"

Lizzy remembered that crisp fall day when Peter had sauntered over from his table at the coffee shop and struck up a conversation. It had been the first time a man had been so forward before, the first time she had let down her guard and flirted back.

"I haven't had much experience with men," she began. "When Nana and I came west, we were broke and I was newly out of J-school and all we had to live on was her meager Social Security. I finally got on at *The Banner* but you know what beginning reporters make and I have to admit, your dad was pretty tight with his money."

Martin winced. "I'm sorry."

"Don't be, nature of the beast. I had a couple of part-time jobs as well. By the time I got on at the mayor's office, Nana needed assisted living, so I did some freelancing on the side—although if you tell Nana all this I will cut out your tongue."

Martin crossed his heart and held up his hand like a Boy Scout.

"Needless to say, I never had much of a social life."

At this, Martin frowned, then deftly turned over her hand and ran his thumb around the inside of her palm. The simple movement caused her breath to quicken and feminine places to tingle. With her other hand, she subconsciously tightened the robe at her chest.

"I met Peter at a coffee shop one day." Lizzy paused to clear her throat, watching his thumb massage the fat part of her palm, then slide up to the soft skin at her wrist. "I had only slept with one man before and he was a friend, someone I had asked because I didn't want to be a twenty-three-year-old virgin."

Martin glanced up, and meeting those blue eyes only made Lizzy melt more. "What happened with him?"

"Nothing." Poor Ron. They had been such wonderful friends until that awful night. "It was awkward. First time, you know. It wasn't pleasant for either of us and it ruined a good friendship."

"I'm sorry to hear that." He started circling her palm again and Lizzy searched her mind to remember what they had been talking about.

"And Peter, what was he like?"

Lizzy huffed, thinking back on how easy Peter had seduced her. "He was a blonde, blue-eyed charmer. He flirted with me, said nice things I wanted to hear. Then he took me for a drive in his car in the Hollywood Hills and lured me into the back seat on Mulholland Drive."

The seductive circles on her palm halted. When she looked up at Martin, he cringed. "Shit," he whispered. Martin moved his hand away and sat up at the edge of the bed, then sighed.

"Martin, if I overacted last night, I didn't mean to. I think we're moving a little too fast. You scared me."

Martin shook his head and grinned sadly. "I scare myself."

She wasn't sure what that meant, and before she had a chance to ask, he turned and faced her. "I'm not going to convince you to do anything you don't want to do, Lizzy. I promise you that."

She trusted him. She wasn't sure why – with those sensual eyes and a body to die for she shouldn't—but she did. "Okay."

"I'm not Peter," he reiterated. "You can trust…"

His entreating eyes shifted, emanating a different emotion. Guilt, perhaps? Suddenly, a shiver ran up her spine.

"I need a drink," Martin said, rising from the bed. "Want some?"

He didn't wait for an answer, picked up his glass from the floor and headed into the kitchen. Lizzy most decidedly needed more champagne. Regardless of whether Martin resembled Peter or not, he was definitely an enigma.

MARTIN RETRIEVED the bottle of champagne from the refrigerator, pouring himself a glass and shutting the door with his foot. While he gulped down the sparkling alcohol, hoping to calm the conflicts raging inside him, the lottery ticket stared him in the face, as if mocking his attempts at seduction.

Five million dollars, he thought as he remembered those numbers she had so skillfully collected several nights earlier. And she sticks it on her refrigerator door underneath coupons for Frosted Flakes. There was humorous irony here, but he wasn't in the mood to laugh.

He had to tell her she won, had to clear the air between them, ask for a cut and move on. Otherwise, there was no future for a relationship, and there definitely would be no newspaper.

Yet, he recalled the sadness in her eyes when she spoke of her limitations with men, of how Peter had taken advantage, coaxing her into the backseat of his car, no less.

"Shit," he repeated, thinking back to his callous comment the night before. He didn't want to seduce Lizzy for a lousy half a million dollars. He wanted to make slow, passionate love to her. Again and again. So what the hell was he to do?

Lizzy entered the kitchen, took the bottle from his hand and filled her glass, then refilled his. "You're mad I didn't take a drive with you last night? That you think I'm comparing you to Peter?"

"No." Martin rubbed her upper arm, forcing himself to stop at her neck. He itched to caress her face, to kiss her again, but he had to set things straight. "Lizzy, there's something I have to tell you."

Lizzy drank half her glass than tilted her chin up. "You're married and support three kids."

If Martin hadn't felt so tortured inside, he might have laughed. "Not even close."

"You were with another woman tonight, which is why you were so late."

He extended his fingers, unfortunately exposing several ink-stained fingernails. "My mistress is a forty-year-old machine that I despise. You have nothing to worry about with her."

She emptied her glass, then took one of his hands in hers, tracing his lifeline with the tip of a moist finger. "Nana says you have a good heart."

Martin remembered that Lizzy said Nana could read a person by holding his hand. When he delivered the gumbo Sunday night, Martin was careful not to come in contact with her grandmother, afraid the old woman might discover his deceptive intentions. He really should have laughed off such a concept anyway, but living with his intuitive mother taught him anything was possible. Had Nana taken his hand during the night? He honestly didn't remember. "What else did she say?"

Lizzy's finger paused where the lifeline curved into the wrist. "You were right. Two kids and a dog."

When she smiled, he felt a rush of relief that they were back to being friends. Was he really falling in love with this Cajun sweetheart? At that moment he suspected as such, wanted nothing but to drag her back to that comfortable bed and make love until sunrise. But the lottery ticket beckoned him from the refrigerator door. Right next to his recent editorial.

Martin was ready to ask again what Nana had said, but he turned to make sure his eyes weren't betraying him. Sure enough, she had cut out his last opinion piece. He grinned, feeling like a schoolboy realizing the girl he liked took an interest.

With his attention distracted, Lizzy released his hand and poured them both another drink. "Can I ask you something personal?"

An alarm sounded. Enemy territory, Martin thought. A place where no man should enter. No matter what a man answered to a woman's question like that, it would likely be wrong. But he found himself agreeing, anything for his girl. "Sure, what?"

"If you could describe me in five words, what would they be?"

Definitely dangerous waters. He sought to paddle to shore as fast as possible. "Adorable in a bathrobe. Five words."

"Four. Bathrobe is one word."

"Is not."

"Is so."

Grabbing the bottle of champagne, Martin headed for the living room. Anything to change the subject. "Where's your dictionary?"

Lizzy leaned against the wall, watching him search through the mess, that familiar fearful look flitting across her eyes. "In the bedroom."

Damn. He had managed to get them off that bed, which was driving him wild with longing, and now he was sending them back into the bedroom. Why had he gone down this silly road anyway? Who cares if bathrobe was one word or two? Only two journalists.

He was about to surrender the fight when Lizzy marched off toward the bedroom. He heard pages shuffling, then a snort of triumph. "It's one word," she yelled out to him.

Martin followed her, watching her scour a dictionary while perched on the edge of the bed. Her fine brown hair curved around her chin, framing the delicate oval face he so wanted to cover with kisses. When she tossed her hair back, a long stretch of neck beckoned to his lips. "The word originated in 1902, imagine that?"

Martin knelt in front of her, placing his glass and the bottle on the floor and removing the dictionary from her lap. "Why do you want me to describe you? I told you once before you're perfect."

Lizzy pulled her hair behind both ears and pouted her disapproval. "I'm not perfect."

Martin couldn't help himself. He slipped a hand around her cheek and kissed her, letting his tongue savor her lips now tingling from the champagne. "Okay, description number two," he whispered. "You're delicious."

When he paused in his kissing, Lizzy pulled away and stared down at the buttons of his tuxedo shirt. Whatever words she searched for, he wasn't delivering them. "Funny. Witty. Intelligent." Still, no reaction. "Cute in socks?"

Something wasn't right here, and he doubted it had anything to do with him. "Again, does this have something to do with Peter?"

Lizzy exhaled and closed her eyes. "He said I was unlovable. That I was cold."

Martin felt the hairs on the back of his neck rise. "He's an asshole, Lizzy. Haven't you figured that out yet?"

She twisted the bathrobe tie into a knot. "Nana said the same thing."

"Nana said you were cold?"

"She said that I'm scared of commitment so I don't let people into my heart. That I'm too guarded with men."

Martin joined her on the bed, sitting by her side. "First of all, you're not cold. And if you have any doubts to that fact, there are parts of my anatomy at this very moment that will prove otherwise."

When she gazed up wide-eyed, he nearly laughed, but the matter was anything but humorous. The tightness in his groin was killing him for sure.

"Second, Nana grew up in a small town in Louisiana, where everyone knew each other. And their parents. And their parents. If a man wanted to ask your grandmother out, chances are she knew his sock size."

Lizzy grabbed her glass from the floor and downed it in one gulp. "Yes, but..."

"But, things are different with us, Lizzy. We live in a big city where we don't know our neighbors unless an earthquake strikes. You have every right to be guarded. Look at how Peter turned out."

At this, she grew silent, her shoulders relaxing. Martin took the glass from her hands and refilled it with champagne. "Now take me, for instance. You know my parents, worked with my dad. You've met my siblings, read my inner thoughts in those diatribes I call editorials."

"Your piece in *Rolling Stone* was amazing."

He paused pouring himself a glass and met her eyes, twinkling from the effects of the champagne. "You read my article?"

She took the bottle from him and emptied the remnants into her glass. "It's on the Internet."

For a rare moment, Martin found himself speechless. She liked him, that much was clear, otherwise she wouldn't have taken the trouble. And he found that knowledge sparking his emotions like the firecrackers popping outside on the street. He leaned in close. "I wear size ten socks."

Lizzy rested back on her elbows, tossing her bangs from her forehead. She was a bit inebriated and no longer caring what Peter had called her, and that made him glad. "I know all about you, Martin Taylor. Your grandfather founded the newspaper and your great grandfather founded the town. Maxwell Taylor named it for his wife, Helen."

MARTIN PLACED his glass on the floor and stretched out on the bed, facing her across the quilt. "Who was named Helen because she was born on August eighteenth, the feast of Saint Helena.

187

Family stories have it she was born with a cross on her forehead, also a sign of the patron saint."

Lizzy's eyes widened. "Don't tell me you're Catholic too?"

At this, Martin laughed. "Father Wesley might not agree with you on that one. I'm not much of a churchgoer."

She fell back on the quilt and closed her eyes, a smile still playing her lips. "Don't tell Nana or you'll never hear the end of it."

Martin leaned close to whisper in her ear. "Now you have to marry me."

She giggled and the sound made his heart stop beating. He knew what endeared him to this woman, the fact that they could laugh together. Like the bathrobe she wore, she was comfortable and sexy at the same time. And he wanted her madly.

But the laughter soon died and the sadness returned. "What else aren't you telling me?" Martin asked, pushing loose strands of her hair from her eyes.

She hesitated, staring at the ceiling and chewing on her lower lip. "It wasn't just about being guarded. Peter said I was cold because..."

"Because why?"

LIZZY SWALLOWED HARD, screwing up her face in a frown. "Because I never had a... Because I never experienced a... Because when we made love I never..."

"Had an orgasm?"

Lizzy turned a deep shade of purple, but nodded, reaching up and grabbing a pillow that she pulled over her face. She moaned in embarrassment, and Martin felt a rush of anger stronger than when he felt like murdering the printing press. "I'm going to kill him. If I ever meet this man, I'm going to rip him to shreds."

"It wasn't his fault," Lizzy mumbled from underneath the pillow. "These things happen."

"Like hell."

One side of the pillow lifted and Martin found an eye examining him. He grabbed the bottom of the pillow and slowly pulled it from her face.

"Lizzy, women don't always climax when they make love, as opposed to men who explode if you blow in their ears. But, it's a man's responsibility to make sure a woman is fulfilled. I assure you, no woman has ever left my bed wanting."

Her embarrassment disappeared and a curiosity took its place. She leaned on her elbow again, more interested in the conversation then the fact that the ties of her bathrobe fell open. "Aren't you being a little smug? I mean, every woman?"

She was a little drunk and he should have taken that into consideration, but at that moment all Martin could think of was taking Lizzy to a higher level. He placed a hand at her cheek and moved so close he could smell her familiar lavender scent. "I want to give you a New Year's present."

Her eyes narrowed, then widened with understanding. Then she smiled nervously. "I don't think that's…"

"Necessary? You're twenty-seven and you're an orgasm virgin."

"I…" Lizzy's face lighted with a grand smile, one born of nervousness and embarrassment. Martin could almost feel the heat of that blush. "I don't think we should go there."

MARTIN CUPPED HER FACE, letting his thumb brush the highpoints of her cheek. "Why not?"

"Because I'm not ready for this."

He didn't believe her, although he certainly believed her fear. Making love to Lizzy was a dangerous step, one he was equally afraid of considering it meant a commitment he was not able to make. But, he was on a mission. And if it was the last thing he did that night, he would send her to heaven.

"Lizzy," he whispered. "I promised you tonight that I would not do anything you didn't want me to. But you have to trust me on this."

She started to speak, then stopped, but he read the confusion and conflict in her eyes. Martin deftly reached down and removed a shoe, then tossed it against the wall, knocking the light switch off.

"Got it on the first try," he whispered, planting kisses along her jawline. "It's a sign."

She still wasn't budging, locked in that position perched on her elbow, her breath coming in spurts. He pulled back and met her eyes, caressing her face with his bandaged hand. "Trust me."

Dear God, it was the last thing he should have said. She had no reason to trust him; he wanted to rob her of her lottery winnings. But at that moment, as the streetlight sent waves of iridescent hues about the room and Lizzy's eyes reached out to merge with his soul, Martin knew he had to win this battle.

He also realized he was falling in love.

CHAPTER 14

She knew she had way too much to drink, but his hand felt so good on her cheek and his breath so warm on her ear. What he suggested was absurd, yet Lizzy longed to know exactly how he proposed to deliver this New Year's present. The thought of those large hands caressing her body sent shivers of pleasure through her. But their proposed love-making was a bridge not easily crossed.

"I can't," she whispered.

Martin smiled, brushing the back of his bandaged knuckles against her cheek. "Can't what? You don't have to do anything."

Another blush made its way up her neck and she felt her cheeks burn anew. The glow of the streetlight reflected in Martin's eyes as he gently pulled her elbow forward so that she was flat on her back.

"Martin..." She tried to right herself, but his lips, hot and inquisitive, stopped her objections. She began to object to those sensual kisses that robbed her of all logical thought, but when his tongue delved into her mouth, exploring, teasing, she wanted only to meet him halfway. Never had any man kissed her this way, as if he threw his body and soul into the experience. When he cupped her cheek and delved deeper, then retreated and nibbled at her lips, Lizzy melted on the spot.

She let herself relax, extending an arm up and around his neck, urging him down on top of her. Then their tongues danced in wild abandon while her hand dug into his blond locks and she pressed hard against his chest. Good thing he had removed his jacket for she could feel the taunt muscles beneath his crispy starched shirt and that wide expanse of chest felt so wonderful against her breasts.

Her breasts? She paused and gazed down at the open robe that exposed her tank top and pajama boxer shorts, her nipples brazenly standing at attention. She thought to slide the robe back across her exhibitionist chest, but Martin instantly slid a hand underneath the hem of her top, purposely letting his fingers linger over her stomach, encircling her belly button.

His hands were as warm as they were large and felt so incredibly welcome against her bare skin. When he began kissing her again, leading a hot trail down her jawline to the soft spot beneath her earlobe, she relaxed again, leaning back into his chest, while his hand moved to her lower back and pressed her closer.

Someone moaned, she wasn't sure whom, and suddenly his hand was underneath her tank top. While those probing fingers massaged their way up her back, his mouth moved downward, grabbing small pieces of skin between his lips, his tongue teasing, tasting her in places she never imagined. All the while a fire burned deep inside her, causing her hips to move of their own accord, pressing upward against his leg.

It was definitely Martin who moaned that time, shifting his body to place a leg between her thighs, then sliding that wondering hand down to her bottom to press her closer. As her bathrobe fell completely open and his hand caressed her exposed leg, Lizzy pulled it over his, suddenly realizing the extent of his arousal.

With her leg wrapped around his body, Lizzy turned to place kisses on his face, enjoying the heady scent of his aftershave and the feel of his newly shaven face. She copied his movements, biting pieces of skin all the way to his earlobe. When she began to suck on the fat part of his ear, while her hands ran up the front of his shirt, brushing his nipples, he gasped and pulled away.

"Darling, you're going to drive me crazy." He held her by her shoulders, as if afraid she might kiss him that way again. "I'm doing this for you, remember?"

Lizzy removed her leg from his, feeling rather embarrassed by her bold moves. And here she had been the one to demand they move slowly. "Sorry."

Martin released her arms and let her fall back on the bed. "Don't be, angel," he whispered, his ragged breath hot against her cheek. "But if I'm going to do this according to plan, I need to have some of my senses intact."

She thought of the bulge in his trousers and felt guilty that she had agreed to only achieving her pleasure. Or had she agreed? Really, the whole thing was preposterous. She was getting ready to tell him as such when she recalled his last words.

Angel. He had called her angel, the same loving name her father had bestowed upon her as a child. While her better judgment screamed in agony, her heart filled with the idea that Martin cared for her, that maybe something solid and real could happen between them.

But, no matter how sentimental her heart had become, her head had the final say. She had let a few hot kisses turn her head. Just like she had with Peter.

She slipped from his warm embrace, missing the contact as soon as she did. "We shouldn't do this."

"Do what?" he asked, ignoring her actions. In one deft, sensual move, he slid the fabric of her tank top up and over her breasts. She gasped as the chilly air hit her nipples, but in seconds a hand provided warmth, taking her breast in its enormous palm while his thumb circled her nub in lazy, repetitive motions.

"You really have the greatest breasts," he whispered heatedly just before grabbing her lower lip with his teeth.

Thankfully, her mind disappeared, no more warnings to be issued. She tilted her head back and closed her eyes at the contact while her phantom hips began moving again. With every circle of his thumb, a string seemed to pull at her insides, building her desire, aching for release.

When he took her nipple between his thumb and forefinger and squeezed, Lizzy thought she would come undone. This time, the moan she heard was hers, its sound frightening her in its intensity. Had she had that much to drink, that she would lose all semblance of control? Or had she wanted this all along?

Martin kissed her soundly, his mouth seeming to suck her tongue into his, which she gladly offered. Then he paused, his eyes searching hers, before he kissed her lightly on the nose.

She thought he had a change of heart, but then his mouth descended to her breast, his tongue teasing her nipple as waves of pleasure poured over her. When his teeth took their place and he began to suck while his hand kneaded her breast, she lost all control and wrapped her leg back around his waist, feeling every inch of his desire press against her own.

Now, she was on fire, her body eager to meet with his. With one hand threaded through his fine hair and the other on his thigh, urging him closer, Lizzy thought she would burst if they didn't make love instantly.

Martin never left her breast, but he moved his hand to her leg and removed it from his, keeping it bent at the knee. Then he quickly slipped a hand down the front of her boxers, cupping the core that wanted to ignite upon contact.

A wave of intense desire seeped over her as his index finger began exploring the opening of her femininity, and with each entrance the passion intensified. He moved one finger inside, then two, then removed them both tracing circles around the opening, round and round, as his tongue continued to do the same with each nipple.

Surges of electricity traveled up her spine, cutting off her air, causing her skin to tingle and burn. The passion heightened as each time a bolt of energy emerged, and again her hips pulsated against his hand, eager for more, demanding more.

Suddenly, as Martin suckled hard at her breast, he moved his thumb forward, searching for that magic spot. While his fingers moved deep inside her, he caressed her nub and all pleasure she had known took on a whole new meaning.

Lizzy's back arched as wild fires seared her flesh. With one hand tightly gripping the back of Martin's shirt, Lizzy extended the other and held fast to the iron bars of the bed's headboard, gasping as waves of passion pulsated through her. She thought she saw stars, or a bright whiteness fill the room. Perhaps it was the champagne, but a bliss like no other filled her soul and she let it take her away, carrying her to a place like no other.

Wild spasms raked her repeatedly, new ones carrying her higher until she reached an apex, her body spent. "Stop," she muttered in a pitiful whisper.

Martin removed his hand, but he continued kissing her until he pulled the tank top back into place. Wrapping the robe around her and tying it at her waist, he relaxed against the pillow next to her, gently pushing her hair from her face. "You can let go of that headboard now."

Somewhere in the deep recesses of her mind she heard him speak, felt the bed tilt as he moved closer to her head. She released her hold on the iron bar, as well as the death grip on his shirt, then exhaled loudly. Suddenly, as the air rushed from her lungs, her insides fell apart like the stuffing on a rag doll when a seam is unthreaded. Lizzy took one look at Martin lying next to her on her pillow and broke into tears.

Martin expected many things after what had just transpired, but tears weren't one of them. Lizzy wasn't simply crying, she was sobbing hysterically.

He hated when women cried, hated feeling so helpless to make them stop. He wrapped his arms about her and pulled her into his chest, but the weeping continued unabated. He tried caressing her hair, patting her shoulder but nothing seemed to help.

"I'm sorry," Lizzy managed between sobs.

"Don't be sorry," Martin whispered back with a grin, "just stop."

The flood slowed some, and Lizzy grabbed a tissue from her robe pocket and blew her nose. "I don't mean to cry. It really wasn't that bad."

Before he had a chance to digest and retort to what she had said, he saw the corners of her lips twist up in a smile. "I'm kidding," she said, wiping her nose on her sleeve. "Believe me, I'm kidding."

His ego felt bruised no matter that she joked. What on earth had he done to start her crying spell? He had only meant to introduce her to carnal pleasure, not cause her pain.

She breathed deep, sobs still popping up like hiccups, but for the most part Lizzy appeared to have it under control. "It's like when I was hit from behind in my car," she said. "I didn't see it coming. The jolt scared me so much I start crying uncontrollably."

"So, my lovemaking skills can be compared to whiplash?"

He felt her smile beneath his hand as he caressed her cheek, planted kisses on her forehead. "Earth shattering moments can knock the emotions from you," Lizzy whispered, closing her eyes as his lips touched on her eyelids. "God knows that was a shocker."

Her body rose and fell one last time, then she relaxed against his chest, nesting comfortably with one hand over his heart. Maybe it was best she had become emotional for it took his mind away from the pounding in his groin, a need that demanded to be fulfilled. He shifted on the bed to try to relieve the pressure, then exhaled loudly himself.

"What about you?" Lizzy seemed to read his mind. "This wasn't a fair exchange."

"I'm fine." Lie of the century.

She propped her chin on his chest and tried to make out his eyes in the darkness. "We can make love if you want to."

Martin cupped her cheek, then kissed her long and deep one last time. When he broke away, he paused to savor her sweet lavender scent. "I made a promise and I'm going to stick by it." He coaxed her head back on his chest, running his fingers through her silky fine hair. "Just please don't cry again."

"I'm really sorry. I don't know where that came from. I've never had an experience like this so I guess I blew a head gasket."

Head gasket? He delivers her first orgasm and she compares it to an engine? "What's with you and car analogies."

She buried her face deeper into his chest. "It was wonderful, absolutely amazing. I can't believe that I've been missing that all these years."

Martin thought of how she reacted to his lovemaking, throwing her leg across his and taking charge. The recollection caused the swelling in his trousers to intensify. "That's what you get for sleeping with the wrong men. Angel, you are anything but cold."

She turned her sleepy eyes to his. "Really?"

He took the opportunity to plant another kiss on her upturned nose. "Really. Again, I have more than enough evidence to prove that theory."

Lizzy lifted herself on an unsteady elbow. "Martin, I…"

He pulled her back into his chest, holding her there with his hand on her hair. "I gave you my word." His tone sounded cold, gruff. He wanted to assure her that his needs didn't matter now, but his body seemed to insist otherwise and it showed in his voice. "I'm fine. Go to sleep."

But Lizzy, in her champagne-induced, orgasm-hazy state, surprised him. She reached down and placed a hand on his arousal. "Good God, it's huge."

Martin instantly grabbed her wrist. "Let go."

But Lizzy refused to obey. "Shut up, Martin, and kiss me."

He should have had more resistance, but when her fingers wrapped around him and her thumb found the tip, he lost all control. He felt his eyes roll back and his breathing halt as her lips began a hot trail down his neck and her fingers worked their magic. Lizzy held his life in the palm of her hand and Martin gladly surrendered.

CASSIE PACED her tiny jail cell, trying to keep from crying. She had done enough sobbing that night to fill the Hollywood Bowl, tears that had gotten her into this mess. She had to regain control of her senses, had to appear calm when Martin arrived. Her brother hated seeing women cry and she wanted to spare him that agony, especially since he broke off his date to come bail her out.

He had sounded so sleepy when she called his cell phone. More than likely he had spent the evening with Lizzy Guidry and Cassie had robbed her brother of one of life's few pleasures afforded him. The knowledge that she ruined Martin's night made the tears come again. This time, she was helpless to fend them off.

She was useless, a waste of human space. She couldn't make films, had no other talents to offer the world, and now she was about to embarrass her family with bankruptcy. And worse.

The last thought hurt the most, turning her tears into sobs. How would she explain this to her family?

She heard the door to the outside open and the voice of her brother talking to the deputy.

"Where's Dave?" Martin asked the man.

"In Vegas. Getting married."

Cassie watched Martin frown at this news and she knew what he was thinking, but that explanation would have to wait. One good thing about the whole mess was her mother wasn't here to witness her downfall.

"She was weaving on the road," the deputy explained. "She said she had only one drink at her party, but it's New Year's Eve and we can't take chances. We had to bring her in."

Martin gazed up at Cassie, those warm blue eyes smiling at her through the bars. With his hands tucked in his pants pockets, her brother looked so amazingly handsome in his tux. Cassie started to speak but felt the rush of tears, so she sucked in a breath and waited for the moment to pass.

"My sister doesn't drink much," Martin told the man. "If she said she had one drink, it's true. Why don't you give her a sobriety test? That will clear everything up."

The deputy turned his back to Cassie and leaned close to Martin, but Cassie heard his words. "I would have but she wouldn't stop crying long enough."

She saw Martin wince, then run a hand through his tousled hair. The deputy opened the door to the cell and let him through and Martin sat down on the cot next to her. Their shoulders touched and Cassie was thankful for the warmth he offered. He took her hand and squeezed.

"What happened to you?" she asked, staring down at the bandage.

Martin sighed. "No, Cassie. The question here is what happened to you."

She bit her lower lip to rein in her emotions, but it didn't help; the tears came anyway but thankfully only streamed gently down her cheek. "I'm sorry to have you come out here in the middle of the night. I never meant for this to happen."

Martin placed an arm around her shoulders, letting her lean her head into the curve of his. "Of course, you didn't. But why were you weaving?"

"I was crying." Suddenly, a burst broke forth.

She felt Martin tense. As the oldest of the three, he had spent half his life watching their mother cry waiting for their father to come home. She knew how much Martin hated tears, mainly because he had been helpless to ease their mother's pain. No son should have endured the responsibilities Martin had, or the heartache, yet her big brother took care of his family without regret or complaint.

Now, he was taking care of her. Again.

"Why were you weaving?" he repeated. "What made you cry?"

Cassie took a deep breath. She had to tell someone or burst from the anxiety. "I have to declare bankruptcy."

Martin pulled her far enough away to look into her eyes. "What are you talking about? You said the bank offered you a long-range payment plan."

SHE STARED AT HER SHOES. "I lied."

"But how?"

"I used four credit cards to make my movie. I have thousands of dollars on them and after the reorganization I still can't pay them off."

Martin removed his arm and rubbed his eyes. She knew what he was thinking, that selling the newspaper would solve all their problems. Yet, Martin had made a promise and Cassie was sure the conflict between his father's pledge and his living family was tearing him up for sure.

She decided to change the subject.

"There's something else, something worse."

At this, Martin turned his grim smile her way. "What, that you're gay?"

If he had wanted to shock the tears from her, the man did his job. "How did you know?"

Martin rose and stretched, then looked through the bars at the sleeping man in the neighboring cell. "You never dated. I used to think you were just defying the old man, since he was always trying to make you into some delicate feminine creature you obviously weren't."

Cassie felt the buried anger rise through her veins. Her father had bought her prissy dresses with bows and ribbons, then argued with her over her choice of extra-curricular activities. Dad wanted her to try cheerleading and go out for homecoming queen, things he could brag about to the community. They were Taylors, descendants of the founding father, and he wanted to show them off every chance he could. Didn't seem to matter that the Taylors were actually Trägers, poor Germans heading west with nothing but the clothes on their backs to avoid social condemnation in their East Coast town because they were immigrants and Catholic. She doubted Maxwell Taylor cared if she were homecoming queen or not.

"I thought so too," Cassie said, thinking back on how she refused to wear any dresses to school, how her mom used to bring her to the mall to exchange them for overalls. The writing was on the wall even in high school.

"Is this because of Holly?" Martin asked. "I saw how well you two got along."

Cassie closed her eyes, trying to forget the shock in Holly's eyes when she kissed her at the stroke of midnight. She had never kissed a girl before. She had assumed Holly felt the same way. How could she have been so wrong? Cassie wanted to crawl into a dark hole and die.

She felt Martin kneel before her, taking her hands in his. "It's okay, Cassie. It's not the end of the world."

"Isn't it?" His vision began to blur as tears filled her eyes. "How am I going to tell the family?"

"Tell us what?"

They both looked up to find Paul being ushered in, his enormous frame stretched tight by a too-small tux. Despite her pain, Cassie smiled at her two saviors, one stylish and handsome who hadn't the sense to let a bad thing go and one who wouldn't know a plaid from a stripe who could solve any problem. She adored her brothers, was thankful to have them in her life. Suddenly, she felt ten times better.

"It's nothing, Paul," Martin said casually as Cassie's twin entered the cell. "Cassie's declaring bankruptcy and finally coming out of the closet."

Paul, in his usual psychotherapist demeanor, took the news in strike, as Martin suspected he would. "New Year's is always a good time to clean the slate. Good for you, Cassie."

Staring at the two of them, not caring if she was gay or spouting three heads or sitting in a cold jail cell made her laugh. Go figure her family would only care about her happiness. Truth was, Cassie's only fear was her father's condemnation. And the old man had been dead three years.

She felt Martin's hand in hers and Paul's arm about her shoulder. They sat there, grouped together, while Martin tickled her to make her laugh more. "We love you," Martin whispered as he kissed her forehead. "Whether you wear dresses or not."

"Speak for yourself," Paul kidded, then kissed her as well. "I kinda liked it when she wore that blue number at her graduation. The one she complemented with army boots."

"You know what I think?" Cassie said.

"That it's time to make another film, this one about psychic dogs?" Paul teased.

"I think it's time we bury the old man for good."

A silence fell upon them as they contemplated the implications of that statement, but they continued to huddle, holding each other close. And that was how Olivia found her children, sitting in a jail cell.

"Well, it's a good thing I found the nerve to leave home," she said. "Who else was going to bail all of you misfits out?"

The boys straightened, shocked at the sight of their mother. Just then Dave entered the room and Olivia took his arm lovingly. Cassie could have sworn she felt her brothers' hearts stop beating. She knew Olivia had sought out Dave earlier in the day but the elopement to Vegas had been a surprise.

"Mom, I think it's time you came clean."

Olivia removed her coat and sat on the opposite cot. "Me? I'm not the one arrested."

"No one is arrested," Dave said. "The deputy picked Cassie up for observation."

"Waste of time on his part," Paul said with a snort and Cassie delivered a sharp jab to his ribs.

"Mom, what are you doing here?" Martin asked. "And why were you at the nursing home yesterday?"

Olivia looked sheepishly up at Dave.

"First things first," Dave said. "Let's clear this up and move to a warmer place. How about we all go to The Helena Café and get some coffee and something to eat." He glanced at his watch. "It should be open about now. They open at six."

They all stood, ready to move on as if the family gathering at the jail and heading toward breakfast happened every day. Martin, however, refused to move until he had answers. "The deputy said you were in Vegas getting married. I think we should clear that up first."

Dave glanced at Olivia, who blushed profusely, then held out her hand sporting a modest diamond ring.

"Don't worry," she said. "We're still planning on having a

church wedding. But when you get to be our ages, you get a little impatient."

Tears long gone, Cassie let out a whoop, which startled the sleeping man in the next cell. She leaped into Olivia's arms and hugged her tight. "I'm so happy for you, Mom."

While Cassie doted on her mom, the boys approached Dave, who pulled them both into bear hugs. Then each son embraced Olivia and they all found themselves glassy eyed.

"Do you mind?" the man next to them said. "I'm trying to sleep here."

The deputy rattled the bars on his cell. "Your girlfriend is in the lobby now bailing you out, so you might as well get up."

The man groggily sat up while another deputy entered and opened his cell, a talkative woman close at his heels, her hair ten shades of red. Cassie admired wild hairstyles, especially liberal experimentations with color, but this one beat all.

"You took your sweet time," the man said to the redhead.

"You should be glad I'm here Peter," the woman mumbled. "I almost didn't come, considering how you lied about all that furniture being yours."

Dave urged the group to move out of the holdings and away from the quarreling couple, but Martin paused, studying the man through the bars.

"Peter?" Martin asked as the man walked by. "Peter Dark?"

The man halted in front of Martin, obviously pleased someone recognized him. Now that Cassie got a better look, she knew him from television, one of those hunky actors from a soap.

"Yeah, I'm Peter Dark," he said proudly.

The poor sod didn't see it coming. In one flash, Martin slammed his fist into that perfect nose and the man fell back into his cell and on to his cot, out cold.

CHAPTER 15

*L*izzy woke in a fog, her head pounding. She sat up on the bed, wondering why she was sleeping in her robe, a lap blanket spread across her body.

Then she remembered.

"Oh no, what have I done?" Lizzy fell back against the pillows trying to piece the evening together, hoping it wasn't as horrific as she thought. The party was lucid enough, including Martin smashing a drunk Anthony Billers in the face. What happened after drinking several glasses of champagne failed to materialize clearly, however.

She had changed her dress and they had ended up on the bed with the bottle, that much she remembered. Somehow Martin had convinced her she needed a...

Lizzy gulped, thinking back on her embarrassing revelation that had led to his fingers working magic on places he had no business touching. He had done more than touch too. Recalling what he did to her breasts made her tingle violently all the way to her toes.

But that wasn't the worst of it. If memory served her well,

she had brazenly unzipped his pants. She didn't want to think of what happened next. Her cheeks burned from the recollection.

She pulled a pillow over her face, cringing at the image. She had never acting that way with a man before and certainly never done that. She had been so naive and shy with Peter, never so much as offering a kiss without him making a move first. Yet, she had slept with Martin, allowed him to bring her to ecstasy—twice! The second time more embarrassing than the first.

Lizzy threw the pillow off the bed, knocking over a lamp. People went to hell doing things like that.

She had to grin though. She had taken the initiative for once, allowed herself to be part of the lovemaking and not simply a recipient—or, in Peter's case, an observer. Martin had awakened her repressed sexuality and she gladly paid him back, fired up by a new bravado. She didn't know which had been more fulfilling either, the taking or receiving of pleasure, both glorious, including the second time around when he had pressed his tongue against her...

"*Mon dieu*," she said bolting up, her body burning from the thought. Good thing he didn't use tongues on a first date or she would have disintegrated in the parking lot of that fruit stand on Highway 126. That nice lady at the cash register would have called 911 for sure.

Lizzy pressed her fingers against her lips and giggled like a schoolgirl, imaging those sparkling blue eyes laughing at her right now, those enormous arms encircling her with their warmth. They were comfortable together, like an old married couple, which made everything all right. Martin wasn't like Peter at all. She could wake up next to Martin and not worry about the condition of her hair or the smudges of makeup. What had Martin said about spending nights with women? That he longed to be with someone whom he could wake up in the morning with bad breath and a boner?

The silence of the apartment slipped into her thoughts, infiltrating her bliss like a computer virus. Slowly, the knowledge spread until she knew exactly what had transpired. They had shared frenzied lovemaking last night, but now he was gone. Back to the comfort of his own place.

"I hope to someday find the woman of my dreams whom I will enjoy spending the night with," she remembered him saying. "But until then I will prefer the comfort of my own bed, and waking up in the privacy of my own home."

"Shit," Lizzy said, grabbing her aching head in her hands. She did it again, fallen for a man incapable of making a commitment. Or at least one with her.

And the truth was, she really liked Martin. Liked him bad. For a few blessed moments before she realized she was alone, she had imagined being in love with him, imagined them making love again. And again. But, obviously, he didn't feel the same way.

"Stupid girl," Lizzy moaned to herself. "When will you ever learn?"

Lizzy crawled back into bed, pulling Nana's hand sewn quilt around her. While the sun peeked above the horizon, sending an orange glow into her bedroom, she cried herself to sleep.

THE SUN PEEKED between valleys in the western mountains, casting soft shadows about the coffee shop located in what used to be the "old section of town." The ancient café, once the resting spot for train and wagon travelers heading north to San Francisco, was all that remained of the original town. Even so, the coffee shop filled with memorabilia, historic photos and used license plates had to be moved several hundred yards when the commuter Metrorail linked Santa Helena with downtown Los Angeles and all points south.

Like most towns in Southern California, uprooted by the

constant stream of progress and growth, one had to hunt for the historic connections, and the Helena Café was a good example in the Santa Helena Valley. But as Martin gazed at the pictures on the wall, one showing a proud Maxwell Taylor with wife Helen and their firstborn who would later create the town's inaugural newspaper, he felt the connection pull down through the generations, like a strong rope refusing to break.

A bond with the past was one thing, however. Relating to the living was another. As he glanced around at his siblings, sharing in their mother's long-overdue happiness, he thought of what Cassie had said, that maybe it was time to bury the old man. Maybe it was time to cut the cord.

"And what about you?" his mother said, breaking him from his thoughts. "What party did Cassie pull you from?"

"He was pretty wrinkled by the time he arrived," Cassie offered, sending her mother a wink. "Think it might have something to do with a certain Elizabeth Guidry."

Martin remembered how peaceful in sleep Lizzy had been when Cassie had buzzed his cell phone, and how comfortable he had felt lying next to her, serenity he'd like to feel more often. He would be there now, possibly initiating another round of lovemaking, this one more interactive, if not for his sister crying on the other end, begging for his help.

He grinned into his coffee, raising the cup before his face to escape the scrutinizing eyes of his family. Lizzy had surprised him. He had only wanted to bring her pleasure, deliver her to new levels of ecstasy then allow her some sleep, but she had caught him off-guard, returning the favor before he had a chance to object.

Martin was used to taking care of people, used to seeing that other people's needs were met. Having someone look after his was a new experience, one he wouldn't mind repeating. Maybe that's what made a good relationship, being partners in all aspects of life. He really couldn't say, having spent his life picking up gorgeous women and giving them wild nights of pleasure, then slinking away to his condo not caring if he ever saw them again.

He wanted to see Lizzy again. He missed her scent and the silky feel of her hair at his cheek. He missed her crazy sense of humor and the way she abandoned all control when she climaxed, nearly bringing the bed down with them when she grabbed the headboard. And he missed having the last say. Before the night was over and she slipped into a blissful sleep, Martin had taken her back to heaven in a manner that even surprised him. The last thought made him smile like the Cheshire Cat.

"Dear God," he heard Paul say. "He's in love."

He gazed above the rim of his cup and saw all eyes pinned on him, but he was through denying it. Besides, the more he objected, the more insistent his family would be. They loved to tease.

"Of course, he's in love," Dave said. "Why do you think he belted that guy in the other cell. That was Lizzy's old boyfriend, a man who left town last week with all her furniture."

"How romantic," Cassie said. "You hit him because he wronged your girl."

He wronged her all right, but Martin wasn't just thinking of her furniture when he plastered his knuckles into the actor's nose. Reminded of the feel of Peter's face Martin winced, looking down at his bloodied bandage. "I will never look at a western or an action picture the same way again."

Cassie rolled her eyes. "We're thirty-five miles from Hollywood and you didn't know that it's all an illusion?"

"He was blinded by passion," Paul said, and the twins shared a good laugh.

"Leave Martin alone," Olivia admonished them. "I've met Lizzy and she's a wonderful girl."

.   .   .

"I'VE MET HER TOO, MOM," Paul said. "She's great. The first one he's brought home that I approve of."

"And she's from Louisiana," Dave interjected. "They both like that horrid coffee and chicory and put way too much spice on their food."

"So, when's the wedding?" Cassie asked.

Martin put his cup down and gave up. Too bad his family didn't know she was also Catholic and a devoted granddaughter. And worth five million dollars. They would have a field day with those pieces of information.

Instead of thinking of a happy life with Lizzy, images of the lottery ticket dangling on her refrigerator came back to haunt him. Lizzy had been right; complicated problems were easy to solve. Watching the delighted faces around him light up at the prospect of him finding happiness assured him of that. Each one at that table would benefit from him selling the newspaper, including himself, and his future would likely include more days like this one, surrounded by family and friends, instead of ones nurturing a printing press and finding snippets of love in one-night stands.

Yet, he still couldn't find the strength to give up hope on his father's newspaper, to abandon the idea that Lizzy would cash in her ticket and allow him to meet that payment.

He had to talk to her, confess all and let Lizzy determine his fate. He loved her, that much was obvious. But he had four days before the bank deadline and one way or another he had to clear the air between them.

The waitress arrived with a pot of coffee and several menus. "Sorry this has taken so long, but we had to call in our substitute cook. The head guy had a little too much to drink last night and we don't want eggs in our orange juice."

Olivia accepted the menu, but she leaned toward Martin. "Why don't you go call Lizzy and ask her to join us for breakfast?"

Paul looked up from the breakfast specials and nodded his approval.

"She must be wondering where you ran off to," Cassie said.

"I told her where I was going," Martin said, although a fear nagged at the back of his mind. After Cassie had called, he had shaken Lizzy awake and explained the situation. She had opened her eyes slightly and muttered an approval, but Martin wondered if she had heard him at all.

"Oh yes, please do," Olivia said. "I want to tell her the news."

Martin was halfway out the booth before they finished urging him on, which brought about another round of laughter. He heard them discussing wedding plans all the way to the deserted waiting area. Martin flipped out his cell phone and punched her number, leaning against the community bulletin board. He couldn't wait to hear the sound of her sweet voice again.

LIZZY HEARD the phone ringing in the midst of her horrible dream. The policeman was at the door again, but the doorbell ringing suddenly became the phone, startling her from her sleep. She pushed aside the quilt, fear still surging through her veins. Who would be calling her at such an early hour, unless it was bad news?

"Hello?" she answered breathlessly.

"Hello sleepy head." Martin sounded so chipper on the other end, like he was thrilled to hear her voice. Before she had a chance to digest that he had deserted her, she reveled in its sound. "Hello yourself."

"Hungry?"

Food? The man wanted to discuss food? In an instant, her reflector shields emerged. "I don't think so."

A pause ensued, allowing the hurt he inflicted to return full force. How dare him leave her like that, than call to see if she wanted to have breakfast? Then she thought of the printing press. What if he had left to attend to the paper? "Did the newspaper come out okay?"

"Yeah," Martin answered. "Imagine that? Mac never called. Some days miracles happen."

For a few blessed days, miracles had repeatedly arrived on her doorstep. Some in the shape of couches and tables and one in the shape of a blonde, handsome man. But today wasn't one of them.

"Lizzy, you did hear me when I said I was leaving, didn't you?"

She refused to hear excuses, feared more heartache. She only wanted to climb back in bed and hide from the world. So this was what came of removing walls, she thought.

"Martin, I think we should take a break for a while."

Another pause followed, but Lizzy could hear his anxious breathing on the other end. "What's the matter?"

"Nothing's the matter." She wiped a tear away, clearing her throat to hide her emotions. "I think this is all going way too fast and we should slow down, that's all. I told you last night I wasn't ready for..."

"You said a lot of things last night," he offered. "But in the end..."

"That's just the point. In the end, I let a little champagne cloud my judgment and act foolishly. We've only known each other a few days."

He sighed heavily and she pictured him rubbing the bridge of his nose like he always did. "We've known each other for over a year, Lizzy."

As a silence fell between them again, and the kitchen clock ticked away the seconds, Lizzy thought about what Nana had said, that Martin had written that editorial to get her attention. She thought about him asking her to coffee last year and wondered if their attraction had roots.

Stop it, she finally admonished herself. He left you in the middle of the night, a clear sign she meant no more to him than Chartreuse Magenta What's-Her-Name. If anything, the man was interested in her breasts.

"I need time," Lizzy said.

"How much time?"

God, if she was only a flirtation and romp in the sack, why didn't he say fine and hang up? Why prolong her agony this way, unless she trampled on his precious ego? "I'm going to Sacramento for a conference this week. I won't be home until Saturday."

"Saturday?" She heard something akin to panic in his voice. Surely, the man who couldn't wait to return to his cozy bed could wait until Saturday to see her again.

"Let me come over," Martin said. "I need to see you. I have to talk to you."

"No." Fear, so warm and familiar, prickled up her spine as if the policeman was now banging at her door. "Holly and I are going up today to catch the sights before the conference starts tomorrow."

Again, an anxious silence, the clock's ticking rattling her nerves. Lizzy looked up to see it was only six a.m. Where was he at this hour?

"Lizzy, about last night..."

His silky voice pleaded with her to listen, but Lizzy couldn't stand any more torture. She wanted so badly to say yes, to rush back into his arms, but she couldn't make that mistake twice. His actions had said it all. Now, she needed to move on.

"Martin, I have to go."

"Wait," he practically shouted. "Can I see you when you get back?"

She didn't know why she agreed, maybe because no matter how much he hurt her, she still missed his smile, those azure eyes, those lips. "We can have lunch on Saturday."

Martin exhaled. "If that's the best I can do."

"No, that's the best I can do."

Lizzy placed the phone on its cradle before he had a chance to convince her otherwise. It was best this way. She would leave town for a few days and give them space. If nothing else, on Saturday she would face him with renewed strength, able to fend off that irresistible Taylor charm.

But she couldn't help feeling defeated, crushed that Martin didn't love her back. She slid to the floor, wrapping her arms about her and setting free her tears. For the first time in her life she had found hope of being loved. And in a split second, it had disappeared.

MARTIN LEANED his head back against the array of business cards attached to the community board. He might have winced at the pushpin biting into his scalp but his head was already pounding. For the first time in years he had felt happiness and now it was slipping through his fingers.

She mustn't have heard him when he left, failed to understand that he was leaving to rescue his sister. That was the only explanation for her cold rebuke. Or maybe she was having second thoughts about their relationship. Perhaps it was the champagne talking last night and not her true feelings.

No, he saw the way Lizzy looked at him, was certain that she cared. Why else would she have done what she had the night before, considering what little experience she had with men?

Trust issues. First her parents dying. Then Peter and his deception. He didn't blame her for being scared, for being cautious when it came to men, but damn it, he wasn't the enemy.

Was he?

"Shit," Martin said, kicking the trashcan next to him, which caused another part of his body to ache. He was the enemy, wanted to pilfer half a million from her lottery earnings. Who was he kidding? She opened her heart and soul to him the night before and he wanted her to join them for breakfast so he could ask for a loan. What would she think of him then?

What was he going to do? Saturday was too late; the balloon payment was due Friday by four with no hope of an extension. Either he marched to her apartment and spilled his guts, begging for her forgiveness as long as she forked over the amount or...

Cassie stuck her head out of the booth and looked his way. "Are you coming back or not?"

The cell phone buzzed and Martin instantly recognized the number, causing his headache to intensify. But he slipped his thumb over the power switch and turned it off, then sauntered back to the group.

He noticed Paul's arm through Cassie's and his mother's arms about her shoulders. Apparently, his sister had come out and realized no one cared what her sexual preference was, only that she find happiness. She simply beamed.

Looking around at his family before him, he realized they all glowed with happiness: Paul with his new practice and the start of a new life, Olivia newly married to Dave, a dear man who had held a torch for thirty years, finally realizing his dream. The only one left out of the equation was Martin, who only minutes before imagined himself perched toward bliss. Was happiness to be an illusion he would only dream about as he trudged away keeping the newspaper alive?

He thought of that night in Santa Barbara, when Lizzy had

rested her head against his chest. "If you don't like what you do, you can change your circumstances," she had told him.

Was it that easy? Was it simply a matter of letting go?

"Sweetheart, are you okay?" Olivia asked.

"I take it Lizzy isn't coming," Paul added. "That's too bad."

Martin stood at the edge of the booth, like a preacher looking down on his congregation. "No, Lizzy's not coming. She has to go to Sacramento today."

It must have been his tone, for his family looked upon him with sympathetic eyes, as if they guessed the conversation he just had. But Martin didn't want pity. He wasn't about to let Lizzy slip away, wasn't about to give up his life for his father's dream. He would change his circumstances, no matter how painful that might be, and no matter that it meant reneging on a promise.

It was time to bury his father.

"I have something to tell you all," he said softly. "I've decided to sell the newspaper."

CHAPTER 16

*D*ays passed with little more than pleasantries spoken between Lizzy and Holly, all starting with a deathly quiet ride to Sacramento. Usually the two chatted endlessly about everything from men to clothes, but neither seemed to have the energy to initiate a conversation.

Lizzy preferred it that way, preferred not speaking about Martin. She worried, though, that Holly might be conflicted about her sexuality and uneasy about discussing it. Lizzy thought to broach the subject, but how? If she had been in a better frame of mind, she might have found a diplomatic way of doing so, but Lizzy's spirits were somewhere in the vicinity of her toes.

They did a few tourists things on Tuesday, then Holly complained of a headache so they went straight to bed after dinner. On Wednesday they split up, attending different workshops, then later separate parties to get the most out of the municipal conference.

By Thursday, however, Lizzy couldn't take the silence any longer. Returning to their hotel room, Lizzy found Holly dressed in cocktail attire, heading out.

"Where are you going?" Lizzy asked.

"San Jose's having a big party in their suite. Thought I'd check it out, talk to that guy who's proposing a similar restructuring of his fire department."

"Good idea."

Holly nodded, then grabbed her purse and headed for the door. Lizzy moved in front and blocked her passage.

"Holly, can we talk?"

Holly averted her eyes. "Now? The party just started."

"Can the party wait?"

Still staring at the ground, Holly paused, dropping her shoulders. "Sure, what's up?"

Lizzy leaned against the wall, praying she would look at her. When she didn't, Lizzy ploughed ahead anyway. "Look, slap me if I'm out of bounds here, but I can't stand to see you like this. You've been moping for days, and I could be completely wrong, but if you're gay and not telling me, I'm going to slap you."

It all happened so quickly, the words emerging before Lizzy could string them together delicately. Suddenly, her accusation was lying on the floor between them.

After several seconds, Holly moved backwards, sitting on the edge of the hotel bed with a sigh. Then she dropped her head into her hands, looking defeated in her finest attire like Cinderella realizing her limitations.

Lizzy sat down next to her. "Holly, we've been friends forever. Why didn't you tell me?"

"I never told myself," she mumbled to her feet. "Why should you be the first to know?"

She still wouldn't look up, her long hair falling down, hiding her face. She turned her feet sideways and pushed out of her high heels. "I despise these shoes."

Lizzy reached down and picked up the black pump. "So, if you come out, can I have your high heels?"

She didn't mean to be flippant at a time like this, but they operated better when they used humor, always had. Holly finally raised her head and smiled, one eye looking briefly her way.

Lizzy took the opportunity to put her arm around her friend. "I don't care, if that's what you're worried about. And if you're thinking of what people think, you live in Southern California, for goodness sakes."

Holly leaned into her shoulder. "It's not that."

"What is it then, your family?"

Holly buried her head inside Lizzy's shoulder. "My family's cool. Doubt they will care."

Lizzy searched her mind: Tom, the people in the office, her friends, all non-judgmental people.

"I humiliated someone," Holly whispered. "Cassie Taylor tried to kiss me at the New Year's party and I freaked."

"Seems to be a running problem with the Taylors."

Holly glanced up, her eyes narrowing. "You're in love with her brother, aren't you?"

They were talking about Holly, weren't they? Suddenly, Lizzy didn't want to discuss heart-to-heart problems anymore. She stood and pulled off her business jacket. "How about we call down for a pitcher of margaritas?"

"Lizzy." Holly had a way of saying her name that sounded like a mother reprimanding her child.

"We could go down to that Mexican restaurant on the corner. You're dressed. All I have to do is…"

"Lizzy." Now Holly was standing, blocking her way into the bathroom. "What happened?"

She really should talk about it; the pain of it bottled up inside her ached to be released. "He kissed me too, and I freaked," she muttered with a grim smile. "Only he did more than kiss and then he left afterwards."

Holly only grasped part of that statement. "I hope you finally got laid properly."

Lizzy rubbed her forehead. "Well, no and yes."

She felt Holly grab her arm and pull her toward the door as she leaned over and picked up a pair of comfortable shoes. "Definitely need margaritas."

The Mexican restaurant was packed with conference attendees, which suited them fine; the noise level could easily drown out any embarrassing conversation. They chose a secluded table and ordered a pitcher of margaritas on ice, extra salt. Then they both dove madly into the chips and salsa.

"So please tell me you finally had an orgasm."

Lizzy glanced up at the giant sombrero above their heads. "Don't beat around the bush, Holly. Just come out and say what you feel."

She shook a chip at her. "You needed one."

Lizzy leaned across the table and stated the obvious. "Well, so do you. And right now, I'm one up."

Holly buried her face in the enormous glass.

"You're going to get a headache drinking that fast," Lizzy told her.

"I don't care." She wiped her mouth with the back of her hand. "Lizzy, what am I going to do?"

"Didn't it ever occur to you before?"

Holly mulled a chip around in her mouth. "I always had these feelings, ever since I was a kid, just never let myself accept them, you know? I thought my problem would be solved when the right man came along."

At this, Lizzy choked. "Seems to be an epidemic among women."

Holly moved her glass aside, then reached across the table and took Lizzy's hands. "Lizzy, I'm gay. But you're not."

"Sounds like a old routine from Saturday Night Live. What are you, Chevy Chase now?"

She tugged at her hands. "I'm serious. You have a good man

staring you in the face. And if he did what I hoped he did New Year's, then you better hold on to him."

With one good jerk, Lizzy removed her hands. "He left me, Holly. We had our romp and then he left."

Her friend shook her head. "I loved it when they left."

Lizzy folded her arms and gave her a look. "He said he preferred sleeping in his own bed, but that he would love to spend the night if he found the right woman." Suddenly, something was obstructing her air. "Apparently, I'm not it."

Holly took her hands again, but this time they offered sympathy. "Maybe it was the newspaper. Cassie said her brother practically lives there and he has endless problems with that press."

"I don't think so."

"Maybe it was something else."

What? She had spent three days raking her brain to find some semblance of hope that she had made a mistake. "I'm not it, plain and simple. He just wanted to fool around."

"Fool around? You make it sound so juvenile."

"Well, we didn't actually, you know." Holly dropped her hands, one eyebrow rising. "I told him I wasn't ready for that but he insisted on doing the other thing. Which, thank you God, he did twice."

Lizzy thought back on the evening and felt her cheeks burn anew. How could a man who made love so easily and so passionately not care? And he had called at six a.m. to ask her to breakfast, meaning he could have returned home only to change out of his tuxedo. There had to be something there between them. She knew deep down she couldn't feel this way alone. Or was it only useless hope?

"You have to talk to him," Holly said. "At least hear his story."

Perhaps Holly was right. Obviously, the way Lizzy suffered since Monday, she had feelings for the man. If she searched her soul hard enough, she might even admit love for Martin. That meant something, even if he did reject her in the end. She had to confront this new emotion, if only to see if it was reciprocated.

"And you?" she said to Holly. "You need to call Cassie."

Holly shook her head and took another long drink. "I can't."

This time, Lizzy took Holly's hands. "If there is anyone in the world who understands what you're going through, it's Cassie Taylor. And for all you know, she's probably sitting somewhere with her friend drowning her sorrows in a margarita."

Holly looked up sheepishly. "You really think so?"

"I really think so."

With that out of the way, Holly wasted perhaps two seconds before blushing, excusing herself and bounding out of the restaurant to their room to make a phone call. Left with the pitcher and her painful memories, and feeling that her problems were much harder to solve than with a simple phone call, Lizzy made good use of the tequila.

MARTIN PAUSED at the counter of the Mini Mart, wondering how to explain his predicament.

"Lottery ticket, Mr. T?" Jeff asked.

How many tickets had be purchased over the last three years, Martin wondered. And how many times had he failed to get one number? He imagined two new schools being built on the money he donated to California education.

"No thanks, Jeff."

"Are you sure? The jackpot on Saturday is twenty-one million."

BY SATURDAY, *The Banner* would be Taylor history. Little good winning the lottery would do him then.

"Even remember your numbers. I can whisk you up a ticket in two seconds."

Martin waited for the perusing couple to move toward the beverage cases, then leaned across the counter. "Jeff, do you remember that night last week when I came in and Lizzy Guidry bought the last ticket?"

The clerk laughed, wiping his hands on the front of his apron. "She got you there."

"Yeah, more than you know."

Jeff's eyes widened. "Huh?"

Martin leaned closer, motioning for Jeff to do the same. "She won."

At first, Jeff reacted as if Martin was telling a joke, then his countenance shifted to puzzlement. "Are you pulling my leg, dude?"

"Trust me," Martin said. "She won. Around five million."

"Holy shit," Jeff exclaimed.

Martin glanced around to spot the couple's whereabouts, thankful they were arguing over a brand of beer. "The thing is, Lizzy doesn't know. And she isn't talking to me right now, so if she comes in here, will you be so kind as to let the woman know of her winnings?"

Jeff's mouth gapped open and Martin wasn't sure he understood, but the clerk nodded. "That's radical, man. Five million dollars."

Five million dollars that could have saved his newspaper, Martin thought before sending the image away. He made his decision, and he had to live with it, but he couldn't help feeling regrets.

"And Jeff," Martin added. "Don't tell her I told you or that we talked, okay?"

Jeff nodded, and again Martin wondered if he understood. Martin planned on telling Lizzy if they resumed their relationship. Hell, he would make damn sure that they did. But, depending on how long that took, it was best Lizzy knew she had millions waiting for her.

"Sure man," the clerk said. "I won't say a word."

"Great." Martin tapped the counter and moved out of the way of the couple. "I'll see you around."

"Are you sure you don't want a ticket today?" Jeff called out to him as he headed for the door. "It's not like you to miss buying one."

Martin opened the door and looked back at the college student who had greeted him every Wednesday and Saturday for months.

"No thanks, Jeff. Won't be seeing you anymore."

THE PHONE RANG INCESSANTLY and Lizzy wondered in her haze why Holly wasn't picking it up. Then she heard the shower running and reached out a groping hand to find the offensive beast.

"Elizabeth Guidry."

"You're a constant professional," the voice said. "You can't even relax on a business trip."

Lizzy forced her mind to clear, but someone was playing trumpets inside of her skull.

"Dave?"

"Hey, Sweetpea, I'm sorry to bother you but we need to talk."

She struggled to right herself, thankful for the headboard to rest upon. "What's up?"

"Well." Her old friend paused, and she could almost hear him smiling. "I have something very important to tell you, but I want to tell you that in person. Your grandmother already knows but she's sworn to secrecy."

"So you called to tell me you don't want to tell me something?"

Dave laughed while the room tilted and Lizzy wondered

how many margaritas she consumed the night before. Or that someone had convinced the government that tequila should be legal.

"It's about Martin."

Suddenly, the air cleared and the pounding halted. Lizzy was wide awake. "What about him?"

"He hit your ex-boyfriend."

Lizzy leaned forward, wiping the sleep from her eyes. "He did what?"

"His sister got pulled over on New Year's, by mistake, something about her being upset and weaving on the road. Martin was at the jail clearing things up. Next thing we know, Peter's girlfriend comes to bail him out and Martin lands a fist to the guy's face."

Lizzy shook her head to make sure she was hearing right. "He was at the jail on New Year's Eve?"

"MORE LIKE NEW Year's morning. It was close to dawn. By the way, we missed you at breakfast."

Holly emerged into the room wearing a towel around her head and whistling Dixie. Between the conversation on the phone and the image before her, Lizzy thought for sure she had gone mad from tequila overdose.

"There's more," Dave continued. "Peter wants to bring charges against Martin. His nose isn't broken, but he got two black eyes from the hit and he can't work until his face clears up so he could bring a nasty lawsuit if he wanted to."

Holly sensed something was amiss and paused at the foot of the bed, eyebrows furrowed. "Something wrong?" she mouthed.

Lizzy wished she hadn't drunk so much the night before. "Peter's threatening Martin?"

"I've struck a deal with your ex," the sheriff said. "If you drop your charges against him, he will drop his charges against Martin."

"Yeah, sure," Lizzy was quick to say. "I don't want Martin getting into trouble."

"Well, Martin doesn't know about this, so this will be our secret, okay, Sweetpea?"

"Okay."

"When are you coming home?"

Until two minutes before, Lizzy dreaded coming home on Saturday. But now she couldn't head south fast enough. "I should be home by this afternoon."

Holly gave her a puzzling expression, then the edges of her lips lifted. "You go girl," she mouthed.

"Stop by the police station and we'll process the paperwork," Dave said.

"Okay."

"Love you pumpkin."

Lizzy's heart constricted. Dave was a father of sorts, and she certainly loved him as family, but they had never said so verbally. Now that she thought about it, how long had it been since she told someone besides Nana that she loved them? "I love you too, Dave."

"Make sure they get me now, if I'm not here. I have something important to tell you."

"I will."

"Bye Sweetpea."

Lizzy hung up the phone and looked at Holly, so many things floating through her brain.

"There was a good reason he left, wasn't there?"

. . .

LIZZY FOUND a smile spreading across her face. "He was helping his sister."

"Oh my God." Holly sat on the bed. "She told me about that last night, but I didn't piece it together."

Holding her head so it wouldn't fall off, Lizzy swung her legs over the side, realizing she was still in her business clothes. "Wouldn't have mattered. I don't even remember getting into bed."

"Obviously," Holly said, laughing at her state of dress.

Lizzy quickly joined her, but she was on a mission and explanations would have to wait. "I have to go home." And with those words, she trotted off to the bathroom in search of the coffee maker, thinking of a blue-eyed dream waiting at the end of the Golden State Freeway.

LIZZY SPED through the San Jacquin Valley, then drove across the Grapevine, a steep incline through the mountains that marked the entrance into Southern California. When she spotted Lake Pyramid and the interpretive center, she knew she had to take a break. For one thing, she desperately needed a pit stop. More importantly, she needed a Diet Coke to take the edge off her hangover.

"We have a great display here if you're interested," the man behind the counter said. "On one side we explain the water systems of California and on the other, it's a reproduction of native habitats."

On any other day Lizzy might have taken him up on the offer. How one government could move vast amounts of water around such an enormous state, one created from desert and containing the country's largest population, continually amazed her. But she needed to get home.

"Don't have time," she told Mr. Lopez. "Maybe on the next trip."

"Well, at least stop outside on the porch and take in the view. We have free telescopes out back."

Lizzy paused, thinking a quick stretch might do her good. She decided to check out the lake view.

When she emerged on to the deck, the scope of the scene before left her breathless. A Pacific storm had raged through the night before, blowing away the smog and haze and leaving behind a vivid blue sky spotted with puffs of billowing clouds. The mountains were turning green and soft because of the rains but their stark, rugged tips still countered the mellow sky. And beneath it all lay placid Lake Pyramid, a manmade body of water created as part of the massive California water system.

She gazed through the telescope and examined the island at the center of the lake, thinking how fun it would be to explore it in the summertime. She really needed to get out more often, discover the treasures such as this one lying in her back yard, one hour north of Santa Helena.

Truth was she never considered California as home—more as a stopping place for a transplant—and she treated her life accordingly. Gazing at the beauty before her, and at the myriad families running about the deck, those of many nationalities and just as new to the state, Lizzy realized how wrong she had been.

All she had to do was let go, embrace her environment, accept the inevitable. She loved it here, as much as Nana did. She had to stop reliving the past and what she left behind. It was time to plant roots for the future.

Time to let love into her life.

Lizzy felt a hand on her shoulder and looked up to see Mr. Lopez handing her two cans of soda. "You left them on the counter."

"Thanks." She gazed at the scene before her, one of those rare days that forced even laid-back Angelenos to pause and stand in awe. A day when one could see forever, where the horizon seemed limitless.

"It's magnificent here, isn't it?" She didn't know if Mr. Lopez remained at her side, and she didn't care. Today, the sky whispered promises of happiness and she planned on grabbing her share.

"It's a slice of paradise," she heard him say behind her. "Just don't tell anybody. Then they'll all want to live here."

She turned to find the older man grinning.

"Too late," she said, smiling back, then walked through the door the man held open for her.

Paradise, Lizzy thought as she headed for home. The car clock showed one o'clock as she passed exits for the Los Padre National Forest. Forty-five minutes and she'd be there. And the first place she would visit would be *The Santa Helena Banner* and the warm arms of one Martin Taylor.

CHAPTER 17

"It's time," Cassie called out to Martin. "Paul is bringing the car around and Mom is finishing some paperwork. We should be ready to leave in about ten."

Martin heard his sister, but he couldn't gather the strength to answer. He sat in his father's enormous leather chair, staring at the myriad pictures on his office wall.

Maxwell Taylor watching his son William break ground at the original newspaper, his wife Helen by his side. William Taylor and family praying with the community after the attack on Pearl Harbor. Theodore Taylor shaking hands with then Governor Reagan. His dad with Governor Jerry Brown and Linda Ronstadt. His father standing proudly next to a new printing press, before it became obsolete.

A whole wall of accolades and accomplishments, but where was Teddy's family? Somewhere through the generations his father had failed to make that connection, failed to realize the importance of being happy. In the end, Theodore Taylor worked himself into a heart attack, leaving behind a guilt-ridden, miserable family.

"He represented his community well," Martin said to Cassie.

For some reason, he felt inclined to defend his father from all that was about to happen that day. "He produced a damn good newspaper."

He felt Cassie's hands on his shoulders as she gazed at the photographs over his head. "Yes, he did. And he was lucky to have you to appreciate that."

"He was a good man, too, even if he failed at fatherhood."

Cassie stood silent for a moment, shifting her feet. "I suppose you're right. I've been so angry all these years, mostly at feeling less of what he expected of me. But, you know, that's my problem. I loved dad and I know he did the best he could do. Some people aren't meant to be good fathers." She reached down and pressed a cheek to Martin's. "Just like some people aren't meant to be publishers."

"Thanks a lot."

He felt her smile against his cheek. "You're a great writer, Martin. Go back to doing what makes you happy. It will all turn out well in the end."

Martin knew selling the paper was the right thing for everyone involved, but nothing said or done that day would alleviate his pain. "Give me a minute, will you Cassie?"

She turned her head and kissed him, then gave his shoulder a squeeze. "You did a marvelous job, Martin," she whispered. "Dad couldn't have done better."

If only that were true, Martin thought as Cassie left the office. He couldn't help thinking that no matter what befell the old man, he would have found a way to hold on.

Martin rose and moved toward the window overlooking City Hall and the Towne Center. In a matter of hours he would be a millionaire, all his financial worries blown away like the dark rain clouds of the day before. But as the sun warmed his face through the glass, all Martin could feel was defeat and despair.

Suddenly, two arms snaked around his middle and a familiar

head rested against his back. "I'm sorry," he heard Lizzy whisper.

Was he hearing things? Martin turned and found Lizzy before him, her hands still wound around his waist. He spent no time gathering her up in his arms, inhaling her scent and relishing the feel of their bodies entwined while her hands encircled his waist, pulling them closer.

"I missed you," he whispered into her hair.

"I missed you, too."

He held her tight like a lifeline, raising his left hand to run through her silky fine hair, grateful for whatever force had sent her home a day early. He closed his eyes, his body absorbing every inch of her, and his anxiety rushed out in a sigh.

Lizzy pulled away and studied his eyes. "What's wrong? What has happened?"

He lifted his bandaged hand to her face, grateful the cloth left his fingers free to touch the delicate rise of her cheek. She captured his hand in hers and pressed it into her lips, but her eyes continued to examine him.

"Is it the newspaper?" she asked. "Is it in trouble, like that reporter said?"

Martin wanted to evoke a brave face, but he hadn't the energy. After a week of filing papers, meeting with everyone from appraisers to bank executives and getting little sleep in the process, Martin wanted to head to the ocean and disappear. Maybe it was better this way. The more exhausted he became, the easier it would be to let the newspaper go. But what was he going to tell Lizzy now? He hadn't the strength to lie.

"Martin?" she asked again, clearly worried. "Is there something I can do?"

In that blinding instant, Martin's spirits lifted. She still held the key to his newspaper's future with a tiny piece of paper sitting on her refrigerator door; all he had to do was ask. Was it fate interceding here? After all, Lizzy had walked into his office five minutes before his mother and siblings were to head downtown to inscribe away the family legacy. If there ever was a sign, this was it.

Martin moved his lips, ready to explain all that had happened between them since that fateful night in the Mini Mart and beg to be loaned half a million dollars, but the words refused to come. Her searching eyes held something new that day. They gazed upon him with unconditional love, something Lizzy didn't aspire to easily, and he felt that power surge within him, renewing his spirits.

He had gotten this far, convinced himself of what was best for him and his family, how could he consider retreating back to that damn lottery ticket and his deception? The one thing that had carried him through the week was the future he might have with her. The house in Ojai. Two kids and a dog. Even writers inheriting failing newspapers were allowed the American Dream.

And Lizzy? She gazed upon him now with a renewed trust born of what he hoped was a deeper love. How could he detour her now, knowing how far she had traveled to reach that point?

Martin smiled, tracing the curve of her cheek with his thumb. "If you want," he said, "you can make me dinner. I have to go downtown now for some business, but I'll be back around six or seven."

Lizzy kissed the base of his palm peeking out from the bandages. "I'll make you a jambalaya."

Martin sighed, exhaling whatever last-ditched, quilt-ridden hope had reared its head with her arrival. Then he delivered the kiss he had wanted to bestow on her since the day she turned down his offer for coffee, standing in that very room in her seductive red sweater. Martin took her face with both hands and kissed her slow and steady, a passion originating from the depths of his soul. He felt its power return tenfold, giving him hope that things were about to finally get better.

When he pulled back after what seemed an eternity, Lizzy stumbled a bit, grabbing his arms for support. But he saw in her eyes what he had been hoping for, that elusive emotion that had been plaguing him all week. The one that taken alone brought heartache and despair, but combined with another delivered happiness and bliss. Taking one last look upon her sweet face, empowered with the realization that she loved him back, Martin kissed the tip of her upturned nose.

"Martin," he heard Cassie say from the door. "It's time."

Lizzy seemed to break from the trance he had placed upon her, glancing from sister to brother, sensing the anxiety permeating between them. "Martin, are you sure there is nothing...?"

Martin kissed her again and hugged her one last time, soaking up her love for what was to come. Then he grabbed his jacket off the back of his chair and pulled it on. "Make it spicy," he said to her with a wink, then headed out the door.

HER HEAD REELING from the kiss Martin delivered, Lizzy found all activities difficult, including concentrating on what ingredients to buy for her jambalaya. If that man didn't love her back, she thought gazing at the numerous rows of celery, he was the world's greatest actor.

"Need some help?"

Lizzy turned to find a grocery clerk eyeing her indecision at the produce section. She peered inside her basket and found only rice. How long had she been standing there, a silly grin upon her face?

She grabbed a celery stalk, not caring if it was organic or pesticide laden, wide and thick or short and long. "Too many choices in California," she told the clerk. "How do you expect a person to decide?"

Somehow she managed to find the other items without his kiss interrupting her logic again, including a nice Merlot and a loaf of French bread. She thought to stop by City Hall, or visit Nana at the nursing home, but jambalaya took time and it was already close to three o'clock.

When Lizzy arrived at her apartment and was greeted by a living room stocked with two lives of furniture, her hope of a pleasant evening faded. She unloaded her groceries and started the process of dinner, but couldn't help catching the disorder out of the corner of her eye through the kitchen's pass-through.

After sautéing the sausage, onions, peppers and celery, she knew she had to do something. She picked up the phone and began calling a variety of non-profits until she found one willing to send a truck that afternoon. Then, after finishing the preparation of her jambalaya, she called Nana.

"Hein?" her grandmother said in her typical Cajun accent.

"I'm making a jambalaya."

"Where are you?"

"Home." Lizzy wiped her hands on her apron then pushed her bangs out of her face. "But you can't have any until tomorrow."

Nana paused and Lizzy almost laughed knowing her grandmother was busy studying the possibilities. "Does this have something to do with that newspaper man?"

"We have a date." Lizzy beamed thinking of what may lie ahead. "I'll save you some, though, bring it over for lunch."

"Don't bother," Nana said. "If that man wants to do what I think he wants to do, you probably won't eat that meal yourself until lunch tomorrow."

"Nana," Lizzy said, feigning shock. "Are you saying I should sleep with this man?"

"I didn't say anything about sleeping."

Lizzy leaned against the counter, not sure she was really having this conversation with her grandmother. But then nothing should shock her after hearing Nana talk about making love to Pawpaw all those years ago.

The phone buzzed in the midst of their conversation. "Nana, I have to let the Salvation Army in. They've come to get some items."

"Have a good time, *'tit monde,* and don't worry about me. You come visit when you come up for air. And bring that cute newspaper man with ya."

"Will do."

Lizzy paused, the words stuck in her chest. Then she remembered that amazing kiss and it gave her strength. "Nana," she said softly. "I'm in love."

She swore she heard Nana crossing herself. "That's wonderful, *chèr.* I'm so happy for you."

"You were right. I really needed to stop guarding my heart and allow myself some happiness."

"Oh sweetheart," Nana said through her emotions. "Your mama would be so pleased right now."

A sharp pain raced through her, but this time Lizzy welcomed it, letting the tears welling up in her eyes be tears of joy, instead of fear and pain. "I know she would."

She heard a knock on the main building door, reminding her to get off the phone and let the men enter the building, but she couldn't resist handing Nana one last tidbit of good news. "And Nana, he's Catholic."

A gasp ensued on the other end of the line. "I done told you he was Cajun."

Laughing, Lizzy said her good-byes and buzzed the men up. Within minutes they loaded her furniture on to the trucks, leaving behind the living room that Martin made, except for her Ikea coffee table, CD and record collection and the stereo she bought as a teenager.

By the time she rearranged the living room to recreate a harmonious apartment and place candles and place settings on the table, the clock rang six. She quickly made a salad, turned off the stove, pulled off her apron and ran for the shower.

Six-thirty. She tugged on her bathrobe and dribbled water down the hall to look out the front window and make sure Martin hadn't arrived yet. So far, so good. Now all she had to do was blow dry her hair and get dressed and hope he wouldn't arrive in the meantime.

Two-thirds through drying her hair her luck ran out and a knock sounded at the door. She fingered her hair in place, then headed for the door. Martin stood before her every bit as handsome, but his eyes were dimmed and he carried his jacket over his shoulders as if heavy weights hung within its pockets. Something was wrong here.

"What happened?"

Martin said nothing, let his eyes drift over her, smiling faintly when he recognized the familiar bathrobe. "Dinner took longer than I expected," she explained.

She moved out of the doorway, letting him enter the apartment, and still he said nothing. Outside of lunch in Santa Barbara, when she had insulted his manhood, the defiant editorialist had never been at a loss for words.

"Martin, what has happened?"

He paused in the hallway, gazing at the living room and apparently liking what he saw. "The place looks great, but what did you do with your furniture?"

She wasn't ready to admit she gave up part of her life relying on him to fill that space. He had said she could keep the furniture, but their long-term commitments were still unspoken. "How do you always get in?" she asked, changing the subject. "You never buzz."

"I did buzz." When their eyes met, he appeared exhausted. "But there's always a neighbor around coming in."

She slipped her arms around his waist and he wasted no time pulling her close. "Something happened. Are you going to tell me?"

"Later," he whispered into her hair. "Can we talk about it later?"

She remembered her conversation with Nana and shivers raced through her thinking of what they might do beforehand. Still, Lizzy was Southern and Cajun and there were formalities to follow. Plus, she wanted to know.

"I have to reheat the jambalaya but it won't take long." She pulled away far enough to look into his face, but she refused to relinquish the grip she had on his shirt. "I have a Merlot breathing. Why don't you pour yourself a glass, I'll go get dressed and then we can talk about it."

"Merlot?" Martin asked, his humor returning. "He tugged at the tie of her waist, a sly gleam twinkling in the blue depths of his eyes. "I don't need no stinking Merlot."

Suddenly, the world shifted into fast forward and formalities were tossed out the door. Martin gathered her up in his arms, kissing her soundly while he flicked off the hall lights with one hand. Her arm reached over to lock the front door, while they inched toward the bedroom in each other's grip, his mouth hungry on hers. She heard Martin's jacket falling to the floor at the same time she felt the quilt beneath her knees. And with one blinding movement, he tugged at her waist and her bathrobe disappeared.

"I guess dinner can wait," she managed through his ferocious kisses.

He paused, letting a lazy hand sweep over her exposed flesh as he nibbled on an earlobe. "Is the stove on?"

"No." She shivered as his fingers slid across a breast and a thumb encircled a nipple, then pinched it gently.

Yes, dinner definitely could wait, Lizzy thought when his hand massaged, squeezed, kneaded and teased and he raised a knee between her legs, causing a brush fire to blaze and send fire lines across her body.

She grabbed at his shirt but the dang thing wouldn't budge

from behind. Now that she thought about it, he had way too many clothes on. "This isn't fair. I'm always naked and you're always fully dressed."

Martin raised up an elbow, grinning down at her as his blond hair fell about his forehead like a teenager. "I can remedy that easily."

He raised himself on his knees and nearly ripped the shirt off, one button skipping across the wooden floor. Then he slid his belt free, pulling it slowly out with one hand extended like a striper.

"Tease," Lizzy said.

Through the soft light of the street lamp filtering in the bedroom, Lizzy watched the lines of his face deepen with a grin. He unbuttoned, then unzipped his pants, but instead of removing them, he reached for his wallet.

Lizzy rose on her elbows, feeling rather vulnerable lying there naked while he rummaged through his wallet. Then she realized what it was he was looking for. While his focus was on a condom, she reached for his pants and a piece of anatomy that was glad to see her.

"Stop it," he muttered, "or I'm going to explode right here."

Lizzy ignored him, enjoying the feel of him taunt and extended. "Then hurry up."

Martin opened one side of his wallet, then another, his body tensing. "No." He searched another pocket and came up short. "No," he said with more frustration.

With one quick movement, Lizzy grabbed the wallet and sent it the way of the button. "Bedside table. Top drawer."

Martin leaned forward, pressing his body against hers until they were back lying on the bed. The soft blond curls gracing his chest tickled her breasts, causing her to ignite all over again.

"Expecting someone?" Martin teased, kissing her neck while his hand reached over and grabbed the condom from the bedside table.

"Actually, it's a leftover, but I was hoping to get lucky." Lizzy slipped her hands inside his trousers and briefs, pushing the fabric away and gripping his behind. Martin nearly bolted upright as her fingers snaked their way down toward his thighs and squeezed.

"Hell, woman, for someone inexperienced you sure know how to drive a man crazy."

She suddenly felt embarrassed and thought to remove her hands, but they fit so well around him. "I can't help it. You feel so wonderful to me."

"Well then," he said breathlessly, his trademark charm emerging, "let me help you."

In an instant Martin removed his pants, then nestled himself inside her legs, his arousal pressing hard against her core. While one hand slammed the table drawer shut, he nibbled on her lower lip.

"You're a wonder at multi-tasking," she mumbled.

"You have no idea," Martin said, as one hand pressed her bottom against his erection and his mouth slipped down to embrace a breast.

The world took on a new dimension as his tongue danced upon her nipple. Waves of pleasure washed over her, each new current more powerful than before as he sucked and stroked, then teased her gently between his teeth. She grabbed his bottom again, slipping her fingers around the thick muscles of his thighs and pressing him closer.

She didn't know how he did it, but Martin broke away from her breasts for an instant to rip the condom open with his teeth, but he was soon back at work, his tongue hot upon her nipple and one hand slipping the condom in place.

"You must have made a good journalist," she said through the haze of passion.

He paused, moving up to her face and brushing the hair from her eyes. He still moved hard against her and her hips responded in kind, begging for a union, but for a moment their eyes sought each other's. "I'd rather be a good lover to you," he whispered.

Gazing into that sea of blue, Lizzy let the waves take her away. "You already are," she said, pushing her hips toward his. "Just finish the job before you drive me crazy."

Still watching her face, Martin moved deftly until he stood poised at her entrance, teasing the soft folds that greeted him. Inundated with sensations, Lizzy moaned and reached a hand up to grab the headboard, then Martin slowly moved inside and began the dance.

It was more than a union, rather a blending of souls. They rose and fell together like the ocean, his hands still exploring her body, bringing pleasure every place he touched while he plunged deep within her. When Martin pushed forward on his knees, grabbing her bottom and delving deeper, Lizzy felt the world tip and the seas pour off the other side. He pulled out one last time, teasing her entrance, circling. Then in one deep thrust, he pounded back inside and Lizzy slipped off the edge.

Spots of white light flitted across her vision and she heard him moan with equal pleasure as her body pulsated from the climax. The spasms continued and she held on to the headboard for balance as they both rode the waves of bliss together. Finally, she let go, reaching for his face, his back, and the comfort of his embrace. He held on to her with equal force, still shivering from the impact of their lovemaking.

As the energy subsided, she expected him to offer up some humorous comment, but Martin became unusually still. He held her tight as their bodies remained locked together, his face buried in her hair.

Lizzy reached up to touch his face, to gauge his reaction and found his cheeks moist. Suddenly, Lizzy realized Martin was crying.

CHAPTER 18

"*I*t wasn't that bad," he joked, a smile teasing his lips.

She might have found that funny had she not been so frightened from his tears. Not from the man who hated to see women cry.

"I can't explain it," Martin said, sliding on his back and resting an arm over his eyes. "I haven't cried in years, not even when my father died."

Lizzy turned into him, letting their bodies reunite side by side. "I know the feeling."

He opened his arm and Lizzy nestled into the crock, laying her head against his chest. She could hear the heightened rhythm of his heart, feel the blood surge through the veins in his neck. "I've never felt this way with a woman before," he whispered.

Lizzy let her fingers explore the blonde curls on his chest, the lines of his chin, the sharp rubble of new growth on his neck. "I know. It's only been a week and I feel like I've known you..."

"Forever."

His composure returned, he began kissing her face repeatedly as if he couldn't absorb her fast enough. His hand cupped her cheek, threading through her hair lovingly. "We work well together."

Lizzy closed her eyes and savored his kisses, while their bodies melded into one. "An understatement." They fit together like a puzzle.

"We came together," he said with a grin. "Think of how wonderful that is. Now, you'll have to marry me."

As he moved a hand up her back, the raw edge of his bandage tickled the skin in its wake causing her to break out in shivers. "Sorry," Martin said. "The doctor wanted it on one more day."

Lizzy reached back and captured his injured hand, then kissed the inside of his palm. "I heard you gave Peter not one, but two black eyes."

"How did you know?"

She turned over his hand to study the extent of his injuries. "Dave. Did you break anything?"

"Nah. Did Dave tell you he got married?"

Lizzy propped her chin on her hand above his heart. "What?"

"I probably shouldn't have told you." Martin reached up and caressed her hair but the effort seemed to tire him. It was clear he was running on fumes. "He married my mother. They eloped to Las Vegas on New Year's Eve."

"Well I'll be damned."

"Said it was all on account of you."

"Me?"

His hands stilled and a sigh escaped his lips. His heartbeat lessened and she could feel fatigue replacing the euphoria they once shared. Lizzy looked up to meet his eyes, which were glazed over from exhaustion. She kissed the tip of his chin, then returned to her comfortable spot at the base of his neck, waiting for him to continue.

"Something about you leaving a sweater at my mom's house

and my mom meeting Nana when she brought it to town. She'll explain it all the next time you see them."

"Wow, that was fast."

Martin tensed. "Yeah, it's been a wild week."

She wondered if he knew the half of the week it had been. She decided to find out. "Did you know my best friend is in love with your sister?"

At this, Martin laughed. "Cassie confessed everything the night I got her out of jail. We had a coming out party afterwards."

He lifted his head slightly and searched for her eyes in the darkness. "You did know I went to the jail on New Year's to bail her out, didn't you? I told you where I was going and you replied."

That night she would have signed her soul to the devil had he asked, but she was doubtful she'd have remembered it. "No, I didn't. But it's okay. I know now."

"Ah Lizzy. Is that why you wouldn't come to breakfast? Why you insisted on us taking a breather?"

Lizzy reached up and touched two fingers to his lips, which he quickly grabbed with his teeth and savored with his tongue. "You're here now. And I'm here. What more do we need?" She slid her moist fingers across his bottom lip. "Unless, of course, you're going to slip away to the comfort of your own bed."

She felt Martin's lips curling up at the edges but his eyes were shut and his breathing slowed. "I'm not going anywhere," he whispered slowly as fatigue consumed him, but the words sent shock waves down to her soul. He was hers for the night and he might be hers forever. Tomorrow would be a brighter day.

Before Martin gave in to sleep, he hugged her close, his face buried in her hair. "I'm so glad you're here, Lizzy. So glad you came home."

She heard the desperation in his voice, still wondered what

tragedies had occurred that day, if indeed they had. Before she could inquire more, Martin slipped away, delving into a deep, peaceful sleep.

LIZZY WOKE before the sun made its usual wakeup call into her bedroom, slipping from the warmth of Martin's arms to get the coffee started. She pulled on her bathrobe, then headed for the kitchen after kissing his stubby cheek.

She had risen earlier in the night to move the jambalaya and salad into the fridge and to cork the Merlot. The French bread was ruined, as stale as a brick but perfect for the makings of *pain perdue*, or Cajun French bread. All she needed was more eggs and creamer. And perhaps another package of condoms.

Lizzy giggled like a schoolgirl thinking of all that had transpired, of how much they had complimented each other, fulfilled each other's needs. "We work well together," he had said. "Now you have to marry me."

He had joked about it before, but Lizzy imagined anything was possible now. She was a changed woman, with the future beaming before her.

But still, she needed creamer and no future was possible without her coffee and chicory. She would put on her jogging pants and sweatshirt and hike down to the Mini Mart before Martin had a chance to wake up. If she gathered up her nerve, she'd even ask the clerk to sell her a package of condoms in case Martin woke with a hunger. Heaven knows, she was starving.

Lizzy tiptoed out the door, enjoying the crisp breeze as the sun kissed the horizon good morning. After two blocks she entered the convenient store, smiling as she thought back on the night she and Martin had fought over a silly lottery ticket.

"Hey Lucky Lady."

Damn, Lizzy thought. Jeff was there. How would she find the nerve to ask him for condoms? "Hey Jeff."

"Have you seen Martin lately?" the clerk asked.

"Saw him last night, why?"

"Then you know. Wow, that is so totally awesome."

Lizzy had headed toward the beverage cases to pick up creamer so she couldn't make out Jeff's face or why he was so pleased with her meeting Martin. Had he known about their relationship? She couldn't fathom how. Having picked up the creamer and eggs, she moved toward the counter. "What do you mean? Know what?"

"Man, the lottery. They told us we sold the winning ticket but I had no idea it was you."

She was still confused. While she tried to piece together what he had said, she recognized his Surfers 58 T-shirt from the night she had beaten Martin to the lottery machine. What had Jeff said about the ticket and where did Martin fit into this?

"Jeff, what are you talking about?"

"You did see Martin, didn't you?"

Suddenly, Jeff look guilt-stricken and a fear coursed through her, stealing her breath. Something was terribly wrong here; Lizzy felt it deep within her soul. "Jeff, what's going on?"

"Didn't he tell you?"

"Who? Tell me what?"

Jeff threw his hands above his ears and cringed. "Oh man, he told me not to tell you. I mean, he said to tell you, but not to tell you he told me to tell you."

She placed her items on the counter, then grabbed the latest copy of *The Banner*, trying hard to remain calm. "Why don't you start from the top and tell it to me straight."

Jeff shook his head, knowing he had plunged into deep shit but couldn't find a way out. "He'll kill me."

Lizzy sucked in a breath. "Who will kill you?"

"Martin."

Her heart ached at the sound of his name and she dreaded what was to come, but she had to know. "Why?"

Jeff suddenly appeared confused, as if he had no idea what was happening or what any of it meant. "I don't know. He told me he probably wasn't going to see you soon so if I did, to let you know you won the lottery. But not to tell you he said so."

Lizzy swallowed hard, but the lump refused to budge. "I won the lottery?"

Jeff relaxed a little. "Five million dollars. That night you were in here and you were so pissed."

"Five million dollars?" she practically shouted.

"Yeah." Jeff reached behind the counter and placed in her hand a ticket similar to the ones he sold, only this ticket reported the winning numbers of December the twenty-sixth.

Lizzy immediately saw the fifty-eight, the two numbers of her birthdate and her age and thought the other numbers looked familiar, but her mind was busy contemplating all the scenarios. She heard Jeff ring up her purchases and felt him place a bag in her hands along with more congratulations, but all she could ponder was five million dollars and a reason why Martin would want to keep his knowledge of this jackpot a secret.

THE SUN HIT Martin's face about the same time he realized he was alone. Not only was her side of the bed empty and cold, but only the sound of cars passing by on the street and a distant door closing could be heard in the lonely apartment. But he called her name anyway. "Lizzy?"

He smelled coffee brewing and that was a good sign. Martin rose and pulled on his pants, then grabbed from Lizzy's chair by the bed an oversized purple sweatshirt with Louisiana State University emblazoned on it. Pulling it over his head, he caught her scent, making him hungry to touch her again.

"Lizzy?" he asked no one as he entered the living room, hoping she was around some corner. The place was deserted, but appeared a hundred times better than the first day he entered the apartment when only bookshelves graced the walls. His father's pieces fit amazingly well next to a couple of items of Lizzy's. And he had a matching chair that would look great beside her bay window overlooking the street. He made a mental note to bring it over that afternoon.

He paused at her CD collection, digesting her taste in music. She liked pop country, Cajun and zydeco, a variety of folk and an eclectic range of rock and roll, from the Beatles to The New Pornographers. But she especially craved BeauSoleil, a Cajun group who dabbled in mixing music forms, his personal favorite band. Martin then perused her books, glad to see she enjoyed mysteries along with her Hitchcock. He'd have to introduce her to some of his cherished authors.

On the way to the kitchen, Martin studied the photographs lining the bookcases: Lizzy as a child with her parents in New Orleans, a 1940s portrait of what looked to be Nana, a similar one of a man proud to be dressed in his finest suit and a group shot of the whole family with a young Lizzy, all of them standing next to a shrimp boat with "LeBlanc Shrimping" printed on the side.

Pictures of family, much like the bookshelves at his mother's place.

Another whiff of coffee assaulted him, as if the coffeepot called his name, and Martin headed for the kitchen to answer it. He poured himself a cup and leaned against the sink, enjoying his favorite brew.

He wished she would get home. Already he ached to hold her close. In a few hours he had to head back to *The Banner* and begin the transition, but for now he only wanted Lizzy. While he sipped his coffee, he caught the lottery ticket out of the corner of his eye, mocking him from its place on the fridge. He still had a lot to explain.

He heard the key in the lock, waited anxiously for her to

appear. But when Lizzy entered the kitchen and placed a bag on the counter, she didn't seem as eager to see him.

"What's wrong?"

Her eyes expressed a mixture of shock and fear, her shoulders tense. Martin glanced down at the bag to see where she'd been and noticed the Mini Mart logo. He grimaced, fearing what may have transpired.

"I won the lottery," she finally said. "But I guess you already know that."

All his happiness came crashing down and the fatigue he experienced earlier returned full force. He didn't know where to begin so he merely nodded.

"How long have you known?" she asked incredulously.

Martin exhaled, wishing he had explained it all the night before. God only knew what she thought of him now. "Since that first night."

"The first night?" Her eyes widened and she held up the piece of paper that announced the winning numbers, glancing at the real ticket on her refrigerator. He could read it in her eyes that she wondered if it was all a dream.

"I tried to tell you," Martin began, but he knew it was a lie. When she looked back at him with accusing eyes, he decided to come clean. "Actually, I wanted you to find out on your own."

"Why?"

He heard it in her voice, that fear that he might be as big a turd as Peter. He wanted to grab her, shout that he wouldn't break her heart no matter what his original intentions, but she had to hear the truth. She deserved as much.

"I needed half a million dollars to save my newspaper," Martin began, grimacing at the pitiful sound of his words. "When I saw you at that press conference and knew you didn't know, I thought I could get on your good graces so that when you found out you'd won, you'd lend me the money."

He sighed, looking down into his coffee cup. "I thought I

could charm you into liking me. I thought I could buy you dinner, help you get your car. Then have you pick up a newspaper or check the website and realize you're a millionaire. You'd be so indebted to my kindness, you'd want to help me out."

He placed the cup on the counter, afraid to look at her, apprehensive to see the hurt and animosity in her eyes. Yet, all these motives seemed so far away, as if another person had thought them up. He spoke the truth, but was it how he felt now? Absolutely not. Surely, after everything they shared she would realize this.

"The truth is, Lizzy, I tried to tell you again and again but something always interfered. And that was okay by me."

Their eyes met, hers watchful and curious. "I wanted to be with you," he said heatedly. "And I knew that if you found out about the lottery, I might have my money, but you might not want to see me anymore."

Lizzy attempted to speak, a frown playing her forehead, but Martin grabbed her upper arms. "I tried to deceive you, and you have every right to be mad at me and never want to see me again. But I love you, Lizzy. And nothing is going to change that. You can kick me out of your apartment right now and be justified in doing so, but I'll be back. You can't get rid of me this easily."

He still expected anger and hurt, but Lizzy's eyes softened as if filled with pity and regret. "Why didn't you tell me?"

Something else was running through her mind, Martin could feel it, but he couldn't comprehend what. "I tried to…"

"Not hard enough."

A tear slid down her cheek. "Martin," she whispered, swallowing hard, "you lost your newspaper."

Confusion set in, but before he could sort out what was being said, she pulled a copy of *The Banner* from her bag, the top headline announcing the sale to the *Los Angeles Daily Times*.

"You should have told me. I would have gladly given you the money. All of it."

Martin fell back against the counter, relief coursing through his veins. This time, Lizzy took his hands and pressed them close to her chest, tears lingering on her eyelashes. "What do I need with all that money, Martin? You should have told me."

Martin reached up and captured her face, realizing what an amazing gift he had been given. "Someone special told me one night in Santa Barbara that if I didn't like what I did to change my circumstances."

Lizzy leaned forward, resting her forehead on his. "Oh Martin."

He placed a finger at her chin and lifted her eyes to his. "Only that meant making a choice." He kissed her lightly on her freckled nose. "And I chose you."

She finally smiled, albeit faintly, sending Martin more hope than he dared imagine. But she still looked upon him with regret. "Your paper…"

"My father's paper," he said, feeling confident about his decision for the first time. "And it's no longer my concern."

He slipped his arms about her waist and pulled her close, reveling in the feel of their bodies joined again. "The only thing I care about at this moment is getting you back into that bedroom."

He was ready to deliver one long, all-encompassing kiss, but Lizzy pulled back. "There is still one thing I need to know," she said, her mouth a breath from his.

Martin wanted so desperately to taste those luscious lips. "What?"

"Why did you write that editorial?"

Martin sobered, thinking back on all he had written that past week. "What editorial?"

She gave him a caustic look. "The one where you called me a name."

"Oh God." Martin cringed. "Are we back to that?"

Lizzy tugged her hands at his waist, a determined look in her eye. "Just answer the question."

Another one of those moments, he thought with dread, where women expected men to say the right thing. But what was the correct answer? Why had he written that editorial? Right now, he barely remembered the subject matter. He couldn't forget linking her to the sanitation department, but why had he included her in the first place? It was about the District Attorney's nephew joy-riding on the Santa Helena back streets and the mayor's refusal to reprimand him. Lizzy was only doing her job by releasing the mayor's statement to the press.

Her finger tapped impatiently at his side, while her chin turned upward. She expected an answer, but for the life of him he couldn't fathom why he had written what he did. He attempted to say as much, claiming temporary insanity, when he blurted out the first thing that came to mind. "It got your attention," he said with a shrug. He braced himself for what was to come, but amazingly Lizzy smiled broadly.

"I said the right thing?"

Lizzy nodded, then pulled her arms tighter behind his back. "Yes, you said the right thing."

She leaned forward to kiss him, but now it was Martin who pulled away. "How much exactly did you win?"

She gazed up at him with a skeptical look. "Five million, two hundred thousand and some change."

"Hmmm." He nodded his head thoughtfully.

"Why?"

"After taxes, I'd say we're worth about the same amount of money."

"You're a millionaire now?"

Hard to believe, considering he had trouble making payroll

only days before. "What are we going to do with all this money, Lizzy?"

She laughed, shaking her bob haircut in the process. "I haven't a clue."

Lizzy moved her hands up his chest to encircle his neck, then leaned her body forward so their lips were close to touching. "Who cares? I've got everything I've ever wanted. Right here."

Martin sobered looking into her sweet brown eyes. All the world was his as well. "I love you, Lizzy," he whispered, his lips skimming hers.

"I love you, too," she whispered back.

In an instant, her feet were off the floor and they were headed back to the bedroom.

"I STILL DON'T KNOW why we are here," Nana said, gazing at the breaking waves off Santa Barbara's pier. "I thought you were going to show me y'all's new house."

"We are," Lizzy said, helping her grandmother walk to the edge. "We're going to head over to Ojai in a few minutes."

"I was hoping to get my nap."

"You slept on the way over here. How much sleep does one person need?"

Nana huffed. "When you get to be my age, you'll find sleeping is a long overdue luxury." She sent Lizzy a sly grin. "You'll understand this when you have children."

Lizzy rolled her eyes. Now they were on to children. It hadn't been a week since she and Martin admitted love to each other and Nana was already making wedding plans. Of course, at the rate they were going...

"Need some help?"

One week and his voice still sent shivers racing down her

spine. Then Martin's breath was hot on her neck, just before he stole a kiss beneath her earlobe.

"Yeah, he certainly can help."

Martin gave Nana a scrutinizing look, one hidden behind a smile. "What are we talking about now?"

Lizzy used her free arm to snake through his elbow. "Never mind."

"Offspring," Nana said, poking Martin with her cane. "And give me a blonde, blue-eyed one. That would be a first for our French family."

Lizzy started to object, but Martin leaned forward and kissed Nana on the cheek. "I'll do my best."

"Okay," Cassie said as she joined the group, followed by the rest of the family. "Why are we here?"

Olivia sent her son a knowing smile. "It's a symbolic ritual."

Paul turned from the railing, eyebrows raised. "A what? It's not another one of your New Age things, is it Mom?"

"It's a little too simplistic for your educated mind, Paul," Olivia explained, placing a picnic basket at her side. "But it must be done."

"I thought this was a lunch to celebrate our new additions to the family," Cassie said. She reached over and took Nana's hand, which surprised Lizzy as much as it did Nana. Cassie usually avoided Nana, fearful of her grandmother discovering her nature and disapproving, Lizzy thought, which was absurd; Nana might be critical but never prejudicial. Somehow one day Cassie figured that out and the barrier had broken down between them. She appeared happier than ever.

"It was a lunch to celebrate our good fortune," Dave said, holding Olivia tight. "But outside of upcoming weddings," he turned to Lizzy and winked, "we have another kind of celebration."

Nana looked her way.

"Not me," Lizzy told her.

All eyes turned to Martin, who grinned beneath his sunglasses. "I wanted you guys to share this with me because if it wasn't for all of you..." He paused and glanced down at Lizzy lovingly, "I wouldn't be here today."

Martin reached inside his coat pocket and removed his work cell phone, then with an enormous thrust, cast it into the open sea, the sound of *Hotel California* drowning beneath the surf.

A chorus of cheers erupted and Olivia opened a bottle of champagne and poured them all a glass. "We shouldn't be doing this," Dave said, looking around. "This is public property."

Nana jabbed him in the ribs. "What are you worried about? This isn't your jurisdiction and that boy isn't going to write any more scathing editorials."

"True, but Dave is right," Olivia said. "So let's make it a quick toast."

They all raised their glasses toward the incoming waves and the setting sun, Martin placing an arm about Lizzy and holding her close.

"To our new and expanded family," Olivia said. "And the happiness that brings."

They all toasted each other's glasses, then took a sip, but Martin had one last toast to offer.

"To scathing editorials," he said with a broad grin, casting his eyes to Lizzy. "And the California State Lottery."

RECIPE

Martin's Seafood Gumbo

1/2 cup vegetable oil

2/3 cup flour

2 large yellow onions, chopped

2 green bell peppers, chopped

1 cup celery, chopped

1 pound shrimp (about 30-35 shrimp), preferably wild Louisiana shrimp

1 pound crabmeat

1 dozen shucked oysters, liquid reserved

Crab pieces, if desired

2 (32-ounce) boxes seafood stock

Salt, pepper and/or Cajun/Creole seasoning to taste

2 cups cooked Louisiana rice

Green onions, chopped, for garnish

Directions: In a large soup pot, over medium heat, mix the oil and flour for a roux, stirring constantly, being careful not to let the roux burn. Keep stirring until you receive the right darkness of roux. The color and time it takes to finish the roux will depend upon your preference but a light roux is preferable for a seafood gumbo.

Add to the pot the chopped onions, bell peppers and celery, known as the "Cajun Trinity," and stir. Cook over medium-high heat until the vegetables are tender or until the onions are translucent, about 5 minutes. Add the seafood stock and oyster juice and bring to a gentle boil, then simmer, uncovered for about 30 minutes. Add the shrimp and cook for 5 minutes. Add the oysters and crabmeat and cook for 5 minutes. Add additional salt, pepper or Cajun seasoning to taste. Remove from heat, serve gumbo over rice and garnish with chopped green onions.

Note: A cast iron soup pot works best. You can also make your own seafood stock, but we listed boxed seafood stock that is easily found in grocery stores. Also, Walmart sells Guidry's Creole Seasoning mix—the "Cajun Holy Trinity" of onions, bell peppers and celery—so for those who want to save time, substitute Guidry's.

AUTHOR'S NOTE

Author's Note

When I was a young girl my mother would sit on the edge of my bed and sing songs to my sister and me. Our favorite was *Let the Rest of the World Go By* by Ernest R. Ball and J. Keirn Brennan. It became even more poignant when this Louisiana girl moved out west and met my husband in Los Angeles and our favorite getaway was a little "nest" near Santa Barbara, a sweet artist community called Ojai.

Here are the main lyrics to the song, recorded by so many people over the years, including Pat Boone, Connie Francis, Willie Nelson, Ringo Starr and even Jed Clampit. It was also included in the film *Out of Africa* and in the 1944 film *When Irish Eyes are Smiling*, in which Dick Haymes sings the tune.

Let the Rest of the World Go By
With someone like you,
a pal good and true,
I'd like to leave it all behind and go and find
some place that's known,

to God alone,
just a spot to call our own.
We'll find perfect peace,
where joys never cease,
out there beneath a kindly sky.
We'll build a sweet little nest
somewhere in the west
and let the rest of the world go by.

ABOUT THE AUTHOR

Cherie Claire grew up in south Louisiana, with mud between her toes and a rabid love of Mardi Gras parades. Born in New Orleans, she couldn't help but write about her unique, colorful state. Cherie is the award-winning author of The Cajun Series of historical romances, the Cajun Embassy series of contemporary romances and a paranormal mystery series featuring New Orleans ghost sleuth Viola Valentine. She's a Holt Award finalist, a Romantic Times Reviewer's Choice Award finalist and received the Louisiana Press Women Book of the Year. Read more at https://www.cherieclaire.net/.

ALSO BY CHERIE CLAIRE

Also by Cherie Claire

The Cajun Embassy

Ticket to Paradise

Damn Yankees

Gone Pecan

The Cajun Series

Emilie

Rose

Gabrielle

Delphine

A Cajun Dream

The Letter

Carnival Confessions: A Mardi Gras Novella

The Viola Valentine Mystery Series

A Ghost of a Chance

Ghost Town

Trace of a Ghost

Ghost Trippin'

Give Up the Ghost

The Ghost is Clear (novella)

Ghost Fever

Ghost Lights